ALSO BY ADAM THIRLWELL

THE FUTURE FUTURE

THE
FUTURE
FUTURE

Adam Thirlwell

FARRAR, STRAUS AND GIROUX
NEW YORK

Farrar, Straus and Giroux
120 Broadway, New York 10271

Copyright © 2023 by Adam Thirlwell
All rights reserved
Printed in the United States of America
Originally published in 2023 by Jonathan Cape, Great Britain
Published in the United States by Farrar, Straus and Giroux
First American edition, 2023

Library of Congress Cataloging-in-Publication Data
Names: Thirlwell, Adam, 1978– author.
Title: The future future / Adam Thirlwell.
Description: First American edition. | New York : Farrar, Straus and
    Giroux, 2023.
Identifiers: LCCN 2023014910 | ISBN 9780374607616 (hardcover)
Subjects: LCSH: Female friendship—Fiction. | France-—History—
    18th century—Fiction. | LCGFT: Historical fiction. | Humorous fiction. |
    Novels.
Classification: LCC PR6120.H575 F88 2023 | DDC 823/.92—dc23/
    eng/20230331
LC record available at https://lccn.loc.gov/2023014910

Our books may be purchased in bulk for promotional, educational,
or business use. Please contact your local bookseller or the Macmillan
Corporate and Premium Sales Department at 1-800-221-7945, extension 5442,
or by email at MacmillanSpecialMarkets@macmillan.com.

www.fsgbooks.com
www.twitter.com/fsgbooks • www.facebook.com/fsgbooks

1   3   5   7   9   10   8   6   4   2

For Alison
For Rosa Sailor

Contents

One

I

It all began with writing. One evening a pamphlet had found its way into the hands of a woman in Paris. The print of this pamphlet was smudged. Beneath the title was a fuzzily reproduced picture of a woman semi-naked in a bed – a notorious image of the woman now reading the pamphlet itself. Neither the copy nor the original image looked like her at all.

A pamphlet can be very small and elusive, like a piece of code. She looked at it for a long time, trying to understand it – for so long, in fact, that she was now late for a party. She didn't know who had written this pamphlet or made the image on its cover or published it. It had been produced across the border. It was one of an emerging pornographic series, printed in avant-garde cities – in London and Antwerp and Geneva. It seemed to be an international project, something samizdat and 24-hour.

She threw the pamphlet away, then continued to stare at it in the garbage, among the newspapers and magazines and bills and cancelled cheques and messages. It was impossible to look away.

Centuries and centuries go by, but everything happens in the present moment.

Then she came to a new conclusion. She retrieved the pamphlet, and went out into the night.

2

Her name was Celine. For the last few months a series of anonymous fictions had appeared, attacking her sexual life, her habits and her politics – along with many similar pamphlets about other women she knew. But it was the pamphlets about Celine that, for reasons she never entirely understood, became modest bestsellers. Soon she was transformed into a sign, or character. People wanted to know *what would happen next* in the ongoing series.

Above everyone the sky was blue then pink, then pink then blue. It all seemed gentle. In the open windows of tea rooms appeared jasmine scents and lavender. On the outskirts of great cities grew deep forests and minute mushrooms. In the oceans octopi were disporting themselves underwater, letting their many arms/legs trail deliciously and gather information. All over the planet pirates traded with other pirates. And meanwhile many people believed they knew Celine without knowing her at all.

At first Celine had read every pamphlet as soon as it appeared but very soon the words upset her too much. She tried to explain her feelings to her friends. It was like everything was dirty or spilled, she said. She felt like the world was blurred. She didn't exactly know what she meant by these phrases. When she was young she had thought that the world would be one large cosmos opening up to her in a sequence of exciting scenes, and it now turned out to be very narrow and dismal and impossible to move inside. She continued to go out to the parties but preferred to stay in her bedroom, with the curtains half drawn. Meanwhile she relied on her friends to give her little paraphrases of the texts that were written about her, that were now piled up in her house. The words emerged from nowhere, like insects. It was as if paper wanted to smother every surface – console tables and beds, the counters of bars and the refreshment areas of spas and saunas – and it was a very upsetting feeling. Her house was filled with the stink of paper – vanilla and dusty.

The girl in the stories about her was not a girl she knew.

Celine's education had trained her to please other people. Her mother and father were from a small country across the border. She always disliked her parents' immigrant nervousness and caution. They were intellectual but also anxiously conventional. She was often criticised by them, for her spelling or her arithmetic – in the same way, she presumed, all girls were criticised minutely. They taught her to enjoy the surfaces of things and she had never liked this kind of training, in fact she had tried to reject it. And now it was being argued in these pamphlets written by men that precisely because of this training she was superficial and even dangerous.

It seemed that the other women who found themselves written about in this way didn't mind being public. They just assumed that this was normal or at least irreversible, as if the voices of their parents or the voices in their heads were now operating in the outside world as well, and this was a development anyone could have predicted. So that maybe it was only Celine who found the situation unjust or even terrifying – as if, she once tried to explain, she had suddenly realised that she was living in some story about monsters where it turned out that everything was scripted *by the monsters themselves*. The only form of resistance she had so far imagined, however, was to dress with an increased sense of alertness, her private idea of armour. She'd started to sew little slogans into the sleeves of her dresses – fragments like AS IF or IF YOU MUST – or to add extra folds and loops, multiplying a system of false openings.

In one of these punk outfits Celine now entered the party, and looked around for an ally.

3

Why didn't Celine do more? she often thought. But it was a world, like many worlds, where your power seemed defined by your relations to other people. For a woman, this usually meant your husband. But Celine's husband was Sasha, a minor but murderous fascist – the personal secretary to the chief minister.

She had married Sasha a year ago, when she was eighteen and he was forty-five, and before her wedding she had met him just once, accompanied by their parents and fifteen lawyers. But still, after these early meetings she believed that she loved him. His sense of humour in private was goofy. They both enjoyed playing draughts. But ever since the pamphlets began their conversations had become more difficult. They argued more often, little dialogues about money and sex and time. The more the pamphlets increased, the more separately they lived. Sasha started sleeping at his office. He ordered in food and crates of wine while he had his meetings discussing the ongoing international wars. There was a rumour that he slept with anyone.

In other words, her husband was an absence. And her parents were elsewhere, in the countryside. Her mother wrote her letters, saying how quiet it was and how they were all thinking of her while they did their sewing and their reading. Her father's lectures at the university were being postponed for a semester. In her letters back to them Celine left the pamphlets unmentioned. She couldn't see her parents as a little shelter, something to take with her in any weather. They were something she had left behind long ago. It was as if her loneliness were an object, or as if she had turned into an object and this object was called loneliness. The only constant presence near her was Cato. Cato was chubby, morose and fifteen. He had arrived in town a few months earlier with a diplomatic retinue from an Indian republic, and Celine had asked if he wanted to stay with her as a personal assistant. She had somehow given him the name Cato, and an extravagant salary. He had quickly developed his own way of speaking her language: a kind of patois of his own that mixed high art with unusual mismatches of register. At night Cato worked on his memoirs of the women he observed – notes which he safely left anywhere in the house because no one could read the script in which he wrote or understand the words themselves. And this was lucky, because the illegible words were little insults, questions of relative attractiveness, revolutionary philosophy . . .

Instead of a husband or family, Celine had her friends: Julia and Marta. They messaged each other every hour, small sentences and notes. It was a way of offering each other hope.

The universe disintegrates into a cloud of heat, it falls inevitably into a vortex of entropy, but within this irreversible process there may be areas of order, portions of existence that tend towards a form, in which it might be possible to discern a design – and one of these was this story of Celine and her friends.

4

Celine found Marta beside the ice-cream bar. She showed her a glimpse of the latest pamphlet, which she then concealed very fast in a hidden pocket.

– Oh: *yeah*, said Marta.

They went to hide behind an imported tropical plant, for private conversation.

Celine loved Marta because she was small and intense, her fingernails were often black with mud and paint and other dirt, she had a filthy sense of humour, she had features that were elongated and outsize but also magically alluring, and she smoked even more than Celine did.

This new pamphlet, said Marta, described a list of pornographic affairs between Celine and various celebrity women, government ministers and assorted minor characters. There was also a lot of politics, she continued, like bribery and extortion and a conspiracy against the government. And it ended with an agreement between Celine and several Jewish billionaires to negotiate with foreign powers and take control in America, which they then celebrated, added Marta, in a variety of truly barbaric sexual positions.

Celine thought she might be sick – not so much at any single detail of this picture but because there were so many more images of her in other people's minds than she could bear.

– Don't carry on, she said.

– I mean, that's kind of everything, said Marta.

An empty moon was orbiting at a vast distance from their planet, the same way the conversations continued orbiting.

– I grew up among women, a man interrupted, speaking very close to Celine.

His breath smelled sourly of chocolate.

– I am *hyperalert* to conversations between women, he added.

– But you've never heard that kind of conversation, she said. – By definition.

– But I can try, he said.

Everyone loved pleasure. And perhaps the gruesome man talking to her was sincerely attentive in his feelings towards women, but Celine doubted it. Increasingly, to Celine and her friends, pleasure seemed complicated.

Celine escaped into a side room, which had a few vases arranged on the floor for women to piss in. She began to piss too. It was a difficult operation and some splashed on the rim, staining the edge of her dress.

Someone she loved once said to her: It looks like a party, it feels like a party, it smells like a party. But don't get it twisted. This isn't a party. This is *power*, baby.

Celine started to cry, then stopped herself. Then she went back into the room.

5

The following night, Celine was in her apartment with Marta and Julia. The general climate outside was an intense heat. Celine was in an old vest and leggings. Julia, who tended to wear the costume of the ultra-feminine, was on a sofa, while Marta gave her a new hairstyle with many ties and pins. They were practising their usual hobby – which was trying to understand the world. They sometimes did this with Tarot cards, sometimes with conversation. And Celine was half observing Julia and wondering at her look, the elongated length of her body and her hair and her pale attractive skin, how she disguised herself for men in these floaty dresses when really she should have been standing there with a riding crop or chain.

Then Sasha interrupted, and it was as if all the pleasure disappeared immediately – the way a room disintegrates at the end of a disco party when someone turns the strip lights on and all the plants are crushed.

– The fuck is this? said Sasha.

He had a pamphlet in his hand, and they were all so badly printed and so smudged that it was impossible to see if this was a new one or an old one.

– Is that the most recent one? said Marta.

– Can I speak with my wife? said Sasha. – This is family.

– What's that? said Celine, ignoring him.

– It's new, he said.

– How new? said Celine.

Then Sasha grabbed her by the throat and smudged the pamphlet up beside her face, as if this might help her to read it. It was very rare for so much violence to be so present in a room, it made everything claustrophobic, like they were all crushed up against a wall. He began to recite, or paraphrase – it was impossible to tell. She tried to speak but he was holding her too tightly round the throat and she felt frightened partly because of what Sasha was doing but also because of the violence of the words being quoted at her. She had become used to never hearing the words in which she was described and the effect now was very ugly.

When Sasha finished there was a bright red ragged line around her throat. She tried to pick up an old cigarette from the plate where it was slowly unravelling to ash but her hands were shaking too much. So Marta took this stub and relit it and placed it in Celine's mouth. There was so much tenderness in this little gesture that it made Celine briefly courageous.

– Wait, do you mean that you *believe* this? said Celine.

In reply, Sasha punched her in the face above her cheek. The shock of it was almost as major as the pain inside her eye and her soft skull. She felt unbalanced and understood very vaguely that her legs were failing to support her until she suddenly found herself collapsed on the floor. Very slowly she got back up, holding on to the leg of a sofa, then the silk of its cushion. There was an old Tarot card, lost underneath a chair. Her ear was very sore, she touched it, and there was a light smear of blood on her fingertip.

Sasha was breathing very fast. He said that it was humiliating, or he was humiliated, or she was humiliating: she couldn't hear perfectly and didn't want to ask him to repeat the sentence. For some moments he stood there, breathing. Then he left the room.

Slowly Celine walked over to a mirror. She was also

bleeding from the corner of one eye, and from the retrospect of a long-distant future it would seem to Celine that this moment when her reflection stared blankly back at her was the moment when she discovered the basic law of her cartoon world – that anyone suspended above a void will remain suspended until made aware of her situation, at which point she will fall.

There was a purple mark on her cheek. It was shapeless the way a spider or spit is shapeless.

– Hey, look, said Julia. – Your psychotic husband dropped something.

Then she picked up a piece of paper and handed it to Celine.

6

Celine had always asked herself why she didn't do more. It seemed that everyone assumed there was nothing to be done. But around her many men thought that they could make plans, many men everywhere were plotting and conspiring and making moves, and Celine felt that she should be able to make moves too. She just needed to make calculations.

In the morning Celine received multiple messages from Marta – telling her that she was not unhungover, that she wanted to kill someone, and that she was coming over immediately to discuss their major operation.

Marta had grown up in the outer provinces on an estate in a kind of swamp land. Her father was very rich but dead, her mother was therefore very rich but drunk or depressed or both, and as a child Marta shot rabbits and deer and listened to thunderstorms. Then she was adopted by her aunt, who lived in a larger house in the countryside and taught her the rules of behaviour. When they met, Celine had immediately loved her. She wasn't someone, thought Celine, who would ever *swoon*. Marta was exacting and pitiless and for these qualities alone Celine would have adored her, even without her garish and brutal beauty. Also Marta was extreme in her care for her friends. In a society made of words and images circulating and recirculating, all devoted to disinformation, it was very difficult to find any personal safety, and one minuscule form might just be this intense form of friendship between two women.

– I am going to die, Celine said. – Why doesn't he love me? What am I meant to do?

– You won't die, said Marta.

– What does your husband say? said Celine. – Has he said anything? Did he speak with Sasha?

– You want to talk about my *husband*? said Marta.

– I like the dress, said Celine.

Marta was wearing a very bright outfit, with outsize rainbow sleeves. She looked very young, thought Celine, even though she was older than her. This was possibly their problem – that they were all so very young, or seemed so. To be that young made people think you could be attacked forever. There was so much hatred! It was all there, waiting for them, expressed in strings of words, and maybe this hatred was the reason why they could not see the sunlit cosmos they were expecting, but only corridors and dead ends.

Marta smiled, took off some layers, and ensconced herself in bed beside her friend. There was a stale gateau by the bed which she ate.

– What do I do about these people? said Celine. – I need to do more.

– You can't worry about what misinterpreters think, said Marta.

– But don't you care, said Celine, – when people talk about you? I can't bear it. It feels like death, it feels like a transformation. And then for it to be my *husband* who is angry –

All language was disgusting, said Marta. But people seemed to adore it. It was like how everyone loved reading these novels in letters. As if everything existed in order to end up in words! Whereas most feelings, or at least the most interesting, she said, avoided language entirely. Then Marta leaned over to pour from a bottle into a dirty cup.

Meanwhile the planet continued to be whirled around a zooming sun.

– I want revenge, said Celine.

– You need a handle on them, said Marta. – If you want to scare these men you need something that they want.

– But I don't have anything, said Celine. – My husband hates me. And if I have no husband then I have nothing.

– I'm not like trivialising your pain, said Marta, – but no: I refuse that.

They had the window open. The sound of the courtyards below came up to them: distant parakeets, muffled horses. She had to admit that it was always delicious to lie around in the daylight when the world was working, however depressed you might feel.

– Like: what was in that message? said Marta. – The one he dropped.

– Oh the message, said Celine. – Yeah, the message was from his boss, the chief minister, talking shit about Marie Antoinette. Can you imagine? Also it's written in code. But you know what shows how dopey they are? *It had the cipher with it.*

– Well, said Marta, – so then we have something.

– Why? said Celine. – What can I do with a letter?

– *It's talking shit about Antoinette*, said Marta. – No one talks shit about the first lady. Give it to Ulises.

– Ulises? The little diplomat?

– Sure, the little Portuguese, said Marta. – The one with that funny jutting penis. Sorry, no, the Spanish one.

For a short moment, neither of them spoke.

– Yeah, said Celine. – But we still need more than that. *I need to take control.*

It was so unnerving to lose a world, thought Celine, or even realise that a world could be lost. All the bricks and children and treetops, everything she could see from her window, now seemed remote and distant. In that kind of situation all she had for her survival was whatever was closest to hand. And the persistent pleasure of her life was this back and forth of conversation between friends, perhaps because a conversation was the last remaining place for words to be tender things. She liked the way a conversation could produce unforeseen creatures – concepts she was not sure she believed, or was unaware that she believed – and then suddenly it occurred to her that this beauty of conversation could be improvised for a different purpose.

– What are we best at? said Celine.

Marta raised an amused eyebrow.

– *Talking*, Celine corrected her.

She couldn't leave her husband, because without any money of her own she would be dependent on the hospitality of others. It was true that at any point it was possible to seduce another man and so acquire some influence over him but that seemed a limited and precarious power – to be once again dependent on the whim of a man. Everything therefore, as it always has been for those with no money of their own, and no obvious means of making any, was very confined and limited. But the power that had destroyed her, she was suddenly thinking, might also be the power that could help her too. She had this vision of a group of writers and artists around her who would repay her for entertainment and snacks with their own arguments and fictions – a field of influence, cloudlike and enveloping.

– We need writers, said Celine.

– We don't seem to *have* the writers, said Marta.

– I mean we need *other* writers, said Celine. – We throw parties.

But, worried Celine, it wasn't obvious how she could just throw a party that writers would think was cool. It was always very intricate, the question of cool, and it seemed to interest writers most of all.

– *Writers*? said Marta. – Are you serious right now? Have you never met a writer? We give them alcohol and chicas. We give them *glamour*.

Celine looked at Marta. In the sunlight from the window her old acne scars were more visible. She was very attractive. It was suddenly possible, thought Celine, to feel hopeful.

In the history of the world, said Marta, the most corruptible, the most lethal and most innocent, had always been the writers.

7

There was literature everywhere. The world was a jungle called *writing*. In this world writers became politicians and politicians wrote for newspapers and meanwhile everyone wrote to each other every day, as if an experience were not an experience until it had acquired its own image in words. Words were being printed on newspaper sheets, scribbled on notebook scraps and letters, hoarded in archives, pasted up on walls or bound together in little booklets for distribution in the arcades. The paper they had to use was rough, was heavy and stained and it ripped very easily, but the words themselves, it seemed, were becoming lighter and lighter, quick sketched symbols for catching the universe in a delicate, ineffable net. And the more ineffable a net is the more impossible it is to escape it.

The way this looked in the ordinary world was that everyone was putting on shows, or starting magazines, or developing crazes for particular kinds of writing. Then they went to bars to talk about these shows and magazines, arguing over masthead layouts and font design and the backwardness of current writing. It was the new era of publication, everyone was gradually realising, with amazement, as they walked around in the alleys and woodlands and concert halls – the way you might enter a fashion show and discover slowly and with amazement that the entire decor, even the chair you sit on, is made from flowers. And perhaps from now on there will be no other era – until the solar flares and asteroids at last demolish everything. Stories multiplied very fast, the way germs or spores will emanate from any decaying thing, while outside roamed the calamitous dogs. People wanted to compose their own crônicas, or comment on the writings of other people, only interrupting this writing for more reading, which led to even more writing. It was as if writing was a narcotic or at least an obsession, and no one really thought about the effects of producing so many words – not on those whom the words described, or on those who produced the words, or on a world in which so many words existed.

A world in which writing is everywhere is really a world of reading. Everyone was writing – but this meant that everyone was reading, and then experiencing a deep illness of reading.

And among these words and articles were the libels about Celine and her friends, as well as many other women who found themselves described maliciously as *famous*. Defaming and libelling and stalking and attacking had never been so easy: it was the golden age of psychosis. This writing was all anonymous and the anonymity seemed to confer impunity, like how everyone savaged the house party Celine had been thrown for her seventeenth birthday. It made these writers feel invincible and invisible, and perhaps the two states were the same.

Celine understood all this while still thinking it was disgusting. She had a fear that meaning was shifting, maybe not just shifting but disappearing, and it was happening because there were now no true sources of information. So much information was being put out there in real time, local and non-local information, and all of it was warped. Every sentence extended objects or people beyond their natural habitat, creating images and rumours – the way a shadow might be peeled away from a person and converted into a silhouette.

And yet no one else, by which of course she meant no men, appeared to share her anger, or to appreciate the violence betrayed by this mania for writing. *I mean sure,* they said, if she tried to mention it, *but did you see what they wrote about Antoinette?* It was as if she had been chosen to understand things before other people understood them, precisely by being transformed into deadbeat pornography. To be exposed in this way was to exist in a total abject state – with nothing to protect her from being made up by people less imaginative or intelligent than she was. But this gave her a knowledge that no one else possessed. People seemed to believe that they had the power to determine their own image. They didn't realise, thought Celine, that they were determined by other people and the words of other people.

All the forests and squid and greyhounds had been engulfed by the literary world, the way a serpent will envelop an elephant. This world, of course, exists wherever representations of people are made, and its essence is compromise, terror, vanity, fashion and death – because in the business of representations all value is subjective, and therefore impermanent, and therefore only ever installed by force. But still, the proportions between this world and the other gigantic world are very mobile and delinquent. At any moment, it turned out, the old world could disappear entirely and become little digital strings of symbols, vanishing into the white air.

8

She had planned everything about her first party with Marta and Julia. It took them two weeks. They hired in extra assistants for the night to make drinks or keep bringing plates in from Balthazar, the restaurant three blocks away that everyone liked for its old-school glamour. They made lists of interesting people, they thought about the kind of food you could eat without interrupting conversation. It was an operation and they enjoyed this kind of precise scheming. Like all operations it had its setbacks, of flowers that were sent to the wrong address on the morning of the party, and roadworks that suddenly appeared in front of the house, making the street impossible for vehicles. Then no one could find any ice.

Finally the evening came and Celine sat there on her own with Marta. At first there was just a nervousness in the atmosphere, something tiny but supercharged that made the plates of snacks around them and the bored assistants seem ever so minutely unreal, the way anything seems unreal when the true event hasn't begun – like how people waiting for the boss to join a difficult conference call so that it can start will maintain a sprightly conversation about their children that in fact is anxious and distracted. And when Cato at last emerged to introduce a new arrival it was only Julia, who was family so didn't count as a guest at all.

For some hours the three of them continued to sit there, eating the croissants stuffed with jam that they had ordered. Then they started on the vodka and other spirits.

At about eleven, their first guest arrived. This was Rosen,

a billionaire finance maven. He was a friend of her father, he was said to be Jewish although Rosen himself had never mentioned whether he was in fact Jewish or not, and he lived in the little country across the border because from there it was always easier to move money in and out of different spaces. He was in town briefly and had come to see her, he said. He had no idea that there was a party on. He was delicate and kind and for a moment it was as if her father was there, but somehow transformed into something more solid or more elegant than her real father, and Celine felt hurt by a kind of nostalgia. What always happened when she saw Rosen was that she had to think about his height, because he was tall in a way that she somehow never remembered, so that whenever other people commented on this height she had to redefine her own perception and she wondered if this mismatch was because with other people he could be severe and even brutal, but with her he was only very kind. She was pleased that he was here, she said. He really had only come to say hello, he said. He would just sit in a corner and read.

And he really did. He sat in a corner and took out a book, so that soon it was as if he was not there at all.

Then, just after midnight, the second and also last guest arrived: the celebrated producer Hernandez. Hernandez had a soft good-looking baby face with ever so slightly wild hair. He liked to greet you by taking your face in his hands then kissing you solemnly on the forehead. The effect was somehow horny and paternal and sarcastic, all at once. He dressed beyond his means. Tonight he was in something tight and velvet. He liked women, but most of all he liked conspiracy. He glanced at the empty room, nodded at Rosen, who didn't nod back, then turned to Celine again. It was kind of what he'd suspected, he said. Sasha had been telling everyone that

was thinking that this one was the true one, this one was a fake one. From outside it seemed impossible to understand the reasons for these distinctions.

For instance, said Hernandez, consider the recent careers of two writers: Beaumarchais and Jacob. Jacob was currently a radical philosopher but he also tried scripts and essays and novels too. He was always on the verge of major fame. Somehow it escaped him. They were meant to be friends but Beaumarchais had just written a notorious essay about Jacob, said Hernandez, in which he described Jacob as both cold and cowardly. The purity for which many journalists praised Jacob, wrote Beaumarchais, was really his own pride and fear that prevented him from ever making a move. Celine asked Hernandez if this meant that he liked Beaumarchais more. He wasn't sure, said Hernandez, if anyone could be said to *like* Beaumarchais. He was very clever, but also manipulative. It was often difficult to understand precisely what he was saying because he kind of mumbled. Absolutely devious, selfish, a hustler, he was also capable, finished Hernandez, of great kindness and amiability. Like everyone, he wanted fame.

What he meant, added Hernandez, was that Beaumarchais was basically a void, or maybe a suitcase – whose contents life would gradually unpack.

Celine felt exhausted by the situation she was in, and the failure of her first party, and it was a difficult feeling because it was made of many feelings, not just a sense of fear or lack of safety but also, she knew this, the depression at her vanity being so betrayed.

The next invitation she sent out was to Beaumarchais and his friends.

And so, a week later, a group of unknown writers gathered at Celine's house for her second first party, with the same assistants rehired and the same food transported from Balthazar. These writers did this despite the general fascist disapproval associated with Celine – mainly because they were writers, because they were friends, and because they were so unknown that they were safe from any sense that Sasha's anger could ever hurt them. They all dressed strange – in tennis shoes and dirty shirts, like a person recovering from a long illness.

Beaumarchais was a scriptwriter. His look was broken but hopeful. It often surprised people when they met him how tall and large he was, given how light and miniature his writing appeared. No one would say he was handsome but when he smiled a strange beauty emerged on his face and it was very touching. He was still trying to get his first script made – a little farce of doubles and mistaken identity and unforeseen coincidence. Its production history was upsetting. First the Comedy turned it down, then five other studios. Then Hernandez had taken him on and two weeks later the Comedy messaged that they would maybe reconsider if Beaumarchais could cut the script by twenty pages. After making these cuts the script was sent to the government's censorship bureau, where it had been suspended indefinitely. And there Beaumarchais still was – in development. He was finding it more difficult to get Hernandez to reply to his notes. He kept hearing rumours of Hernandez working with other writers.

It was possible, he thought, that he might die of malnutrition. He was thinking that he was maybe suffering from some inner sickness. He had recently tried to begin journal writing but had stopped because he hated writing as himself, without the multiplication of dialogue.

Maybe this was why Celine liked him, or at least felt sympathy for him. At one point that evening, Celine would remember, forever, she had stood against a wall just listening to the little noise of conversation, observing the group she had gathered. The atmosphere was vagabond and underground, as these men tried to describe unimagined futures or unimagined worlds – and they were very dense, like all group compositions, so that in trying to toggle between them it was difficult to tell where the connections lay. There were just little fragments and clues: *you have to try the narcotics from Martinique – long revolution – it's –*

Everything was departure, leap, cunning, passage, a flight towards the outside.

It was a new style of language for her, and therefore alluring. Beaumarchais, for instance, dolefully explained to her his theory that he couldn't understand why so much effort had been spent in creating him, if that effort was going to be wasted. He was nearly forty, he explained, and he was also a highly precious and fragile being, an object whose creation had required a lot of preparation and education – not only education but travel, even illnesses had been part of this preparation, and he regretted very much that, as she could see, so far this effort had not yielded its potential. He said it with such sincerity and bleakness that Celine realised that she liked him.

– What's the ultimate ambition here? said Celine.

– With me? said Beaumarchais. – It's *on*. Beaumarchais's got something everyone wants, I know it.

– You just need the opportunity, said Celine.

Beaumarchais paused and looked at her with warm devoted gratitude.

– Exactly, he said. – Although first I need a bath and a haircut, and a weeklong nap.

They were obsessed by novelty and originality. They talked violently about everyone else's writing, and she understood that the only thing preventing them from talking violently about the writing of those present was the fact of their mutual presence itself. It was possible that this was only envy and therefore disgusting, but it was also possible that they felt a passionate attachment to literature as an ideal. Maybe, in fact, the two states were the same. They seemed to believe that it might be possible for a work to survive for many years, maybe even forever, as if a work that did not survive was therefore without value, and it was very strange to realise how passionately they believed this, that all value was linked to timelessness. For all of them there was something very romantic in the idea of the future, and they believed that the way of entering a future existence was the production of works. Only a work could exist beyond the timescale of your lifetime. When someone mentioned a novel they were writing Beaumarchais asked if what they were writing was *total all-out writing*. He wanted everything in there, said Beaumarchais, because unless a writer was writing for their life it wouldn't last forever. Someone else interrupted, asking in that case what Beaumarchais thought about form. Oh, form, Beaumarchais replied, he wanted that too. He wanted everything.

It was difficult to tell, thought Celine, if she was acquiring power or not.

II

For some weeks it was just Beaumarchais and his associated crew who came to Celine's house to talk. They all thought of themselves as advanced thinkers, and perhaps in their love of justice they really were advanced – but were unaware that Celine wanted justice most of all. It's always beautiful to be twenty, one of them wrote, much later, in a memoir published after most of them were dead, but to be twenty in this era made people doubly blessed and happy – because to feel that you're forming the future is a very easy form of corruption. The parties they liked were wild. When Celine had imagined this scheme with Marta her vision of these parties was of something elegant and stylish. Instead they always disintegrated into mess and envy and disappointment, floral and striped with failure, and she found that she liked this atmosphere even more.

And then something new began to happen. It was so rare for Beaumarchais and his friends to be part of a scene that they therefore mentioned to anyone they met the large connections they were making. Gradually her parties became a little famous – just famous enough for the celebrity and notoriety to outweigh the danger in people's minds. The room became crowded and acrid. It became difficult to hear what other people were saying. Definitely it was hard to see your friends. You could lose them in the atmosphere. Sometimes you had to just make do with whoever was there, and hope they spoke your language.

An ensemble began to form: something collective and confusing. Into her house came novelists, scriptwriters, starlets, fixers, schlemiels, essayists, collectors, art dealers, academics, agents, librettists, young painters back from travelling, philosophers, singers, scumbag poets. Some of them brought their own food. An émigré soldier from Poland brought his own samovar because, he said, he didn't trust the people here to know how tea was made. It was complicated to speak with him much more because he found the language difficult. He came up to Celine, nodded, and said: *the extreme present*. She found it imprecise or even incomprehensible but also impossible to forget.

It was enchanting and confusing, a park for stories to develop. One night Celine saw Ulises passing by, the little madrileño diplomat Marta had mentioned as a possible useful actor in their plans. Celine whispered something in his ear which in fact he never understood, then took from her dress Sasha's message, with its incriminating talk about Antoinette, and handed it to him – then drifted away, leaving Ulises confused and standing beside a political theorist, in silence, trying to work out how to look at this enclosure from Celine, this piece of paper which he hoped would be some kind of sex message, while the theorist stared at him, morose, his fingers pink with icing from a cake.

When Celine began her parties, she thought they'd be a way of finding writers who would write texts in her defence, or of expressing herself more publicly. She wanted to create her own image so it wouldn't be created by other people. Very quickly she understood that the image strangers had of her was far larger than any image that these writers could invent themselves. But meanwhile she had discovered that inadvertently she had acquired an even greater and more unpredictable power of her own – not a single image but a medium, a place for images to live.

The miniature universe over which she ruled was immensely seductive – the way any nightclub is seductive when only a limited number of people are admitted. On an individual level, people agreed, her parties always seemed to end in catastrophic harm, but collectively they created something beautiful and permanent, because they produced a reality. The conversations created at these parties formed impressions of other people which were indelible, and therefore nothing needed to be *written* at all. Like how one time everybody was drinking until about six in the morning. And when Cato went down to the store to get coffee supplies, Beaumarchais's friend and enemy Jacob stood up and began to recite a monologue from an old script. Even without its sombre beauty it would have been wonderful just for the way he managed to continue, having drunk so much. Jacob was slight and nervous and physically unremarkable and he knew this. He had medium brown hair and a medium nose and medium height and a medium little belly to match. It was a very sad condition for him, he used to lament! He thought it made people not take his writing seriously, this lack of excessive presence, and so he tried to make people ignore this with the drama of his speaking. He was somewhere in the middle of his monologue when Cato returned, whispering that the Americans had just been massacred by the British. When they heard this everyone stood up and left but Jacob, oblivious to the news or simply angry at the loss of his audience, continued to recite. When he fainted – because for the last sixteen hours he had survived on just alcohol and cigarettes – there was only Cato left, who carefully applied a bandage to Jacob's lavishly bleeding head.

So that finally these parties were not just parties for writers and artists but also people who operated in larger areas of the world – business leaders, bureaucrats, insurance backers, fascist enemies of Sasha, bankers, advertising executives, radicals from rich families. Marta and Julia used to stand there listening in the room's heat, with oval sweat marks on the armpits of their dresses and the effect was oddly attractive or at least exciting, thought Celine, who was beginning to enjoy her fleeting sensations more and more. Everywhere inside the room were many words being spoken rapidly.

The party was an art form the way conversation was also an art form, Celine began to think: absolute, demanding – and underappreciated, because it was an art form developed by women. Twenty years later, in upstate New York, destitute and in exile, someone who had also been there said to her that her parties had been so gorgeous because they had been so hyper: everyone talking about border territories and the postal systems and international alliances. She kind of saw it differently, said Celine. Her life at that time, she said, had been a kind of very slow awakening. It was the life of a person waking up and very slowly realising the *setting they were in*.

The parties were night school, said Celine.

12

More time passed, however, and Celine felt her excitement just slightly dissolve. The summer was very hot and it felt like a kind of suspension, as if maybe nothing more could happen or she could achieve no grander effect. It was acceptable, she guessed, but it was also disappointing. Until one evening all this talk suddenly produced Lenoir, the chief of police. It was very magical, this appearance! And she suddenly felt she might have access to the real source.

Lenoir was famous for his repression not only of a city but of himself, but it turned out that this didn't mean he didn't like to watch. And now here he was. He liked to sit alone by the bar, rolling cigarettes. Celine went over to talk to him. He liked to talk about himself, his childhood in the provinces. They were poor but honest and happy, he said. Celine replied that she didn't remember much about her childhood. They weren't rich either, she said. She did remember her mother playing the piano, in a room full of steam from clothes drying on the stove. Exactly, said Lenoir, so she understood. He had put himself through police school by selling scientific magazines. He still went back to see his parents every month.

It seemed that Lenoir liked her.

– I wanted to say, said Lenoir. – I wanted to say how much I support you. The things people write about you. I never believe them.

– Lots of people say that to me, said Celine. – I mean, they say that to me *in private*.

Lenoir seemed upset by her implication.

– If I could do anything, he said. – If I could stop this in any way –

– You're the chief of police, she insisted. – You run this town.

– But they're not *in* this town, said Lenoir. – I mean, the writers.

– So? said Celine.

She seemed to have hurt him, the way men so easily could be hurt by women, like men were peaches. She was used to the situation but it was always unsettling. They looked out over the party together, trying to find peacefulness. A woman was examining a large bruise on her arm, next to her platinum bracelet.

– Do you like it here? said Celine.

– I don't like it anywhere, said Lenoir.

13

It was maybe a week later when Lenoir came back to see her in private. The room was a sweltering twilit cube. It seemed that her image haunted him, that she had made him want to do something for her.

There were many people, he said, who disliked this writing about her, this pornography. He had therefore begun a plan to find the writers who were writing such terrible things. They had noticed certain patterns of distribution in the postal system: little lines between certain booksellers and port authorities. For instance, there seemed to be a particular node of activity coming out of London. They had spies who were saying that there were production centres there. But it was difficult to infiltrate these centres. As soon as one production site was found, a printing press or bookstore, it closed down and reopened somewhere else. So they needed her advice, he said.

– My advice? she said.

It was obvious, however, that for Lenoir this represented a major speech and so he didn't immediately reply. He had brought a giant pale green ice cream as a present. It was already melting and subsiding. He had a matted bandage taped across his forehead. Presumably, Celine thought, it was the kind of thing that happened when trying to maintain a state by violence, whereas the true reason was that the night before, arriving home late from the taxi station, Lenoir in the dark had walked into the jagged corner of a bookshelf he had forgotten about in his new rental apartment, so that there was now a drastic cut above his forehead – drastic but very neat, like he'd been knifed with a stiletto.

– I really hate dealing with literature, he said.

– Who doesn't? agreed Celine.

Her dress felt sticky. A plate of pastries had gone stale. A congealed bowl of pici cacio e pepe was on the floor, being licked by Marta's dog – who Marta had left behind while she went out of town for a while. In packing crates around her was a newly delivered set of porcelain, a series of circles and rectangles, severely painted in an international blue, that was waiting for its arrangements on white shelves. All of this is a way of saying that Celine's thinking was a very abstract cloud in which somewhere she was wondering if perhaps the person she had been needing all along was Lenoir. After all, she wanted revenge that was not just cosmic but also personal.

Lenoir put the warm ice cream to one side.

His plan, said Lenoir, was to send a writer to London: a writer they could trust but also trusted by the pamphlet writers over there. It was why no ordinary police or spook would be useful. The mission was to find the people producing these pamphlets, then buy up every copy and destroy them. The problem, continued Lenoir, was the craziness of writers. They were unreliable. They followed each other's activities in the magazines minutely and also maintained that they only ever worked in isolation. Murderers made more sense to him.

– You should send Beaumarchais, said Celine quickly.

It was as if life was about discovering little meeting points and interfaces between apparently unrelated planes, and one point of intersection right now was Beaumarchais. Beaumarchais? They knew about Beaumarchais already, said Lenoir. He looked disappointed by her suggestion and unpersuaded. Totally, continued Celine. He was a script-writer. He was neither young nor successful. Every writer, therefore, liked him. Also he wanted power and would do anything to acquire it.

– So you should send Beaumarchais, she said.

14

Celine hadn't thought about what other people would do if she became powerful. All her thinking about power had been about how she might acquire some kind of freedom for herself and her friends. She wanted to leave the place expected of her. But now that it was happening she found that it seemed to make her more attractive – new people wanted to know her, but people who had known her for a long time also seemed excited by her in a new way, so that singular events were suddenly happening more regularly and with more intensity.

A few days later, after Lenoir had sent Beaumarchais to London, her old friend Claude came to see her. He was a sci-entist who travelled to distant countries to collect material.

His experiments and theories had brought him into a long dialogue with Celine's father. Celine had therefore known him forever, since Celine was twelve and Claude was twenty-five. He had spent the last years travelling on a voyage into the Pacific Ocean. And now he had returned to the city, famously accompanied by Titere, an emergency interpreter he had befriended on one of the islands he had visited, who was now an exotic and super-charming celebrity.

As soon as Claude came back from this latest trip he came to see her, and it was interesting because she had always felt nervous with him but now it seemed that he was nervous with her. He wanted, Claude said, to see what her parties were like – but he arrived on the wrong day, when there was no one else there. As always, she liked his wildcat energy, however much she found him unreliable. Claude was never stationary. He was restless, perverse, melancholy. He was constantly surprising in his information from elsewhere.

There was something he was unable to stop thinking about, said Claude. He wanted to tell her this story because he couldn't understand it, but maybe she would understand it. At one point in his latest journey he arrived at an archipelago, in the middle of the ocean. It seemed that they had interrupted some kind of violence between different groups on the island, or even entire different islands. It was very unsettling, just being there. He had wanted to leave immediately. Then just before they left, said Claude, a strange event had happened. A woman chose a man and young girl, explained something to them, then led them both onto the beach, in front of Claude and his sailors, where the man lay the young girl down and began to undress her. This girl showed no enthusiasm. Her face displayed no expression.

Meanwhile the woman stood on a high platform strewn with vetiver canes, while looking at a group of islanders, who were standing at a little distance, in the surf. The air was a kind of powder blue, and the line of the horizon was a green blur on the sea. Then the man lay down on the girl. They made no noises of pleasure. There was just a general seriousness, and a continuing unease. He had tried to talk about this with Titere, but Titere would not help him. Titere had only said that any meaning Claude thought he'd perceived wasn't accurate or even possible. In fact, added Titere, said Claude, he didn't think the meaning was intended for him or his sailors at all.

Claude had arrived with a bottle of spirits and a present, wrapped in a linen scarf, and with Celine he was drinking the spirits hard.

Did she understand this? Celine wasn't sure. It seemed that she couldn't presume to understand at all.

But before she could continue to think about his story Claude became distracted by the present he had brought her, which he handed over excitedly – and she extricated from the cloth a small but deadly fish hook, made of bone and metal, delicately engraved. He had been given it as a present himself, said Claude, by Titere, his friend from the islands. And now he wanted her to have it, as his own gift from him. It was ceremonial, he said. It had its own power.

The fish hook was surprisingly heavy in her hands. Immediately she loved it, the way some objects make you love them and want to look after them. She put it on a cushion, then poured herself another drink.

It was as if the hook had some uncanny aura. Her mind was becoming very light and very agile in the presence of this object from another world, as if the object were an antenna. When you are young, she was gradually thinking, everything you know is only known through pictures, but you grow up assuming that gradually you will see everything for real – and it takes a long time to realise that in fact most things, like volcanoes or tigers or planets, will never be known for real at all. And she wanted the real most of all.

So that although she was in general finding the idea of a man's body difficult and appalling it also now occurred to Celine that what she wanted to do was find out what Claude felt like. She moved towards him then kissed him. It was as if it was hardly Claude she wanted, however much she liked him, but a particular sensation of her own, something private and so far inaccessible. Shyly, Claude tried to resist. He wasn't sure, he said. He liked her so much. So unless she was serious about this he wasn't sure. Celine told him not to talk. Then she undressed him as minimally as necessary. Beside them was the deadly fish hook. For a vertiginous moment she imagined it was the other way round, and it was Celine entering his body, pushing something inside him.

Then everything ended very fast.

Afterwards, she tried to think about her feelings. She felt very exposed and sensitive. There were many worlds inside a world, and she wanted to understand these worlds. This was maybe because she was so aware of her difficult position in what seemed to be an increasingly giant network. She was very aware of her own complicity, but she was also very aware of her own powerlessness – and the complication this caused made her long for a kind of passionate precision in her thinking. She didn't want to be casual, she didn't want to be cool – the way she liked Marta's husband for his scientific collection, the serious way he went about it. He had recently begun a correspondence with George Washington, Marta had told her – not so much because of Washington's revolutionary politics but because Washington had promised to send him some bones from a giant animal that he had found in the American forests. He thought this discovery seemed to represent a deeper revolution, and from the perspective of a universe, thought Celine, it was possible that he was right.

15

Celine was a woman who was moving further away, she was the woman who leaves. But it would be wrong to think that this movement was easy or unhampered. All the time she was making her first moves into a new world, or new space, her old life continued to stick to her! – the way a gallant fly will feel its legs tugged back by flypaper.

One night her husband Sasha entered what was once their house, uninvited. Celine was in her pyjamas, talking to Marta. It was the first time Sasha had come to see Celine in some weeks. In this period of scandal and myth he had avoided her completely – sleeping on a sofa in his office.

He was wearing a kind of dark green dressing gown or cape – so dark it looked black, like a sorcerer. It was very beautiful and also made him look wild. Celine asked him about this get-up. Sasha said he was very anxious. He didn't think about clothes. Who ever thought about clothes? Then he changed the subject abruptly.

– So you're fucking Ulises now? he said to Celine.

– Ulises? The one from Madrid? I mean he's very *sweet* –

– I knew it.

– I'm not fucking Ulises. Why are you even mentioning this?

– Yes, why, said Marta, – are we talking about Ulises?

– Because he just destroyed me, said Sasha, – along with the chief minister.

– Define destroyed, said Celine.

– Sacked, kaput, fucked, said Sasha.

– It's probably just a little rumour, said Marta. – *Why do you always believe all this?*

– What do you mean rumour? I just came from the office, said Sasha.

– And both of you are sacked?

– Totally, he said.

No one spoke for some seconds. The presence of the room around them became a pressure of decoration. They were surrounded by the new porcelain service, which had now been taken out of its crates but was piled on various pieces of furniture, still waiting to be put away on shelves: the side plates and dinner plates, dessert bowls and soup bowls, coffee cups and saucers, tea cups and saucers, double-handed cups, jugs with covers, jugs without covers, milk jugs, tureens, ice pails, sugar bowls, tea pots, tea canisters . . .

– But how, said Celine, – could Ulises destroy you? Who listens to Ulises?

– Because, said Sasha, – the chief minister was so stupid he talked shit about Antoinette. Like thirteen seconds before she is about to become the Queen.

– To Ulises? He talked shit about her to Ulises?

– About her *acting*. And not to Ulises himself. It was in a message. He wrote a message saying that if Antoinette tried *very* hard she might be able one day to become a mediocre actor.

– Which is kind of funny.

– He messaged that to Ulises? asked Marta.

– *No*, said Sasha. – In a message which Ulises showed to Antoinette. And Antoinette, who wants to show that no one can fuck with her, showed that no one could fuck with her.

– I mean, said Marta, slowly, talking to Celine, – is it possible that Ulises is in love with you? Ever since you let him lick your –

Sasha stepped forward and savagely upturned a table with six piles of plates, which shattered into irregular mess. It was as if all the air was terrified. Very quietly Marta continued with a dreamlike poise:

– I was going to say *gelato*, said Marta.

Then Cato came into the room, worried by the noise, and was immediately too scared to speak.

– Oh what, you're going to protect her too? said Sasha.

– If I can, said Cato.

His response was modest and therefore beautiful, and it made Sasha lose his sense of his own rage. He just felt very suddenly tired and bewildered by the world, which is a state that can happen very often to a person. He stood there, silent and immobile – while Celine and Cato and Marta contemplated the scene they had just been forced to be part of without asking or even anticipating its possibility.

– But I don't understand, said Celine. – Why are you blaming me?

For a long time no one spoke.

– I lost a message, said Sasha. – It wasn't to Ulises. It was to me. And I lost it.

Idly he picked up another plate and dropped it. He watched this splintering and destruction without animation.

– So now I'm in exile, he said.

– It's just your house, said Celine.

– No, said Sasha. – You don't understand. I can't stay in town, they said. I have to leave town by tonight.

For a long time no one spoke again.

– Do we both have to go? said Celine.

Sasha was very dejected, all his catastrophic rage had gone – and the strangeness, thought Celine, was that this had made him even less likeable, not more, especially in his gothic witchy outfit.

– Do you want to? he said.

– I mean, no, said Celine.

– Then, no, said Sasha.

He paused before he spoke his final sentence.

– I know it was you, he said. – And I will *ruin* you, my darling.

16

Was it strange that Celine felt hyper? The danger she was in made her terrified but it also electrified the circuits. And in fact the more danger she found herself in the more she wanted something larger than just survival.

Malice and misunderstanding constitute every universe, she thought. We say *an innocent misunderstanding* when really all misunderstandings are deliberate. It's very rare to make the effort to understand someone. Most of the time we are angry and dejected and will not understand another person at all, not even in correspondence with someone we love – so that often it's only much later, maybe many years later, when searching through the archive of your messages for something else, that you reread an old postcard and only then realise the hurt a person was trying to express, the love they were offering. No one knows anyone, or at least they try not to. Instead of conversation we have rumour, boato, opinion, journalism, prejudice, gossip: all the forms of language that have no weight at all. And the longer you spend among gossip, which is for most of us the only language we will ever know, the more you inhabit a new realm that has still not been explored enough by philosophy: a realm of neither appearance nor reality but something shimmering and melting, the way the air begins to melt above the tarmac of some desert road. For once you have abolished the true world, as Julia once argued drunkenly at a party, then what world remains? The apparent one perhaps? No! Because with the true world you have also abolished the apparent one. And that makes everything more confusing and much softer.

It now seemed to Celine that if she wanted to survive then everything depended on manic activity. Her desires were expanding. The old systems were dying out but Celine felt that there was nothing to take their place. So people were running in many directions at once. Some people chose timelessness, and these were the artists. Some people wanted power, and these were bankers or politicians. Others wanted the future, and these were visionaries. Whereas the move she wanted to make was to inhabit the present moment as urgently as possible.

But the more she thought about her moves the more the

depth of the force against her was revealed as unexpectedly vast. When she had begun this process she had thought she only needed to resist the pamphleteers and their pornography, but it seemed that the problem was much wider than she had ever imagined: not just hack writers and fascist husbands but an entire arrangement of men talking.

Around Celine that season people continued to talk and talk, and the conversation was always male violence or the prospect of male violence. A new trend was to lock wives away in the country, totally alone, to stop them seeing other people. Of course it was agreed that this was barbaric, but how barbaric were the people who complained about such barbarism! Men everywhere talked about universal values while it seemed that the only universal stories were stories of women being killed or beaten or raped or abandoned. The case that everyone was talking about was a murder trial where an immigrant housekeeper had savagely killed a businessman in self-defence, after he assaulted her when she resisted his attempt to rape her. It seemed very obvious to Celine that no man had the right to judge this woman, however crazed her murder had been, since she was part of a system that was organised by men themselves. Those on whom injustice had been visited forever could not be forced to keep to a certain moral code, and certainly could not be held to that code by the people who caused the injustice. Just as they could not be criticised for moments when they were complicit in what they purported to attack: the way Julia once confessed to her how much she liked it when men hurt her in bed. All resistance would naturally have to borrow from whatever it attacked. But if she ever said this, even to radical intellectuals or poets, they gently explained to her that this was against all moral reason, and that the woman who savaged the businessman was a psychopath who should be eliminated forever.

There were stories that happened to you that could therefore only get told to other women. One night, for instance, in this era when it seemed that day followed day without any difference in temperature or colour, just a total burning haze, and there was no news from Beaumarchais in London, Celine had dinner with Hernandez. She told this story only to Marta and Julia. This was in a restaurant near the river, a maze of little booths and private rooms. Hernandez had written to her, saying he had a proposal. She had tried to meet for coffee one morning. He had said he was too busy. It had to be at night. Hernandez began by saying how much he loved her parties. They were a new kind of world, he said. She was basically a producer, like him. So he thought, continued Hernandez, that they should do something together – perhaps co-host a series of performances, a series of rehearsed readings with star actors. Celine had no interest in this proposal, the business of actors and the outside world either bored her or perplexed her, but she also felt that she needed to politely pretend that it was intriguing. Before she could invent a sentence, however, Hernandez leaned forward to kiss her, so she wildly tried to talk to him about his suit. Instead he held her arm as if to restrain her. It was a very scary situation. She could feel herself ageing or becoming adult and the sensation was upsetting, this feeling of experience gathering inside her body, never to be erased. Please, she said. She didn't want to have to say what she was going to say. Hernandez looked at her with absolute surprise and curiosity.

– Say what? said Hernandez.

– That we are never going to sleep together, said Celine.

However much she meant it she regretted the violence of

this sentence, and would have tried to soften or reduce it, if there had been any way of doing so.

Hernandez stood up. He was very agitated.

– You think you're so unique? shouted Hernandez. – Don't be so fucking pious.

It was very abrupt, the way he changed from elegant to violent, she said to Marta and Julia, when telling this story. And she felt absolutely vulnerable, however much she had been right to reject him, like she was being threatened by a larger power.

All Celine could do was wait for Beaumarchais and Lenoir. But the overall problem, it seemed, the total situation, was much larger than anything Beaumarchais or a police chief could solve. It was a system that expanded. And there seemed to be no immediate solution for a system.

17

This of course took place in a time when everything was happening at the same time, because everything was being connected to everything else by little networks that were voracious and expansive, but not everyone had understood this. Celine was beginning to understand this, some others were understanding this, but many people continued to believe that what happened was happening only to them.

Little systems, however, were expanding everywhere, creating related effects. In America, the Americans were trying to kill the British while also trying to kill some Iroquois and others. But to kill as many British as they wanted to kill, the

Americans needed the Iroquois as allies. There were therefore many crisis meetings, and on the outcome of these conversations which were also negotiations many possible futures depended, not only for the people who seemed most directly involved but also people who at that moment never thought that such events could be relevant to them at all. One of these was a meeting that took place in a forest near the Ohio River, in an overcrowded cabana, between George Washington, an American general, and Louis Cook, a Mohawk chief. Its subject was the future of what some people called America and others called the great hunting grounds. Rain had fallen all day. Inside it stank of goat hides, steaming. Washington was asking for a hundred Indian troops to help in his jungle war. They were there to discover Louis Cook's conditions.

In between them was Montour, the interpreter. Montour was a mischling: half French and half Mohawk. He spoke five languages, including English. Like so many people, Washington had been surprised by Montour's look when he first met him, the way someone can often be surprised when having to correct the virtual image they may have formed of someone else in correspondence. This often happened to Montour. His name seemed French, and in some ways he was French, since his father was a French fur trader, but his mother was Mohawk and so Montour looked Mohawk too.

If he sent the hundred troops, said Louis, said Montour, he wanted the settlers to end their claim on the hunting grounds west of the Hudson. Washington found it difficult to understand why Louis wanted land so much, said Washington, said Montour. They never *farmed* it. The elks, replied Louis Cook, very slowly, were their horses, the buffaloes were their cows, the deer were their sheep, and the whites would never have them. Washington asked Montour what he was saying. It was difficult, said Montour. Then Louis asked to have a private conversation with Montour. They stood at the porch, in the fine rain. The chief was very alive and beautiful, in full blue make-up streaked with red, even if his hairband was a little grimy and his hair was a mess. He wanted Washington to know that the whites were crazy, he said. Recently, seventeen white men rode on horses into a Mohawk village and made for the cabins. Only some women and children were present, because the men were out hunting. First they burned down the huts. Then they killed the women and children. *Civilisation or death* was their slogan, said Louis Cook. Now, if the law were really the law, then the laws would have stopped these people. But they did not. So why should he believe them? What, for instance, about Sycamore Shoals?

They went back into the room. Montour paraphrased all this for Washington. What happened at Sycamore Shoals, replied Washington, said Montour, was in no way his idea. But still, said Louis Cook. These motherfuckers. Washington asked what Louis had just said. Montour replied that it was nothing. Washington, who was easily irritated, began to shout that he needed to know everything they were saying.

Montour was understanding something that Celine, along perhaps with some other small groups of people on this planet, was also understanding. Increasingly in this world, which was a world of expanding systems, Montour disliked his job as an interpreter. He was always having to find a way of paraphrasing, a form of words acceptable to everyone. But he could not. Even the names were impossible. For instance, he had always known the man whom Washington called Louis Cook as Akiatonharónkwen. It made the job very stressful. Washington asked if Louis had also remembered about the bones. Montour didn't understand. The mastodon bones, explained Washington, they found out in the Dry Lick Spit. The ones he wanted for his research. Montour tried to explain this to Louis, who asked why this killer was talking to him about bones. Forget about the bones, said Montour, in Kahnawake.

For a long time, everyone paused. Louis Cook felt lonely, which was a feeling he disliked. What he missed was solidarity. To choose a loyalty was always very hard. Finally, he agreed that they had a deal. As they walked away, he said something to Montour. Washington asked what he'd said. Montour paused, then he translated.

Akiatonharónkwen feared for the future, said Montour.

18

The more power Celine acquired, the more she realised how little she actually had. It was possible, she was discovering, to have power in one context and in another context to have none. To make moves was a very delicate process.

To resist inside this world was too precarious, it seemed, without the protection of a major influence. Power was a collaboration, it was a series of abstract causes and delayed effects – and because this was true, she said one day to Marta, she was starting to think that they needed to make a new move. Even if Beaumarchais came back from London successful, it would never be enough. There would always be violence against them. A new move like what? said Marta. She always felt excited listening to Celine talk because it made her feel that perhaps the world was more available to them and more open to their engagement. It made her hopeful, and she liked hope above all.

Now that the chief minister was gone, said Celine, there was an opening. It was maybe urgent to make the new chief minister someone from their entourage. This all sounded super political, replied Marta, who wasn't expecting such thinking from her friend. She was impressed and almost afraid because it was like she could see her friend hardening in front of her, becoming something unexpected and therefore requiring effort to reimagine. But this was the kind of thinking they now required, said Celine. The true business of self-defence was detailed and long term and exhausting.

For a long while Marta thought about this. She wanted to be equal to her friend and her new hardness. The problem was, she pointed out, that while they knew many people, there were very few who could be said to be their friends. There were very few who could be trusted. And most of these were writers. But what did she think of Rosen, the finance expert? said Celine. It was true that he was the only person they knew who had true success in the adult world, but maybe he was perfect. He was sincere and generous and intelligent, but at the same time he seemed to terrify many men. His height was very impressive. Also, she was thinking, very lightly, without even perhaps knowing how deeply she was feeling this at all, it was as if Rosen were the kind of adult she had always wanted to live among, in her dejected childhood. She loved this idea, said Marta. But then the problem, continued Marta, was how to get him the job. The options were restricted. Their power was all verbal.

– But isn't that enough? said Celine.

Men might have the luxury of plotting with large gestures, with international travel and arms deals, she said. But their own plotting could be equally effective even if it seemed much subtler because they had this medium of their own that was liquid but explosive. And very softly, almost floating, that's how gently the thought emerged, she remembered Hernandez's idea for script readings and performance parties.

They should remember that they owned a scene, she said – and a scene was always alluring to other people. So they should put on a script read. Marta said that she was confused. No but listen, said Celine. What did Antoinette love more than anything? Marta replied that it was kind of obvious she loved sex more than anything. But apart from that, said Celine. Dressing up, said Marta. Role play. And, said Celine, Rosen was always secretly financing scripts. He loved literature more than the deals he did with governments and companies. Therefore, she added, with all the excitement of a major inspiration, this was how they could bring Rosen and Antoinette together. They could act in a script read together, she said, and begin a conversation about scriptwriting, which was what they both loved more than anything, more than love, more than money. Then afterwards Antoinette could do the rest herself, in the board meetings and appointments committees. They just needed, said Celine, to find the right script – but then she was interrupted by a wetness on her slipper and looked down, to see Marta's dog squatting on her haunches, leaving long flat flanks of piss on the carpet in a purely absent-minded fashion, as if she were entirely unaware of the liquid emerging from under her stomach. She looked at Marta, who shrugged.

– She's an animal, said Marta. – She doesn't understand what *inside* is.

Celine tried to concentrate. Beside her were Beaumarchais's reports from London, in his surprisingly beautiful handwriting. What about Beaumarchais, she said, and his banned script? Marta worried that they had no idea if Beaumarchais could write. Had she read his script? Celine shrugged. Maybe there was a reason why it was always in development? She wasn't sure, Celine replied, if anyone could write at all.

Marta smiled, smoothed away a grain of mascara under Celine's eyes.

– You're the belle of the ball, said Marta.

And it was like the atmosphere between them shimmered, felt Celine, the way it shimmers when anything begins to emerge into existence.

19

It seemed that the universe wanted to adapt to this new form they were creating, and give it a home. After a series of beautiful days Lenoir arrived to announce that the pamphlets were over.

Celine and Lenoir went out walking beside the river. The river was a colour. The sky was another colour too. This was what Celine was concentrating on. Meanwhile Lenoir told her the story of how Beaumarchais had done what he'd done in the city across the ocean, and as he spoke he gave her a letter from Beaumarchais where Beaumarchais wrote confused but interesting sentences about how he had begun to believe that what was happening here was in fact a possible and dazzling future for all writing, as if out here in this city words were becoming completely immaterial, with no reference to the real at all, and the images they conjured up were just a mirage, something exorbitant and immaterial too.

All the pamphlets had been burned, said Lenoir. And the connection who had put them onto the producers of these pamphlets – this was the strangest aspect of the story, he said – was an ex-diplomat of their government, who was famous for refusing to say if they were a he or a she. People had tried to find out an answer to this question, apparently, said Lenoir, but without success. Now, various events had led the previous government to see this person as a danger, Lenoir continued, and forbid them to go back home. For a while they had therefore lived in exile, acquiring a beatnik fame because of their ungendered attitude and also because of their poetry, little lyrics that were copied and pasted from person to person. But now this person wanted very much to come back, which was why they had approached Beaumarchais with a deal. In exchange for information on the writings against Celine and all her friends, they wanted permission to return across the ocean and live from then on very simply as a woman.

– It doesn't sound such a crazy story to me, said Celine.

There was a loud noise across the river. Together they looked for it in the buildings opposite. It was just a man on an opposite roof, shooting pigeons with a pistol.

– It doesn't? said Lenoir.

– Not at all, said Celine.

And then they carried on walking.

It was very important to feel happiness, thought Celine, at least when you were able to feel happiness. And this surely was a moment when you might feel that something in the way the universe was organised was being altered in her favour, at this discovery of the pamphlets' destruction, and of her anonymous unknown ally being a person who wanted to think differently about the situation everyone was in, of having a body that other people wanted to own or at least define.

The river was turquoise. The sky was light green and pink. It was very beautiful, and it made her hopeful, as if she could begin activities that she had never begun before, and she felt that more activities would always be possible, in a long and unbroken chain.

20

That evening Celine and Marta opened some fizzy wine which they started drinking from the bottle. Outside there was a tropical rain, making every leaf silken. It was the kind of moment when in the ponds there are frogs emerging with their gelatinous eyes, blinking in the grey light. Everywhere was warm and raining and it made the world inside feel delicate and lovable. An object was a unique and battered thing, inside a drenched environment.

Celine nestled her head on Marta's lap. And Marta draped her own head down, stroking her. Everything was friendly and intimate and accessible.

More and more it seemed to Celine that her conversations with friends were the opposite of conversations with men, where there was always some imbalance of power – whatever other distinctions might be operating – so that as a woman, however much you might have been amused by the man you were talking with, like Claude or even Beaumarchais, you were always having to make sure that you were *likeable*. Celine preferred conversations where there were no constraints at all, and it seemed that if you were a woman then these could therefore only happen between women, and not even all women but only a certain few.

The conversations she liked above all were her conversations with Marta. So perhaps it shouldn't have been a surprise if something extraordinary came out of them, this feral closeness and adaptability.

– Your eyebags are huge, said Marta. – You need some sleep.

– Eyebags are sexy, said Celine.

Marta, with the bottle in one hand, offered her a miniature mirror. Celine stared into it.

– They don't look sexy, said Celine.

And as she said this Marta bent down to kiss her.

It was a modest movement but as soon as it had happened it seemed vast in its implications – but then that's something that happens on this planet, things seem impossible before they happen but then as soon as they have in fact happened they acquire a dense little thicket of meaning and future thinking. Celine's lips felt dry and it was a strange sensation, the difference between the wetness of her tongue and the dryness of her lips. Marta looked into Celine's eyes and Celine could smell her, in a way she felt she had never smelled her before. It was very puzzling, to feel this close to another person, to know them as intimately as she knew Marta, and then to add this kind of physical closeness too. It was at once deeply logical and also uncanny.

They kept on kissing. Then she felt the way Marta's fingers

were touching her, just moving slowly up from her thighs to between her legs, and wanted to repeat what Marta was doing but in reverse, to her.

With Marta she always loved how conversation was so easy, and it seemed that this way, with fewer words, was no different. Everything was a game with insides and outsides. She found that she was pressing against Marta, leaning a hand on her shoulder for support. It was amazing that this kind of pleasure was so available, that they had been living adjacent to it for so long. For a moment she was worried that she might be ashamed – of what she was doing or her own smell, this fragility between two people. Then Marta withdrew her fingers, licked them, grinned. And Celine grinned lavishly too.

What she liked, said Marta, touching her gently between the legs, after they had finished, was the way the hair between her legs went kind of brittle with wetness as it dried. Then she pressed Celine's hand there and did not let it go, and it was as if, thought Celine, with this gesture or this scene they had decided to construct something delicate and precarious but also apparently invulnerable – the way a wasps' nest seems invulnerable, when it's just made out of paper held together with saliva. It was fragile but it was new – and novelty, it turned out, might be a major form of potency. Because no one could destroy something that they themselves couldn't imagine.

21

Meanwhile the performances in theatres and the novels and the epic poems were becoming more and more violent. It so happened that the common obsession of all these art forms was women and it seemed that this wasn't without meaning, since in general all conversations between women about men were developing a new tone: amazed but also irritable. In these conversations they often found themselves discussing a new theory that was being called a theory of the *libertine*. The men believed that they were trying to invent an ideal of pleasure and they thought that this ideal found its expression in novels, in letters, or dialogue, a place where every voice could be heard.

These men thought that they were radical but to Celine it felt like it wasn't enough, or was inconsistent – as if the ideal of transparency concealed something malign. To be a woman had always been to be trapped, but however terrible this condition was it had also been a kind of safety – you were trapped but also cosseted, the way a flute is fitted in its velvet case. And to now try to emerge from that trap turned out to be a trauma of a greater dimension. For of course Celine understood the theory she was supposed to follow. She too wished to pursue happiness in every way possible, but if you didn't want to pursue the desires of other people, and by people she meant men, very quickly this was seen as evidence of puritanism or even misanthropy, and you were suddenly accused of cruelty, as if the very fact that a man felt something for you conferred an obligation to you to nurse him through the pain *because you had caused it*, when of course it was entirely controlled by him. It was true that with Claude she had found a possibility of conversation, because after the one time they had slept together they had been able to establish gently and charmingly that it would never happen again, after she had hesitated when Claude approached her at a party with a drink.

– I know, I know, said Claude. – What's a woman?

– Is this a joke? said Celine.

– Someone who has to say no to men every day, said Claude.

He said it so charmingly that from then on they could like each other without desire, and this perhaps was the best state to achieve with a man.

Still, often now, when everyone thought they were writing about desire and lightness and pleasure when in fact they were writing about pain, Celine felt murderous. One day, reading a new magazine set up by Jacob, his new venture devoted to the urgent and contemporary after the failure of his scripts and poems and philosophical articles, Celine had a premonition.

– Let me explain, she said to him. – I know you want the most modern picture possible. I want it too. But that means I want spaceships and radical politics. And most of all I want the perspective to change. Perhaps also some jokes. Now: *is that too much to ask?*

The fact that Jacob seemed unable to understand was depressing but somehow less depressing than it might have been before, because she was now able to construct a little rickety space of her own, separate from these traps and disasters, which was the space she was constructing with Marta – small scale and improvised. She understood that to many people, maybe everyone, what they were doing would seem perverse, but she disagreed. There was much more perversity, she thought, in all the varieties of abjection men and women developed between each other.

Marta and Celine used to hang out quietly in the countryside. The countryside was always there. It was a place of pleasure. They lay beside a lake, at the foot of trees on soil they shared with invisible mushrooms pushing through the earth. Leaves were little plastic structures in the sky. By the water it was almost noisy: weeds impeded the water's slight movement and made eddying scurries and lifts, while within each tree invisible animals made flourishes and forays. Everything was an arrangement of small voices. And yet, she thought, it was also called silence, because none of the noises were made by people.

The less language they used, or the more they just used language as an amusement, the more happiness they produced. In the light mornings they played a game they had invented, a little thing with words and images. Marta picked up one of the magazines and would show Celine a picture, hiding the surrounding words, and Celine would offer a line to go with it. For instance, a naked man stuck in a window, trying to escape from a bathroom window:

– Feelings? Fuck them, said Celine.

Or a woman talking to a man, naked, from the tousled sheets of her bed:

– You are not a beauty queen, she said.

It was very interesting, watching what the words did to the pictures. Something happened between the two which was neither the picture nor the words but both of them at once.

Celine had lived in a certain kind of world for so long, and to discover a way of rejecting it was both surprising and refreshing – like the way, she once told Julia, you push open a door to discover there's been a rainstorm, and you step out into the amazingly rinsed and electric world.

Their other game was telling their own story to each other.

How did this begin? asked Marta. Celine said that they met at a party, where Marta observed that everything wrong in the world was because of the miseducation of girls, and Celine had thought she seemed so cool. But then what happened? asked Marta. Then they became friends, shrugged Celine, and everyone was always talking about Marta, and that boy, the one with the terrible eye problems. No, it was the dress store, interrupted Marta. They were at the dress store, continued Celine, agreeing with her, they'd been looking at dresses and were waiting for a taxi, it was snowing, the snow was almost black, and Celine had asked if Marta was ever upset by things people said about her, and she'd said no, because no one should ever rely on the affection of other people.

They lay there, talking, sometimes licking each other's faces very delicately. Celine's breasts were micropebbled from the breeze. And sometimes Marta bent down and kissed Celine and each time Celine would think how mysterious it was, this moment when two people moved across little borders or assumptions, the way this friendship also sometimes involved their bodies, too. It required great delicacy to move across these little borders.

– Why do you like me? she said. – I'm basically thirteen. I'm not wearing any socks today. *I woke up and couldn't find any socks.*

And Marta shook her head subtly no, then they began to kiss again and touch until Marta finally looked away so she could concentrate and even while this was happening Celine thought how much she loved this very neat selfishness in the way Marta acted sexually, and did not mind it because it was with the same concentration that she thought about other people. And Celine thought that if there would ever be a true theory of pleasure and of a person who understood pleasure then in some way this would be it: a person who could think with equal ferocity about the pleasure of another person and their own.

22

The working title of Beaumarchais's script that had been so rejected and rewritten it was as if it had developed its own feelings and history, full of loneliness and misunderstanding, was *The Useless Precaution*. As soon as Beaumarchais came back to town Celine asked him for a meeting – to persuade him to let her put on a reading of this script, privately, for their friends.

She made this proposal in her house's soft interior. Little candles spilled orange light in semicircles over the patterned carpets and the ornamental plants. Beaumarchais reached for a doughnut on a porcelain plate but realised that he was sitting very deeply on the softest sofa he had ever known, so that the plate was ever so slightly too far away and to reach it he had to push himself forward through a slowness of cushioning. It added to his sense of disorientation.

Her plan, she explained, was to put the play on here, in this room. Beaumarchais looked around, at the candles and begonias and the mirrors. With Antoinette and Rosen, she added, the most powerful woman and the richest man, in the main parts.

Everything was warm and aromatic and clean in this house and at the same time forest-like. It was all very exciting and confusing to Beaumarchais. He really did believe in art as something that was pure and perhaps even holy, it hadn't bothered him that no one understood or liked the way he wrote, even as it was also true that this hurt him very much. He had grown used to the hurt and the indifference coexisting. The settings in which art had to develop, this cold and eternal thing, were always so much warmer and more charming than the art perhaps ever wanted. And Celine understood Beaumarchais's confusion and also wanted to soothe him. She wanted to do something for him, she said, after what he had done for her. Her basic principle was that you should always help your friends. And she meant this sincerely, however much she had her private crowd of other motives.

Timidly Beaumarchais asked if someone should first discuss this with the censorship bureau. Or even, maybe she might want to read the script first. What if she hated it? he asked. And of course, he added, he would always be very open to any rewrites she might suggest. Rewrites! said Celine. She really felt that people had no idea what a rewrite involved. In her opinion, said Celine, people in his business talked too easily about rewrites. Oh but exactly, said Beaumarchais, who liked her very much. A rewrite sounded like a simple technical exercise but in fact required the highest philosophy. It required definitions of the continuous and the discontinuous, not to mention ethical definitions as well. For instance, any rough definition of integrity would surely mean that a writer should refuse to alter a text they had written for any other reason than their own personal taste. *And yet*, he continued, not wanting to seem too definite, maybe this was too old-fashioned. Perhaps other people could collaborate too, the way he saw Celine as his collaborator? For after all, he finished, there was also something beautiful about rewriting a text again and again, working on it for so long until suddenly its essence became clear: a present moment that required so much time to reveal itself.

It was a confused speech, and Celine liked it for its confusion, because the confusion was the sign of a basic message: that Beaumarchais was wonderfully excited. As so often in a conversation the meaning just leaked out of it, the way milk spreads from a nipple. And Celine was right, but perhaps it is also important to mention that something else was happening inside Beaumarchais's soul, minutely but savagely. He had a very pure soul but also such a yearning to be known that occasionally his soul would find itself in very impure landscapes. As she mentioned Antoinette and Rosen, these celebrities and their vast power, he could suddenly and helplessly imagine triumph, people adoring him, *so much money* – maybe even a house in the country. He pictured a dinner many years later, where a committee member at the Comedy would admit to him that turning that script down had been the biggest mistake the studio had ever made.

And maybe this is natural. A writer is an animal who is often pure but somehow wants fame, all the time, however lethal it may be, because they are also infected with this illness of timelessness. They love language and want to make works where this dark thing is made light but they also want this language to last forever. And so, sadly, a writer is this animal who confuses fame with love.

23

For the performance Celine had all the room's windows and doors opened so that the room extended out to the courtyard – like a little street, an interior that was also an exterior, but with foliage and decoration. It was as if the script could somehow become real and go out into this street and she wondered if this was the kind of art she would always like to see.

In this space it seemed as if almost everyone she had ever known had come to watch. The reason for this excitement was not so much the script as the celebrity cast list. Many worlds combined, and this was a proof of Celine's influence – the deep fluidity of being a multiverse. Some people sat on sofas and cushions. Others stood in doorways, or sat in windows or just outside in the courtyard. A damaged cactus, noticed Celine, had been left behind a watering can. In the centre of the room on a large table were the scripts. There were so many people that it was difficult to see this table, or also, in fact, Beaumarchais – who was sitting beside it, terrified and sweating, in a comically low chair. He was leaking everywhere, sweat emerging from inside him very fast, and that, he thought, was the least forgivable thing a body could do. Antoinette still hadn't arrived. All Beaumarchais could do was listen to the abstract conversation, until finally Antoinette entered the room – and a woman began to cry, as mutely as she could, because she had never been this close to major celebrity.

The situation was overpowering and relentless and Beaumarchais felt very alone. He bowed to Antoinette very low but too slowly, so that he realised as he rose that it seemed he had been bowing to her assistant. He hurried over to the main table to try again.

– Who are you? she said very sweetly.

– I'm the author, said Beaumarchais.

– Ah, she said. – Well, exactly.

Then Rosen arrived and Antoinette turned her attention to him. One mark of Rosen's total wealth was the scruffiness of his appearance. His shoes were surprisingly scuffed. He dressed in sweatpants like a muzhik.

– It's chaos in here, said Rosen.

– I only understand theatre as chaos, Beaumarchais interrupted, before Antoinette could reply. – People who try to control the process, like Jacob, they don't understand that chaos is the only method.

– Who's Jacob? said Rosen.

– He's the author, said Antoinette confidently.

– No, that's Beaumarchais, said Beaumarchais. – I mean: I'm Beaumarchais. I'm sorry.

As so often when writers he disliked were mentioned, Beaumarchais felt a panic of envy descend on him, a little ghost suit that enveloped him and from which his eyes in panic peered out of the raggedly cut-out holes. He was interrupted in this panic because he suddenly felt his shoe fill with iced water. Someone had knocked over a glass. An oblivious and beautiful teenage girl was laughing with her friends. His shoe was soaked.

Rosen was watching everyone very closely. It was in these little digressions that Rosen found people often revealed most about themselves. Look for the spaces, he said to any junior financier who wanted to learn the art of deal-making. Examine the absences.

– Don't be sorry, said Rosen kindly.

– Do you ever feel this? said Antoinette. – You go into someone's house for the very first time, and discover with delight that it has a balcony. So you walk out onto this balcony and look at the city below you. And then you pause there, for many hours, stranded – I mean, you stare at the noise of the couriers below you, carrying so many packages, or the people eating waffles in the streets. And it's almost too entrancing, the amount of activity the world contains.

– Absolutely, agreed Rosen.

There was a long pause. Beaumarchais had no idea how to reply. The first lady had this combination of intelligence, hauteur and total lack of context or education, and it made her very difficult to judge.

24

At first the performance was slow and very awkward, and it interested Celine to notice that this upset her very much, not only for what she was hoping might happen because of this reading, but also for the script itself. There was a version of language that was completely tender, an ideal that so far the universe had not permitted, but this was the version some artists were trying to create in their works – and she understood that in his script Beaumarchais had been trying to achieve this ideal lightness and neutrality, as if it might be possible to think from many positions. And she also understood that it was a version of the tenderness she admired above all things. The more people you could have present in your mind and the better you imagined how you'd feel and think if you were in their place, the more interesting the picture would be and the more language might lose its horror and its evil. Little systems were expanding everywhere but perhaps there was this opposite kind of system, which was a work that had as much as possible inside it. But in this crowded interior there was so much nervousness and anxiety that it was as if the blissful time of comedy in which everything will always be paradise and where the present moment is pure elasticity had been replaced by something slower and heavier, where people either spoke too slowly, with too many pauses between the dialogues, or too quickly, interrupting each other, so that everything was staccato and unnerved. In the audience people began to talk among themselves, quietly but audibly.

– You ever been to prison? Jacob whispered to Hernandez. – The first time they take you to prison it's shit-like-a-squirrel scary. If someone offers you a chunk of soppressata you don't know if you can take it, I mean in case it's doused with poison or stuffed with nails or shit. That's how terrible you feel.

– The fuck did he do this? said Hernandez, preoccupied by his own thoughts. – Do you know why he did this?

– Who? said Jacob.

– Beaumarchais, said Hernandez. – This reading? Why did he agree to it? I would have totally told him not to.

– No one's more corrupt than Beaumarchais, shrugged Jacob.

Then Antoinette laughed because one of Rosen's lines had amused her and the effect of this laugh was very definite and unusual. It was as if everyone in the room at last and suddenly became an audience. No one was fidgeting or sleeping or coughing or writing notes or looking desolately out the windows, but instead a larger truth inhabited this room and even outside in the courtyard, where people were straining to hear so that they had to be very close to each other, and this unusual closeness was something many of them would remember, even many years later, as oddly intimate and erotic.

When it ended Antoinette immediately began to applaud, so everyone else applauded, and it was like little excitements were sparkling everywhere in the bright air. Then she stretched and yawned and together with Celine went to a window for a smoke.

– I love theatre, said Antoinette.

– She loves theatre, said her assistant, who had brought over some cigarettes.

– The only person I know who understands theatre the way you understand it, said Celine, – is Rosen.

– Well, Rosen's wonderful, said the Dauphine. – I hadn't seen him in so long. He should spend more time here.

– He really should, said Celine.

– You know, Rosen, said Antoinette, raising her head a little as she exhaled, to angle the smoke away, – added a real value to his role, which is impressive because the role was already super seductive. I mean, OK sure, the *charisma* of the role belonged to the author, to Jacob –

– Beaumarchais, said Celine.

– Absolutely, said Antoinette. – The charisma is of course the author's, the charisma of the character, but not the charisma with which the role was played, that belonged entirely to the actor, and in fact Rosen had perhaps as much charisma as the author himself. He invented it as he played it.

– You know he admires you very much, said Celine. – I mean, Rosen.

– He's wonderful, said Antoinette. – Everyone says he's Jewish?

The head of the censorship bureau was hovering near them, hoping to say goodbye with elegance and speed.

– Who's everyone? said Celine. – I mean, consider this man here. You know he *hated* this play.

She said this with a bright wide terrible smile.

– I think I'm no I'm just not sure I understood it, he said.

– Everyone says they don't understand a work of art when they want to destroy it, said Celine.

– I don't want to destroy it. Absolutely not, he said. – I just don't get it –

– So they can stage it? said Celine.

– Of course they must stage it, said Antoinette. – Why wouldn't they stage it?

– At the Comedy? he said. – I thought that was agreed?

And Celine realised that at this moment he had no consciousness of lying or even inconsistency. That's how absolute power was and will continue to be – until the planets and the stars at last disintegrate and everything disappears.

25

Here began the little period of total calmness for Celine. It felt like she had acquired some kind of extra family, thought Celine, or at least stability. Because the reading did exactly what she wanted, it was a move that produced many other moves, it was the site of language turning into power – and the degree of its success could be seen in how gently but swiftly its after-effects appeared, as casually as Beaumarchais's little party at Balthazar to celebrate his success, or the announcement that Rosen would become the new chief minister. For this was how a new world always likes to assert itself, however much effort has been required to create it – very gently, and with the apparent minimum of hurt – and it was as if everything was suddenly stable and she wasn't so vulnerable or anxious and at last could sleep more calmly through the night.

Some people felt more part of the world than other people, thought Celine, by which she meant not so much part of the human world but the non-human world – they seemed more part of the sky or the leaves or the plants. One of these people was Marta and another, she was now thinking, was Rosen, and it made her relieved to be surrounded by these people, as if they could support her and defend her against danger.

One night Sasha returned to their house very drunk, his shoes sodden. She asked him why he was so wet and he didn't explain. Instead he just told her that he wasn't really allowed to be back in town. He had come back to get some clothes, he said. Also he wanted to see her. She didn't know what he really wanted and she felt uncomfortable, like she was being forced into a feeling that she had spent so much effort in trying to dissolve or at least leave behind. It was as if something precious to her was being invaded. He pointed at the little fish hook that Claude had given her, this precious heavy object, and asked what it was. She didn't want to show him because she felt an attachment to this fish hook which she could not name, as if no one else would appreciate it for what it was, something outside their experience entirely, but to her disappointment she realised that she did not have the energy to refuse him, not in this kind of interior situation, so she walked over to get it for him. Maybe this complicated set of feelings was why, when she picked the fish hook up, she immediately dropped it, so that for a short moment she couldn't find it. It had somehow bounced underneath a sofa. And then, when she finally brought the fish hook to him, Sasha just glanced at it then abruptly turned and left.

It was about an hour later, when she realised that all her messages from Marta were gone, that she understood Sasha's sudden exit.

But she wanted to stay hopeful and so she refused to let this worry her. She had acted in what seemed like tiny zigzags, thought Celine, but the effects seemed massive enough to protect her – and it felt like with this contrast of the miniature and the massive she was learning a larger lesson about the universe, the same way a historian in a recent interview had said that in writing his history of empire he had been forced to rethink everything he'd thought about *causation*. It turned out that it was a category that was far more invisible and long term than he had thought.

People treated her with a wild reverence. At one of her parties a young writer died very suddenly of a heart attack – and the next day his mother wrote to Celine to apologise, to say how sorry she was that her son had so ruined the tone of Celine's evening. She was deeply sorry, and she hoped Celine would forgive him.

26

At the same time, over the next few weeks, something became more and more hidden between Marta and Celine. At parties Marta floated next to her, kissed her on the forehead, then disappeared. Sometimes they lay in bed together, other times they didn't. Celine found this desire very difficult to understand, the way it could be laid aside as well, like a little box. Everything they did, they felt, was an intense new kind of conversation.

– You know I adore you? said Celine. – I think you are the coolest thing there is.

– *Cool*? Marta said. – Like what do you mean by cool?

– I don't know, said Celine. – Cool is universal.

– So cool will outlast us?

– Of course. It's lasted forever. Cool is an attitude, Marta.

A kind of relief cascaded in the atmosphere. It was possible to think that there might be no more language, or that language could instead become something intimate and different. It was as if inside true conversations there was always a moment when a voice emerged that belonged to none of the people who were in the conversation but was the voice of the conversation itself, and when that happened it was like a little lamp switched on, spreading warm light in a limited space. Other people thought of this as a god emerging or speaking through a person but Celine did not think like that. It was the voice of the conversation, she thought, that belonged to everyone and to no one and to let it emerge and give it space was maybe the most important thing you could do.

Even Beaumarchais seemed to feel this. He was telling her all the time that he wanted a different kind of writing. All the scripts and novels he was seeing were the same. *There must be more to life*, said the cats and dogs of every village in every story – all of them keen to get to the neighbouring village, in which there would just be other cats and dogs lamenting that there must be more to life. It needed a bigger perspective. For instance, said Beaumarchais, he still did not understand how the universe began. There was no space and then there was space. Did this not seem a logical impossibility? And until a work could include this, he was not sure it was worth writing at all.

And meanwhile with her friends Celine felt herself relaxing and this feeling was very new. They had been educated for so long to hide themselves and to see the business of living as a constant negotiation with danger. To be a woman, they had been taught, was to disguise your character so perfectly that it was impossible for anyone to try to understand it. But at the same time as deceiving others you were meant to be able to see through the deceptions of other people – while simultaneously never revealing that you had seen through these deceptions, because it was very dangerous to show that you wanted to understand a person's true nature. Whereas now they had invented a kind of softness, where these questions were somehow not relevant or not true.

But still, it might be very adorable, said Marta. And for the moment might all be true. But swathes of apricot skies were not enough. They were never enough *to be going on with*.

She loved Marta, Celine realised, because of this restless distrust. They shouldn't mistake what they had for absolute power, Marta argued. The ideal state of power, she said, was that it just welled up, like water. Julia said she didn't follow.

She meant, added Marta, that the ideal state was for power to renew itself the way a bubble renews itself, rising from within the body of water to the water's surface. But, argued Celine, if she understood her correctly, almost no one possessed power in that way – most power was acquired vicariously, precariously, from other people.

And well, said Marta, totally. Which was why you could never believe that your power was enough. So what were they going to do next?

27

Celine wasn't sure what the answer to this question was, and it often worried her that she had no answer. She was thinking that there were some people who were able to be inside the world, like Marta, and others who weren't, like her parents. Celine often thought about her parents and whenever she did she felt a kind of cooling. The place she grew up in was a place of limits and of fear and she wished never to be inside that space again. And perhaps she would not but still she always feared the possibility. Maybe she was wrong to fear it. Maybe Marta also was too pessimistic, and from now on, thought Celine, there would be only strings of lights and little pleasures, very ordinary but pleasurable, that couldn't be threatened at all.

For this reason she liked spending time with Rosen. Rosen met with her every week. He was cosmically optimistic. The world talked to him every day, and so he had this habit of dividing its communications into categories. More and more, said Rosen, people thought that they could not just analyse a problem in the era but also solve it – either by eliminating something that seemed to be currently dominating society, like women or Jews or money, or by imagining a future where a goal, once reached, would eliminate all problems instead. Everyone was obsessed with theories of everything, and it turned out that anything could be the key to a theory of everything: your colour or your money or the language you spoke. There was no way of settling which element in the end would be decisive and of course there was no need to settle on a single solution, but still, it somehow lessened the effect of every new theory, said Rosen, that there could be so many theories of the unified explanation.

Rosen instead preferred an ideal of thinking that tried to be equal to the world's expansion. There were the islands in the Pacific Ocean, or the territories of America, that people had only seen as ghostly, to be controlled at a distance. For Rosen, however, they were real and he thought of them as seriously as he thought about anything else. He was thinking of a secret operation in America, he said, a kind of theatrical intervention into their revolution that could be made to look invisible. It seemed like it might be possible to model something on what Beaumarchais had done before, when he had gone to eliminate the pornographers: a little plot of disguise and machination. They would set up a shell company – financed out of Paris but based in London – that would look like an import–export business trading with America. Really, however, it would be supplying rifles to the guerrillas in their war for liberation. He thought that Beaumarchais might run this, said Rosen.

This was how he thought and it made Celine feel safe. Rosen floated like helium or one of the other original gases.

One day Marta arrived looking pale and with dark shadows under her eyes, which was very unusual. It was because a new pamphlet had come out, she said. She was worried that everything was beginning again after all. This new text was a series of leaked messages written by and to Celine. People were finding it exciting, said Marta, because the characters were famous – not just Celine but also Rosen and his assistants – and also because no one had read this kind of thing before, where someone's private messages were let out into the world and you could read people talk about their body the way people you knew might talk to you about your own body, attentively and with detail. It turned out that Sasha, after he had stolen the little series of messages from Marta that Celine had been keeping, had taken them to Hernandez. It had been a while since Celine had rejected the producer, but he had not forgotten the humiliation. Hernandez always loved to hurt. He had a little group of bankrupt writers, and these writers worked on the messages and made their own additions and subtractions. Then they made these fake accounts public.

When Marta brought this pamphlet to them Celine felt a vast tiredness take possession of her. She felt foolish that she had believed it might be possible to make her own moves. But Rosen just found this anxiety amusing. It was nothing, he said. Could they not see this? He encouraged them to look around. And although it was difficult they did also have to admit that nothing, it seemed, was happening in the way it had happened before. The texts appeared, weeks went by, and nothing happened. They became a subject for conversation but no longer harmful or depleting, the way most language was depleting. Her power was finally too much for the language that attacked her.

And when Celine said that, still, it was always important to be more down to earth, Rosen just replied: *I mean, sure, but why this earth?*

28

And then suddenly, without warning, the beautiful season ended for real.

For some time now Celine had been feeling ill almost all the time. Her skin had red patches, papery. She thought this was just anxiety. She tried to medicate. She got high. Each morning her assistant Cato woke her with coffee and she vomited into a chamber pot or any other available bowl. Then Celine tried to sip the coffee while Cato told her whatever stories he was thinking about. Cato liked telling stories which were hardly stories at all – like how his friend's cousin had arrived from the country but had left her bags behind at the station, so was now forced to wear the clothes of her twelve-year-old nephew, or how the woman in the nearby breakfast joint had just discovered that she liked garlic soup after all. Meanwhile Celine checked the eczema on her fingers, the rash above her right eyelid. Cato thought that her afflictions might be caused by her recent suffering. *We all know what it is to suffer*, he said. Celine didn't know exactly what he might mean by *we*. It was increasingly difficult, whenever anyone said *we*, to understand who or what they meant by it.

Then it became obvious what was happening inside her. She went to the little journal she kept, recording her daily

Tarot cards, her conversations, the day's events – trying to find out when she had last had her period. She had noted down nothing, she realised, for the last two months.

Her body had become pregnant. She felt appalled. Outside she could hear a bird and its noise in the leaves seemed inextricable, the same way she was entangled in the world.

It had to be Claude, she thought, but obviously she didn't want to tell Claude. It would represent a total complication of their friendship, and certainly she didn't want him worrying and wanting to care. And anyway Claude was already back on a new voyage into the Pacific Ocean. He was taking Titere home. Instead she started to message Marta, but then she stopped that too.

She had never thought of having children. It seemed too much of a way of limiting your future, and especially of limiting your future because of a man. She always wanted intensity instead. It was possible to say *I am a body* and possible to say *I have a body* and Celine felt that all pleasure consisted in being able to maintain the second statement and not the first. But too often the first sentence was the more accurate, whether in conversation with a man, or in bed with a man, or now, as the consequence of going to bed with a man. To be pregnant was to know that your identity was only a body forever. Perhaps for the men themselves it was possible to imagine the other mode of being, to think that they merely owned a body the way a person might own a greyhound – but maybe that just meant that they were too easily deceived. Maybe the only thing that was true was the brute matter of being a body.

The entire world she had constructed was suddenly absent, and it felt like it was the male world of Beaumarchais and Rosen and Lenoir, or that the men could continue to inhabit it while she could not. Everything had suddenly narrowed to this new perspective, as if she'd been shown into a side room at a party and locked inside.

For a week she stayed at home, not talking to anyone. She kept beside her bed little twigs of ginger, and sucked them before she tried to emerge from the blankets and sheets. They rarely worked. She trusted more in the little fetish object that Claude had given her, that remained beside her bed, the deadly fish hook. She needed the special powers it conferred on her, the way the power of the gods might flow over you, fluid and charismatic.

The air was green in the white rooms.

Then one morning she sensed a familiar perfume in the room, something like fleur de cassie, and when she looked up she saw Marta, who sat beside her on the dirty sofa. Marta was a patient remonstration.

– So whose is it? said Marta.

Celine started to cry. And Marta gently said that of course she didn't need to know, and in this little offer of a gap or elision Celine realised that in fact it was always possible for Marta to help her, because their friendship was something that could alter with each new moment.

– I didn't want to worry you, or make you sad, said Celine.

– You can't make me sad, said Marta.

– It must be Claude, said Celine.

Marta started to roll them each a cigarette.

– Do you remember, said Marta, – that night when we walked out of some party and got into a taxi? And the driver took us to that apartment where everyone was sitting round smoking tobacco and snorting mescal.

– It was all men, said Celine.

– It was all men, said Marta.

– It was fucking dangerous, said Celine.

– But still, said Marta. – Nothing bad happened at all.

– Which is also true, said Celine.

– The shit you get into, said Marta, – when it is two girls on their own.

Then Marta leaned towards her, and her eyes were very large and it felt to Celine that she could float inside these eyes forever, that she could become very small and still be herself, but protected inside the space that was inside Marta.

29

Celine wanted privacy. She wanted to live inside a protected space forever. So Celine decided that she and Marta and Julia would go to Julia's house in the countryside for the summer, so she could have the baby in secret.

But before Celine went, she argued with Rosen in his luminous corner office above the river. Beaumarchais was also there. He had come to ask Rosen how he might get paid by the Americans. So far they had paid him nothing, after he had supervised at least four ocean crossings. Still, thought Beaumarchais, it was important not to seem like he was complaining about this life of business Rosen had gifted him. He found it very exciting. Messages were coming back from America. They were saying that his guns had reached the Mohawk guerrillas, and had won the battle of Saratoga. He felt part of a larger connection.

– You don't know what it's *like*, Celine was saying.

– What what's like? said Rosen.

– To be trapped, she said.

It was as if he didn't know how to continue the conversation. He seemed awkward. He always found it uncomfortable to have to think about problems which he could not solve.

– But you won, said Beaumarchais.

– I'm *leaving*, she replied. – So I've lost.

– But you'll be back soon, he said.

– But I don't want to leave, she said.

– Do you have to? said Rosen.

It was sometimes impossible to speak in any way precisely with a man. It was as if she could see how power was always distributed, its endless circuit, the way you can see the entire electrical circuit of a city when you zoom over it at night. The circuit was very simple. The circuit was men / women, and in some way she refused this, thought Celine. She did not know exactly how, but she refused it.

30

The period that she spent at Julia's house, Celine felt that something was changing. At first she had no way of describing this. The house was a white square in sunshine. For breakfast Celine spread pistachio sorbet inside twin puffs of brioche, then ate it with hot chocolate. She lay in her bedroom, with her fish hook beside her. After some weeks she became exhausted and the heat was terrible. She tried to go for walks in the forest, but the heat was too intense. The smell of pine needles and cicadas was overwhelming.

It was as if nothing could ever happen, while she waited for the grand event.

In town people found it incredible that she was no longer there to be written about and thought about and it made them strangely morose. She had disappeared, they said. Whereas Celine described it differently to herself. She had entered a cloud of thinking.

There was one little space she loved in particular in the forest. She sat there every morning, letting the insects arrive around her, the sound of the gannets fleeing overhead to the sea. Occasionally people would pass by with their animals, or someone would be gathering fruit or mushrooms. Julia had always refused any restrictions on the forest: anyone could enter it and use it how they wanted, and Celine liked this sense of makeshift usefulness.

She felt altered, as if she was now living on the seabed of an ocean of air, and she let herself be a series of feelings, little nuances. It's really terrible how language modifies the world, she was thinking. So much of what's important in a life happens incredibly rarely, sometimes only once, and therefore it's distressing how quickly language has to take it over, our experience, and make it neater and more regular and less abstractly splurged.

Then one morning as she sat there in the forest she began to feel that something was watching her. She looked up. There was nothing there, just the trees and their branches and leaves. Thoughts were occurring inside her and it was possible that this was not even her own thought process, as if different broadcasts were occurring on a single frequency. Then suddenly it felt like she had woken up and a voice was speaking to her. She thought of it as waking up but until that moment she thought she was awake already.

– We need to speak, said the voice.

– Are you sure you mean me? she said.

– Just listen, said the voice.

It was possibly some kind of stress hallucination. This seemed, after all, very likely. She had always been very rational and now there was this mirage – while the light continued streaming in the background.

– So but who are you? she said.

– I was talking, said the voice.

– I'm sorry, she said.

– It doesn't matter, said the voice.

Certainly, something was speaking. It was language, at least: that monstrous thing. But also it was the trees, or the light, or the sun. She knew this very certainly but also slowly, the way bubbles emerge in a glass of water left out overnight.

Before she could listen any more, however, she began to shake violently and could not stop this happening, until gradually she realised that the sensation had faded away.

31

That night the forest caught fire. From her window Celine could see the forest being orange, a sort of vast smeared rushing roar in the distance. She walked outside with Julia and Marta to try to look but the heat was too intense. Everywhere people were running with little buckets of water, cloths, large blankets. It was a communal process, the way the forest had always been maintained as a common space too. A line of workers was holding the flabby leather nozzle of a hose. Where it kinked on the ground little eddies of water were leaking out.

After some hours they all went inside and began to cry, out of some kind of exhaustion and animal terror, then Celine went upstairs, and listened to the emergency services shouting through the night.

The next morning, they went out to see what had happened. They had managed to save large expanses, people said, but some areas of forest were gone. As they walked through these empty patches the sounds were different: clearer and with less background. Everything was reduced and grey and sensitive. A lake was now visible which had not been visible before, from a certain hilltop.

They walked for a little while, then they turned to go back home.

In the burnt grass, an exposed toad was throbbing hysterically, like a terrified heart.

32

That afternoon, Celine started to feel that there was a surge everywhere inside her. They called a doctor, who came from the local town and said it was still too early, then sat downstairs in the living room eating honey cake. Upstairs Celine lay moaning and talking. In front of her Cato was holding a bowl with water, he was swabbing her forehead, her neck.

– I need this to come out, said Celine. – Find a fucking professional.

There was such immense pain that came in flowing patterns then subsided, but even when it subsided there was still pain. It was as if things were being rearranged inside her and perhaps they were. Around her women were looking with sympathy and terror and relief. She realised she knew none of their names. She was too tired to ask who they were. In this way she passed a morning and an afternoon, absorbed in the task of surviving. Then night came and it felt to Celine like an impossible thing, to keep living through this night. In the daytime it was easier – but to continue in the dark, with only candles which were moving in a kind of sinister motion with every air current, was too large and impossible. The fear she felt was very particular, this fear of her own body, its own little borders, something which had seemed so deliberate which was now being opened and reclosed continually and harshly.

There was an inside and an outside and it was no longer obvious how to describe the difference between them.

Then Cato was in the room again, and everything was purple and black in the background, like a Gothic scene. Very gently Cato held her hand.

Then it was Marta.

The next day it was a state holiday in honour of a saint or other notable figure and so it was not a major day, a true day: all the noises were different. It was a morning of echoes, little sounds, buzzing and birds in the leaves, little noises of tools, a person laughing or sneezing. A message was delivered from Claude, from a port in Sumatra or Kamchata, it was difficult to read. Then finally Celine felt something inside her begin to give way, something hard but elastic, it was impossible to judge size, the way it always was for her, to understand the sizes of something inside her. It was coming and coming and Celine stopped thinking, she was absolutely absorbed in this sensation that was very tight and very loose, it was the precise opposite of sex, it was something that went from the inside out. There was only this other self to think about, very definite, the exact weight and shape of her giant body. It was a fascinating problem and one that after many hours she thought might be impossible to solve, or only solve in a way that was terrifying, with too much blood. She could feel wetness everywhere, there were women putting down sheets, removing sheets, and these sheets were stained brown and black and red.

It was impossible that this was natural. It was the most unnatural process she had ever experienced.

Then she felt for a moment very calm, the way she imagined she might feel before she died, or at least the way in novels people sometimes feel before their death – in a way that seems plausible but is perhaps entirely unbelievable, because it is just one of the many experiences that can never be communicated. She heard something screaming and she thought that it was her own voice screaming but it was too faint and too extraordinary.

There was nothing and then there was something.

Celine fainted. When she came to, she saw Marta, then she slept.

33

What Claude wanted to tell Celine was that he now understood that Titere had come back to these islands for revenge. His aim in Europe was to acquire authority, and he had now gone back to use it. It had been a very disturbing discovery. Titere had grown up in this ocean, Titere had told him, wrote Claude. He was born into a very important family. But one day, when he was a boy, he had gone out hunting in the sea with his father. His father took an arrow and shot what he thought was a school of tropical fish. In fact he had misunderstood what he saw and had shot a great shark instead. The arrow pierced the shark in the eye. Something immediately darkened his father's vision, Titere said. When he opened his eyes, it was like looking in a mirror. Claude wasn't sure if he had understood Titere clearly. He asked Titere to explain. He was standing in front of himself, said Titere. One of his eyes was bleeding. And all the noises in the air were suddenly mute. And so everyone, said Titere, became very angry with his father. They pushed him out to sea with his son. They had to drift for a week, then they were allowed to come back. Every time he saw a shark, he sang to it, said Titere, asking for forgiveness. The story was very strange, said Claude. Many elements were incomprehensible to him. But what he was sure he understood was that it was about this time that Claude had first arrived on his island. And so, continued Titere, wrote Claude to Celine, this was why he had decided to join Claude on his journey back to Europe – partly to see other islands and other lands, but especially to collect a series of powerful objects, for him to take back home, to assist him in his project of revenge. Everyone was fighting over who would have power next, and Titere thought it should be him.

When they landed, wrote Claude, they unpacked Titere's trunks from the ship, containing his exotic portraits and textiles and guns – and then they had set off, leaving Titere to make his way up the beach back home.

34

In the countryside, Celine woke up and felt towards the world. The light was yellow or almost orange. Beside her there was a baby sleeping, swaddled, so that it looked like a worm or chrysalis, something inhuman but also deliberate.

She was woozy but more alert than she had ever been. Everything inside her hurt. There was still some blood coming out of her, which was so dark it looked like something that wasn't blood, something inside her that was rarer or at least more rarely seen.

Then Marta and Julia came in. Celine tried to get up, to piss into a bowl on the floor. It took her ten minutes, propped on Julia's shoulder. She walked in a painful waddling motion, like after a long night fucking.

When she came back to bed, she picked up her baby and held her. She was a girl, and Celine felt something almost like fury when she thought about this fact, or at least something fierce and intense. It was an emotion very close to eating – sensual and particular. It was beautiful but it also hurt.

Together they all considered the situation. She had a child, but did not live with her husband. There was one obvious solution, said Julia. Her child could live here with Julia. They could say that she was a cousin. Celine asked her if she was sure. She would have expected Celine, said Julia, to do the same for her. On the other hand, added Julia, she could also take her back to town and just say that she had adopted her. The single important meaning to convey was that the child was only hers.

It was as if everything had suddenly crystallised into this

moment of total solidarity between women: an overlapping arrangement of friendships and desire.

Celine looked at the baby and thought that there was nothing more beautiful or more gentle. She was surprisingly hairy. There were tufts of hair on the tips of her ears. She smelled bitter but also sweet. She was incredibly small. She lay on Celine's breasts, which were oozing a yellow substance that was almost mucus.

She felt like she no longer existed, or now existed in a melted state. Then Celine corrected herself. What in fact no longer existed was the world.

She kept thinking of everything that had happened and it seemed that so much had happened that nothing more could happen. She had aged so much, she thought, and surely could not age any more. She had moved across a border.

Sometimes in the nights that followed she thought she heard her daughter wake up so she propped herself up to stroke her, but then she realised what she had taken for crying or babbling was the noise of a pigeon, or two people talking in the courtyard. Instead her child was sleeping and she had broken in on her privacy. It amazed her, the stillness of her child asleep.

She would call her Saratoga, she told Marta and Julia. And then she kissed her tiny daughter.

35

Some time afterwards, Celine had a vision of a world being destroyed. She could see it all go up suddenly in flames: the newspapers, stockings, pamphlets, theories of irony, dollars, travel guides, bookshelves, recommendations, protons, letters, garters, portraits, enamels, pen-caps, libels, wampum, codes, scripts, glasses, tea cups, pencils, crayons, water, ink, wrist-bones, magazines, coffee grounds. Everything was suddenly unattainable, the way anything is unattainable the moment you see it go up in flames.

Her world vanished and there was only the bare dark.

Then everything was there again: a room, a world, Celine.

Two

I

A few years later Julia finally looked at Celine and said that she was leaving her husband. He was a monster, he ate children, she said. She was bruised and battered. She hated him. She was leaving him.

– He doesn't eat children, said Celine.

She was about to turn thirty and she felt middle-aged. For Celine these years that had passed by, the years of Saratoga's childhood, had been years of a kind of amazed blankness. She thought about Saratoga all the time, and especially her future, because she wanted Saratoga not only to have a perfect future but also a perfect childhood and so she was anxious with an urgency that surprised her about what Saratoga would remember from when she was young. Celine wanted these memories to be beautiful, or if not beautiful then at least not aggrieved or angry, but it was difficult to see into the future.

It was as if Celine had finally emerged after a long night's travelling under the moon and planets and dwarf stars and come out onto a high plateau, and it turned out that what she was looking at was time. There was so much more time in a life, she was discovering, than she had expected, and it changed the way she saw each event. An event was no longer exactly an event, it was something blurred by repetition, the way even her friendship with Marta was now decorated with all the souvenirs of its giant length, and it made events seem almost ugly and she no longer wanted them at all.

It was still true that whenever Marta and Celine couldn't see each other for vino rosso and martini they messaged each other and wrote journals that were also messages, describing their feelings and the feelings they felt when they thought about their feelings. But a slight ennui was settling delicately over them, and it might have been almost comforting, this ennui – like the blanket given to comfort the apprentice yogi in her early-morning meditation – if it hadn't been so sad to find that even something that had once felt so unique and so exciting was itself subject to disappointment.

It would have been so much easier to be a butterfly! Or at least, something with a very short lifespan: a luna moth, or mayfly. Although maybe within the consciousness of a mayfly as their single day progressed there were boredoms and wearinesses too.

The planet seemed just a little less glossy, however much outside there were new trees trying to exist and everyone was excited by the ultramodern methods of measuring rainbows or planets or clouds and Antoinette was throwing manic parties in the government buildings. Everyone now said that Julia was thinner. It made her look electric but also anxious. Her skin was still almost transparent and she still went costumed in an aura of dreamy beauty, but now there were mauve discolorations beneath her eyes. These alterations seemed part of a general change in the atmosphere. Beaumarchais was a celebrity, while Jacob had now transformed his failure as a writer into a passion for radical politics. He wanted to fight for universal rights, he said, and had gone on a major trip to America to advertise this new passion.

Rosen had finally gone back to pursue his business interests outside the restrictions of government bureaucracy. And meanwhile a new friend had been added to their little group, a woman called Izabela, who was from much further east in Europe, and it was at least beautiful that new friendships could still happen, even if most friendships seemed to diminish or become more problematic.

But now there was this new problem of Julia and her husband. Her husband was called Dolan and was a multinational businessman. He came and went across borders very fast. He had made on Celine in many years almost no physical impression.

Celine was just worried, she continued, about acting too fast. Julia scratched an armpit, sniffed it, concentrated again. Obviously women left men all the time, and especially men left women, said Celine. But at the same time it was very possible for women to be unhappy with men or men to be unhappy with women but for no one to leave. And this was sometimes the safest place.

– But, said Julia.

– If you leave him then what do you have? said Celine. – I mean what money?

It was so terrible to be talking in this way! But there seemed no other possibility. While talking about love, they were always talking about money, and maybe money was the entire question underneath every other.

2

This was the situation with Celine. Without Sasha, her separated husband, Celine had no money – except the money contained virtually in their house and other possessions, which couldn't be turned into money at all. Therefore she thought about money all the time. It was the basic cost of being a woman on one's own.

Her largest expense was on Saratoga's teachers. Saratoga was now ten, and still living at Julia's house in the countryside. Celine wanted Saratoga to be as independent as possible, existing in some artificial and wonderful extended family of friends, outside the paternal system. She had briefly told her that her father was probably Claude but she most of all encouraged her to think that she had no father, that Celine had conceived her on her own, and Saratoga seemed to like this mythology. She had come from nothing, said Celine. In the countryside, Saratoga wrote delighted messages back about the decor, about the food, about the lessons and the tutors and the absence of any vehicles.

Meanwhile Sasha's payments came erratically, or punctually but for the wrong amounts. Sasha was still living in internal exile, disgraced. He refused to be divorced. She did not like that the money she had to use was Sasha's money, but she could not avoid it. He never replied to her messages, or only answered them bizarrely, as if asserting some oblique power, maintaining philosophical conversations that made no sense. He had recently read that novel, he wrote to her, the one everyone loved called *Messages*. It was a novel she had once recommended to him but he had never read it, he said. And now, the other night, he found himself reading it and understanding why she loved it so much – and then pitying these poor writers, poor geniuses, whose fate was always to be misunderstood by their contemporaries. Such reflections in no way interested Celine, now that she was inside this new realm of time. Her concerns were all practicalities. She found herself constantly involved in precarious schemes to bring herself extra money, using little loans from her parents as capital. To deal with money made her very nervous. It was the only force that protected her from men, a kind of inflatable cushion that preserved her from their violence, and it could deflate or even disappear at any moment.

3

– But what I'm trying to say, said Julia, – is that now I'm with Lorenzo.

– Lorenzo? said Celine. – The Jewish one?

– I think just Venetian, said Julia. – But maybe, I have no idea. Why does it matter?

– It doesn't, said Celine.

Lorenzo was a recent addition to the story of Celine and time. He was a scriptwriter who wrote adaptations of successful plays. It was becoming more and more important to make a script into an opera. A script on its own was not enough, and maybe this was rational. To be real it needed to be multiplied.

Lorenzo had in fact been born in their city and was not

foreign at all, but his family had moved first to Venice and then Vienna, and he was possibly also Jewish – the way it was possible for anyone who had no obvious identity to be Jewish. So his identity was always in doubt. He had a sleek little beard that was ever so slightly grizzled and dark frizzy hair and the effect was to make him very gentle and eccentric, especially because it contrasted very much with his muscular but undeniably compact body, which he maintained in regular weight training. Lorenzo was back in town to work with Beaumarchais on his latest script. Until this job Beaumarchais had always disliked him. Now he adored him. The project was being produced by Hernandez – the way almost everything anyone had heard of was now produced out of Hernandez's studio.

– Isn't Lorenzo kind of old? said Celine.

Julia did a little shrug and moue, a way of hinting at a conversation she preferred to be simply understood rather than spoken out loud – where Celine expressed her understanding of this urge, to become the erotic masterpiece of an older man, while admitting that it depressed her how common this perversion was, if in fact it could even be classified as a perversion, considering how often it occurred, and where Julia could then assert that perhaps the only way of *expiating* the urge was by fulfilling it. Instead she began a vague sentence, something like:

– The thing about Lorenzo –

But then they were interrupted by Cato. It often seemed to Celine, perhaps every time she saw him, now that she was so conscious of inhabiting a new perspective, that Cato was the only person who didn't seem older at all. He came in to deliver a new set of messages from Saratoga in the countryside.

In any case, added Julia, as Cato began to clear away some old cannoli, people could say anything about Lorenzo. But she knew she would love him forever.

4

That night Julia took Celine to Hernandez's latest production, a show by a celebrity magician, where they could meet with Lorenzo in private and discuss the options for their future together.

This celebrity magician was from the wilderness of central Europe. His shows were extravaganzas. He travelled with his nine-year-old daughter and a cat which he claimed was the incarnation of his dead mother. In his career across Europe he had befriended many celebrities and would tell you this in conversation. He knew everyone, or at least it seemed so – fashion designers, architects, magazine owners, ballerinas – but all his stories ended with *but of course he no longer speaks to me,* or *but of course she disappointed me terribly.*

His new show promised unique methods of visual and theatrical projection. It was a show that came from the future, and the special effects he used were being manically debated. Lorenzo had written an essay on this new theatre of illusion, arguing that whereas it looked like the magician had all the power in fact two codes were always in play, not just one. The virtual reality produced by these illusions was as much a creation of the audience as of the magician. The special effect, he concluded, had a *double essence*, and this phrase had made him famous outside the mini circle of his usual admirers.

Celine and Julia sat down in a box, in darkness. They looked around for Lorenzo's little bearded form but could not see it. Below them, onstage, a gun went off and the magician caught the bullet in his teeth. While everyone applauded his daughter tugged a metal helmet over her head and the magician, standing on a scaffold many feet above her, dragged her up to the ceiling using a giant magnet. Everything was unseen force, spooky action at a distance. It was very unnerving to see that kind of force, even if it did resemble other attractions: the way you could make a man's penis move, for instance, just by a way of opening your mouth. Or the way a room would change its tone and composition because a celebrity had entered it.

The next part of the show was a little interlude, where the magician's daughter played draughts against a mechanical player, a player who seemed to move and think of its own volition. And it was a very beautiful vision, if also a little disturbing, to see this figure make its jerky but definite moves, and Celine could have watched this for hours, but then someone behind them in the darkness said that Julia should come the fuck with him. It was incomprehensible to Celine, this intimate and sudden intervention. Down below on the desolate stage the magician was beginning his new act, he was talking about how the audience would feel very afraid, very anxious, while up here Julia said, very intently, that she didn't want to.

Then all the lights went out.

In the darkness Celine looked for Julia, and Julia looked for Celine. Behind them, Celine now vaguely understood, was Julia's husband, Dolan, the multinational businessman, sweating and stinking. He liked to drink before any heavy conversation. It was difficult to know how to make such a man be quiet. He was talking very fast in English, telling Julia to come back home with him, and Julia was saying that this was annoying, or embarrassing, it was annoyingly embarrassing, that he had to be quiet, very very quiet. It surprised Celine to discover that in private, it seemed, they talked to each other in English, not so much because it was surprising in itself, since Dolan after all had grown up in Ireland and always found English the easier language, but that she had never known this about them before. Dolan dragged Julia by a sleeve and she stumbled over a chair which noisily overturned, and at the same moment a light was suddenly projected onto the stage, illuminating some smoke. Very rapidly Julia started talking, asking what he could not understand about this situation because it was very simple and she was not coming with him. Then inside the smoke onstage a skeleton appeared, which seemed to be waving its arms very gently. *It was here to judge them all*, said the skeleton.

And then, very late, Lorenzo arrived.

Mostly no one likes farce or melodrama, thought Celine, they seem artificial and impossible forms, but they do happen, their little structures of cause and effect do sometimes happen, after all – the way at this moment Lorenzo now entered their box and stood there, not exactly comprehending the situation he had entered. He looked at Dolan and then Julia who made a gesture to Lorenzo which was meant to mean something large and multiple. She wanted in silence to apologise to Lorenzo for this coincidence, to assure him that of course she had no idea Dolan would find her here, that in some way he must have been following her or have

as upstate New York or the Mohawk Valley, Louis Cook was signing off on a message to George Washington. The passage of time and its poisonous effects was a constant preoccupation for Louis, and the way it was emerging from him was the way he wanted to tell Washington a story that had happened lately, while Montour was visiting.

Recently, wrote Louis – in a message he dictated and whose language Montour perfected – a trader had arrived at their village, with a trio of men carrying a canoe piled with kettles. No one welcomed this white man profusely. It was very ragged and strung out, the atmosphere. This was because there was no money left. People were chewing old cigarettes and making little cocktails out of stale rum. This trader, wrote Louis Cook, to Washington, as translated by Montour, was an old agent, but he came with new associates. After the usual little formalities, they began to speak about prices. It had become necessary, apparently, to raise prices. Now Louis had been expecting this kind of move, in the current slump, and so he replied that while he understood this he also needed his warriors to be treated well, and supplied with the things they required. He absolutely agreed, said the trader, but then he was interrupted by one of his associates, who said that he disliked the way the Indians were extorting goods and getting better prices than the white men got. It was as if this man did not understand, wrote Louis Cook, that they spoke his language too and could understand everything that was being said.

For this was a time when terrible things were being said by the Americans about his people, as if they had forgotten everything his people had done for them. Just as Celine had emerged into a landscape she did not recognise, so Louis Cook had emerged into something he had hoped not to see, which was a landscape where something was removed from the picture. He had lost trees and plants and skies. Everything written by the white people was becoming more and more insane, and it seemed to be making them insane, too. He had heard how a white man had happened on a Delaware man outside a stockade. The Delaware man was simply gathering lichen. Do the world a favour and eat a bullet, said the cowboy. Then he shot him in the mouth. It was creating a very bad feeling among his people, wrote Louis Cook. His interpreter Montour, for instance, maintained that the Americans were becoming lawless banditti, bands of murderers and psychotics, and he was saddened that it was making their own people behave badly in return. Montour kept on telling stories of the Thunder, of how the Thunder had told him that the animals were disappearing and the corn was broken because his people kept killing the animals to sell the skins to the white people so they could buy rum in exchange – and the Thunder did not like this.

This was why, wrote Louis Cook to Washington, he felt it was very important to think about meetings like this. Business could still be done in honesty and with carefulness. People could have a conversation, even in more than one language, and he valued conversation with strangers above all things, said Louis, and believed that even if a thing was broken, or not what you expected, it could still be repaired if treated with appropriate care.

6

Or could she say, thought Celine, that while no one wants to succumb to anything as grandly named as destiny people do succumb to it, after all, every day? And this time destiny wanted Celine and her friends to suffer more. It did not think there was enough suffering. It thought there had been too much hope.

Because while Celine received many messages and forgot most of these messages, the message she received the next day from Julia – somehow smuggled out by an assistant in a bag of dirty laundry – was a major alteration to the picture.

Men had come to her house in the middle of the night, wrote Julia. They said that they were just there for her security, that they were taking her to see Lenoir, the police chief, to discuss this business with her husband. Then they transported her across the river, but instead of going to Lenoir's offices they had taken her to a house, this house from which she was writing, Julia continued, somewhere in the city. She didn't know where it was, she didn't recognise anything. She was on the ground floor of an apartment block. There was a patch of garden outside. No one seemed to look after it. There were some old bottles on a heap of mud. She was very scared. She had also added a postscript, where she begged Celine to talk to anyone, then finally little illegible phrases. It was as if Julia could not bear to end the message and send it.

Tiredness was something Celine was feeling more and more. It was as if the golden procession of moments she had imagined for her life had become something that was easily broken down and it required exhausting effort to continue. Would resistance last forever? Would it always be so minute? This kidnapping was a form of intimidation that was definitely frightening, like all successful intimidation, and Celine didn't want to be frightened. But if the police chief really were involved then this was especially frightening because it meant that the violence was in some way regime violence and that therefore the forces they had to contend with were more organised than the usual violence of men.

The only solution, it seemed, would require her to see Lenoir. But she hadn't seen Lenoir for years.

Because of course it often happens that some people remain in your life while others disappear, it is very unpredictable who disappears and who remains and so there is a corresponding strangeness in surprisingly returning to a person to whom you've once been in some way close, but never a *friend*, and whom you're now trying to use in your ongoing resistance to the basic order. There were so many chasms, compromises, little memories, or at least it seemed that way to Celine. It had turned out, as she got older, that some correspondences with other people were little fragile things, hanging off events from fraying strings, and in the absence of the events or circumstances that sustained them they seemed to flutter away, into the turquoise air. So that in returning to Lenoir, for instance, it was difficult to imagine what the right tone would be, now that so much time had passed. They would have to construct a new way of talking, even while being aware of the ruins of the old one. And this was especially a problem because when they had first met her power in society exceeded his, whereas this was not in any way still true, and she didn't know how close he might be to Julia's husband, or how brutal he might seem.

But still, she had determined that she would never allow herself to disappear in silence, especially if this silence were a silence imposed by other people – and so she sent a message to Lenoir which he replied to at alarmingly high speed, telling her to come over whenever she wanted, as if they were still in constant and easy correspondence.

Fearfully, Celine travelled across town to the police chief's bureau, inside the regime offices.

7

The interiors of the office complex were now grand and colourful and improvised. It was as if Lenoir had allowed himself more freedom of self-expression and although it surprised Celine she found herself strangely admiring it. Ageing had given Lenoir a new authority. He picked up a swatch of various colours, little smudges of paint, and asked her what she thought.

– Do you like this? We're repainting. Is it too purple?

– It's green, she said.

– Sorry, that's the wrong one, said Lenoir.

He handed her another, a little stripe of pastel patches. She pushed it back to him.

Celine didn't think that she was the strongest person, or the wildest person, but she had gradually realised that it was possible to achieve what you wanted if you thought about it closely enough and with passion. There was always this moment in a conversation where you wanted something, and even if the other person in the conversation was trying not to talk about it, still, you could always make something overt, however awkward that might feel.

– But so? she said.

– So? said Lenoir.

– What's happening about Julia?

It seemed to make Lenoir anxious, this talking about women and private lives. It was often like this, thought Celine, when women talked about women to men.

– I can't help you, he said to Celine. – I know why you're here. I can't help you.

Some conversations end immediately and some have many trick endings. It isn't always obvious which conversations will end fast and which will end more slowly, just as it isn't always obvious if anyone can be in control of a conversation's shape. Certainly Lenoir wanted this to be over but Celine refused to accept that this conversation would end so abruptly and so she said simply that she didn't believe him. Lenoir looked surprised at this kind of direct sentence, as if he was only used to meetings where directness was usually impossible or at least socially forbidden. It shocked him into a kind of similar directness. It wasn't like the old days, he said. He couldn't operate on his own. There were so many committees now, and plots and counterplots and people being anxious or neurotic about the general atmosphere.

– But still, said Celine. – What's happening?

It might seem like he had power, continued Lenoir, but the reality was that everyone was conspiring against him all the time. Did she have any idea what was happening in here, he said, in this government compound, in all these tiny rooms? *All the money was gone*, said Lenoir. It was amazing how little pity people had for him, he said. Celine replied that she still didn't believe him, and the effect on him of saying this was a kind of aggrieved indignation that made him talkative and expansive, offering recondite information, hints about the sources of Julia's husband's wealth, and Lorenzo's family's background in the ghettos of the Veneto. Did she know, said Lenoir, that Lorenzo's real name was *Emanuele*? How much more Hebrew could he get? All of which combined, he argued, to make it impossible for him to help Julia.

Celine looked at him. She was in a little bubble of thinking that was a way of working out what she could ask for from Lenoir. She needed to travel towards him, in this bubble! It was as if something was flowing between them that was not air but made of feelings, as if she were able to float towards Lenoir and talk to him from the transparency of a bubble, and he could meet her in his own bubble and understand what she was needing. Until finally she settled on a sentence that was as restricted as she could find. She asked him for Julia's address, and without replying but with a sense around him of melancholy and a wish to talk with Celine some more, Lenoir wrote down a location, realised he had misspelled it and crossed it out, wrote it again, nearly crossed it out to start again, gave up and handed it to her.

The way he did this seemed to be a way of erasing the time that had passed since their last meeting long ago, or at least maintaining some little connection to a form of talking they had both once enjoyed.

8

They had put Julia in a side street close to one of the northern canals, in an unmarked government apartment. The weather at this time was a vast stillness: it was hot but the sky was grey. The air was trickling over the water in deep soft swathes. Inside, everything stank of marinara sauce.

– I look terrible, said Julia.

– You look terrible, said Celine.

And it was true. It was as if Julia's usual elongated pale beauty had collapsed into something ordinary and incomplete.

Celine placed a wrapped package of new underwear and a box of fresh eclairs on a chair. It was obvious that no one lived here, that this was some kind of state amenity, and the effect on Julia of spending twenty-four hours in here had been rapid – a kind of high-speed desolation and amazement. She couldn't live like this, said Julia. It was obviously true, said Celine, and she wouldn't have to live like this, but right now she felt it was also important to try to create a less tragic atmosphere, something resembling normal life. But what, said Julia, did she mean by a normal life?

– They've locked me up, said Julia. – How is that possible?

– I'm just thinking, said Celine. – I'm trying to understand what it is we should be feeling.

Julia had a problem which was that her hearing was a little muted, but she had never realised this and therefore treated the obscurity of many conversations as something simply embedded in the world's texture. It was possible, thought Julia, that Celine had said that she was feeling confused, or also possible that she had said that she wanted to know what Julia was feeling.

– I'm in love, said Julia with indignation. – That's what I'm feeling. *And they've locked me up.*

But of course for Celine this was a difficult response in its apparent lack of logic or rationale, and she didn't know how to reply to it – as if in some way Julia was trying to rebuke her for not caring about her imprisonment or not taking her passion for Lorenzo seriously. There was a lot of pain in the room and it was of course important to concentrate on the pain but it was also important to think about ways of escape. The problem was that the only way to think, it seemed, was in this old way of talking. And Celine wanted a new way of talking but had so far not quite found the way she meant. So for a long while Celine said nothing, which meant that Julia tried again to pursue the conversation. She asked Celine what people were writing about her, what they were saying. She was just trying to work out what was happening, said Celine. She needed to talk to Marta about this. All she knew was that Dolan had some arrangement with Lenoir. But what about Lorenzo? asked Julia. She obviously had to talk with Lorenzo too, said Celine. But Lorenzo was an outsider, so –

– This is all so ugly, said Julia.

Nothing could be done by a woman on her own. Nothing could be done by women in any configuration. To act you needed associates and those associates needed to be men. They understood all this while also being enraged, and at the same time even when they accepted this as a set of facts to be negotiated it still wasn't obvious who the associates here should be.

– Do you know how violent my husband was? said Julia. – In the night I'd wake up and find him on top of me. Can you imagine how scary that is? Every time someone praised me in the magazines, it made him more violent.

– Like really violent?

– Super crazy. Knives out.

– I had no idea, said Celine. – Did anyone have an idea?

– Of course not, said Julia. – Every day I had to hide the newspapers, in case they contained something about me.

Celine felt a kind of downcast shame. It seemed appalling that she hadn't known this about Julia, and also appalling that Julia had never told her. It was one of the problems of living among people – that you thought you knew so much about your friends but that it tended to require a catastrophe before anyone spoke sincerely with another person. Human nature was appalling.

A courier delivered a plate of spaghetti alle vongole that Julia had ordered from some immigrant trattoria nearby. Immediately Julia began eating.

– Sorry, I'm eating all the time right now, said Julia. – It's not because I've gone crazy.

She forked up some clams and white sauce.

– It's because I'm pregnant, she said.

9

Celine felt middle-aged. She felt that some things were now out of reach. It was like the present moment was elsewhere, thought Celine. There could be a time when you felt so much part of the present moment that you thought that you and this moment were identical, but then it turned out you could continue and the present moment would just gently move to one side, maybe not even so very far, but far enough away for you to notice a distance between yourself and the soul of things. So that the ballet you were always trying to perform became more and more difficult, you were moving, you were making your moves, but the rhythm you needed to dance to was less audible and more confusing.

Celine's parties were now marked by novelties and absences, they were just a little degraded. But fashion is unique for the strange way it can accommodate many varieties, and so although she was no longer faced with the white light of total celebrity, her glamour was persistent. Her parties, like evenings at all legendary microculture venues, whether voguing joints or communist cells, were diagrams of coinciding and exploding forces: overlapping groups who defined themselves against a network of other groups.

There were now more writers, younger writers, and they were using a new vocabulary like democracy or sincerity, and although she liked these words she never knew if she could use them naturally. Other people around her seemed to have no such reluctance. Since Jacob had come back from his famous trip to America he was writing long articles about economics and true feeling, and these articles were making him admired in a way his previous writing had never achieved. He had even acquired a new look, something trimmer and almost tanned, so that his entirely average appearance was ever so slightly more impressive.

But it was writing like Jacob's that made Celine feel that she was losing something, or moving away from something, because however utopian it might be intended to sound it was still male dialogue, she thought, and like the atmosphere on some demented exoplanet this dialogue distorted every perspective. What he loved, said Jacob to her one evening, explaining his love of the mesmeric trances that were now so chic, was the way a person in one of these trances felt so much empathy for the poor or dispossessed that they felt like a little child. Personally, he thought this also helped him identify with his children. So many unfortunate fathers, he added, were so caught up in their business affairs that they hardly had any idea of the way their children felt.

– Do you know how many children you have? said Celine.

Jacob paused.

– Does anyone? said Jacob.

Maybe this was why Celine was preferring her new friend Izabela instead. Izabela came from outside everything, as if from another era. Her look was absolute gauntness and cheekbone and severity, with long straight ash-brown hair and green enormous eyes, but when she laughed she was goofy and comical. She had a constant supply of personal anecdotes that were eccentric and endearing. One day, Izabela told her, when she was growing up, she had this idea of bathing in milk. And so with a friend they went out to buy up all the milk from the surrounding farms. They dressed as boys, riding donkeys. They left at six in the morning, very early, and visited every farm in the area, asking them to deliver milk. Then that morning they took a bath of milk, and they scattered flowers on the surface. It was the strangest sensation, said Izabela. She'd expected to love it but in fact had found the smell disgusting. So she had never done it again. But still, said Izabela, she liked the memory.

10

After leaving Julia in her house arrest, Celine went for dinner with Beaumarchais. Beaumarchais had become as famous as he always wanted to be but had also made the discovery that to be famous required much more and varied industry than he had expected – it was in fact more arduous, this building work that had to happen on top of the previous building work, than the effort it had taken him to become as famous as he was. It turned out that everyone had a theory of the famous, and this made the moves you could make very vulnerable to misinterpretation and revision. He himself was often hated by people who did not know him, and while she knew this and at least understood some of the reasons, Celine herself still loved him. One reason was that he had never mentioned sex to her and it seemed by now that he never would. And this was deeply relaxing.

They sat together and she let Beaumarchais complain about his life. It was as if no one really understood him at all, said Beaumarchais sadly. He had recently offered a pair of tickets to his latest show to a friend of his, he said. And the next time he saw her, after she had seen the show, she simply looked through him, said Beaumarchais, absolutely looked through him – as if rather than asking her to see a play he had made some colossally ill-judged sexual advance, as if they had been eating in this restaurant and he had invited her upstairs, into a quiet room, where he waited, naked, primed, with implements.

– As if I had said, said Beaumarchais: – But when you said

you liked the forks in this restaurant, *I thought this was what you meant.*

– How long ago was it, said Celine, – since we met?

– How long? said Beaumarchais. – I mean like five years?

– It was ten, said Celine. – We were so young.

– You're still young, said Beaumarchais. – I'm like twenty years older than you. Why are you so sad?

She wasn't sad, said Celine. Then she realised that she was incredibly sad and she explained to him what was happening about Julia. It was a story with many ambiguities and confusions and it took her a long time to tell it, and when she thought that she had finished she realised that in fact you could not finish this kind of story, there were not enough words or not the right words, and so you simply stopped and hoped that something would be left to continue the noise of the words inside the person who was listening.

And perhaps the real reason she liked Beaumarchais was that she could transmit noises and codes and he would receive them and be gentle with the messages. It was insane and appalling, he said. He really hated this regime. She hated it too, said Celine. It was a regime where everything felt impossible. It wasn't surprising if people so loved the new theories of fluids and magnetism, the serums and the potions, because all of these were theories of blockages and magical reversals. But what she wanted above all was to leave this landscape entirely.

This was all true, said Beaumarchais gently, but still, for the moment she had to live inside it. And there was at least one thing that seemed to be admired by this regime, which might be useful to her. Celine asked him what he meant.

– Celebrity, said Beaumarchais.

II

There will be a punishment for being once at the centre of the present moment, thought Celine. The punishment will be how severely you will suffer from then on, when you are no longer in the centre. Beside her there was Beaumarchais and Beaumarchais it seemed would never suffer. But she would suffer because she wanted something that other people did not want, which was to have a soul that lived inside the flow of time, and to live in that state forever.

Whereas Beaumarchais wanted fame and this was a different problem, with maybe different punishments. When she returned to Lenoir's office with him the next day he was very excitable. His presence seemed to make Lenoir excited too. He had come here, said Beaumarchais, to try to find a solution but he wanted to begin with a secret admission. In this affair of Julia and her imprisonment, of Julia sleeping with Lorenzo against her husband's wishes, he was doubly compromised. On the one hand, he was a friend of Lorenzo. But also he had to admit that he had once slept with Julia. Before continuing, therefore, he wanted to hear Lenoir's response.

Lenoir's response was to laugh delightedly.

– I know, I know, it's funny, said Beaumarchais.

– That isn't what's funny, said Lenoir.

It was as if, thought Celine, this kind of conversation would continue forever and it would make her feel dejected. She only wanted a meaningful and sincere life but the conversations she was exposed to were not meaningful, they were cold and abstract and made her feel uncomfortable but apparently you had to bear it because no other tone would ever be possible, or at least it seemed so. The universe would continue to say to her that she was wrong to wish for a meaningful life, or perhaps to look for it in any human conversation. Certainly the birds seemed to be enjoying themselves and that was something. At least that was something, thought Celine. Meanwhile inside the room Lenoir tried to begin the conversation again. Anyway, he said, he should tell them what had happened the day before, about two hours after Celine had come to see him. Julia's husband had arrived, and it was very odd, he said, because he came with his own assistant, a man called Yves, who was recording everything that happened in a notebook.

– Yves? said Beaumarchais.
– You know him? said Lenoir.
– I mean kind of, said Beaumarchais.

Beaumarchais stood up to look for cigarettes in his bag.

Yves was the latest kid who had come to town to make it, said Beaumarchais. He was a lawyer but he wanted to be famous for his writing too. He often hung around with Jacob, discussing political causes.

In fact, said Beaumarchais, lighting a cigarette then moving over to an open window, he'd recently upset Yves very much. This was about a month ago. They'd met at some party and Yves had started asking him about advances. Yves had never earned out an advance on anything he had written, he said. It seemed unlikely he could ever give up his law work. So to try to make him happy, said Beaumarchais, he had said that he was very pleased to hear that Yves had never made a publisher money. Whenever Hernandez sold one of his scripts, continued Beaumarchais, he always wanted to hear that he had lost the studio money. That way he knew he'd got the most money he could.

Beaumarchais stubbed out his cigarette on the window ledge and came back to Lenoir's desk.

He'd only told him this as a way of trying to console Yves, explained Beaumarchais, it was a kind story, a charming story, but it seemed that Yves had listened with poisonous disgust, because he'd immediately gone to Hernandez to ask if this was true. Anyway, he was very ugly, finished Beaumarchais. He was prematurely bald. His face resembled a crumpled frog. Something was wrong with one of his hands, it had this kind of shake or tremor and maybe that explained his inner violence.

– It's the same kid for sure, said Lenoir.

He seemed preoccupied by the portrait Beaumarchais had sketched.

But the amusing thing, Lenoir eventually continued, was that the reason Dolan had come to see him was because he now wanted Lenoir to lock Lorenzo up as well: the lover as well as the wife.

– And what did you say? said Celine.

– I said, said Lenoir, that if I were to lock up everyone who was sleeping with someone they shouldn't be sleeping with, it would basically empty the theatres and the bars and the saunas.

It was like something from a script, said Beaumarchais. Talking of which, said Lenoir, he'd just seen his show. He really loved what he did. Perhaps, Beaumarchais replied, Lenoir would like to come and watch an early rehearsal of the adaptation he was working on with Lorenzo. It was being adapted? said Lenoir. This was wonderful. Although wasn't all opera production controlled by the Jews? Then they talked about Lorenzo, about the actors Beaumarchais was working with. It was crazy, said Beaumarchais, the kind of money this production needed. If you didn't attach the right performers, it never happened. Lenoir seemed very interested in money. It dazzled him, the way it dazzles anyone, and he asked Beaumarchais what was happening with his American money, the money he was owed from that scheme he used to run, and Beaumarchais replied that he was getting nowhere. He had hired a lawyer. He had no idea if he was any good.

In this way two men developed an understanding. It felt to Celine like they were talking very far away. It seemed the opposite of the way two women would do this, thought Celine, to talk in this way about money and business contacts. But it also seemed to be working. Everything in Lenoir was suddenly relaxed. His authority as police chief, it seemed, was nothing when compared to Beaumarchais's proximity to actors.

He had to confess something, said Lenoir. The real comedy in all this was that Julia's husband was right to be so paranoid. Many years ago, said Lenoir, he himself had slept with Julia too. It had happened only once, but he had adored her ever since.

– So let her go with Celine, said Beaumarchais gently.

Everything was corruption, contact, intimacy.

So that it wasn't surprising or against the implicit laws of power that, finally, Lenoir nodded. He let them understand that he agreed without committing himself to anything as definite as language. And so Julia could be released, into the soft and powdered air.

12

It turned out that Celine now needed to consider Yves more closely – because he was soon to become a kind of force field, warping her surroundings.

Yves had grown up in a town in the provinces, where he studied law. He always carried a dusty backpack full of notebooks. He bought all the books he could and when he ran out of money he stole the ones he wanted instead. Every morning he went to cafes to read the newspapers. The news now was always torrential and obsessive. People were updating themselves in the morning, then around lunchtime when the newspapers began again, out of a desire for truth or terror of ever understanding the truth. That summer some riots began happening in his town and they excited Yves very much. They made him feel that it might be possible for a person like him to move in newer circles, and so, inspired by these ideas of revolution and reform he had come to live in the city: to succeed.

It's of course true that many people come to a city from the provinces to be celebrated, it's not an unusual ambition, and in fact from a certain distance there was something similar to both Yves and to Celine: they wanted intensity, and began by thinking that the contemporary was the place of most intensity. But Yves's ambition had a darkly different tone. He was infected with something like the infection of literature. But whereas the fame some writers like Beaumarchais wanted was to make something that would be beyond time, the fame Yves imagined was rather to extend himself as far as possible within the timespan of his lifetime, to make an image of himself that would be known by the greatest number of people. He assumed that the medium he should choose for this was literature, but when he came to the city and discovered that he was only mediocre as a writer, he realised that there was another possibility. He had studied law, after all. Yves decided that his fame would be arrived at through public speeches. He imagined a new model of justice, where anyone could come and plead on anyone's behalf, directly to the people.

Around him, Yves gathered a set of radical friends. Some of these were rich, like Dolan. Most of them were other lawyers or journalists, like Jacob. All of them were lonely. They set up reading groups to discuss their revolutionary ideas, like Jacob's club to defend the slaves in America, which he had begun after his journey travelling through the American South, and these clubs then expanded to societies and resistance cells.

Yves made a world around him, and soon he began to love this frantic city. He loved the juice trucks, the sausage stalls, the breakfast meetings. He loved magazines and wanted to have one of his own. A magazine, thought Yves, might be a little portal through which a fiction could enter reality, and in his case the fiction he and his friends wanted to produce was a constitution. Without a monarchy you had to make something out of nothing, and it seemed very interesting to him that across the ocean the Americans had invented something called *the people*. He wondered if something similar could happen here.

It was as if a new power were oozing into the world, and the medium this power chose, thought Yves, was language.

13

The morning after Julia was released, Yves therefore sat down with Julia's desolate husband to suggest a plan. Dolan shouldn't let these people get away with this, said Yves. Everyone knew what was happening in the police department. There was corruption everywhere. Dolan agreed that it was disgusting. These people had, Yves argued, no sense of right or wrong. They lived without restraint. It was possible that Dolan could not see this, because he had lived among them too long.

The city at this time was very wired because the government had just banned every law court from sitting, after many judicial reviews of its spending forecasts and its war planning. A lot of young men were therefore sitting in cafes, unemployed, and arguing. It had made the atmosphere jumpy and alive with possibility. A person must always be looking for opportunity, thought Yves, the moment at which they find themselves at the edge of the contemporary, and he finally thought he had discovered his moment for action.

Now, Dolan liked Yves because he wanted to support a younger generation and he felt the future would be in some kind of liberal future, but this morning he was still feeling heavy and dejected. The house felt empty. He felt very tired. It seemed so boring, to be one of the billion people whose wife hated them. He had never felt part of his wife's general circle but until now he had felt a kind of pride in this isolation. He had seen it as part of his multinational vibe – the way he was Irish as much as French: too Irish among the French, too French among the Irish. But now everything that had once seemed unique about him felt lonely and aggrieved, and therefore easily vulnerable to Yves's questions and insinuations.

Dolan observed that if these women thought they could do whatever they wanted, they were kind of right, especially if Lenoir was in on this too.

But what he was saying, said Yves, was that this was a new era. Law could conquer everything. And there were two very simple cases they could bring. The first case would be against Julia, accusing her of adultery. The second case would be against Lenoir, for misconduct in public office, with Celine and Lorenzo named as his accomplices. Yves would represent him in both. They would become symbols of society's corruption and injustice. Sure, there were no courthouses at the moment, but this would mean that they had space to first make their case in writing, through a series of pamphlets and other articles.

– Nothing good, said Dolan, ever happens in a courtroom.

– Yes but still, Yves replied.

And this was how the new wave of pamphlets about the meaning of Celine and her friends began. In the weeks that followed, so many words squeezed out of Yves, like some linguistic paste. The atmosphere that leaked from these women, he wrote, was something magical and malevolent. This was the basic message of his series. Women corrupted the whole system, so that everything was confusing, and a man was constrained in every way. He wanted to be himself but everywhere he went, wrote Yves, a man was thwarted.

14

After Celine had become a legend, she felt that there was no worse fate. But perhaps this word legend is too various to be useful, and one way of trying to define it might be to compare the legends of Celine to various legends of someone very different to Celine, legends which began circulating at the same time as her own across the ocean in Hispaniola. They were legends of the man who became known as Toussaint Louverture, the man who freed the slaves, but right now was only Toussaint – and that's maybe what's so perplexing, how quickly legends can circulate but the meaning only reveals itself more gradually.

The first legend people reported was that Toussaint was the spirit of previous resistance guerrillas come back to life – like the slave who had escaped his plantation and hidden out in the mountain forests then moved around the island, who could control the natural world, who taught other slaves how to find the most poisonous roots, how to distil them in tea or wine so that the white people died immediately. Because maybe every revolution had to begin with people dying. The second legend was that Toussaint was a writer, who wanted Literature + Politics + Life. At the dance-hall nights in town he stayed at the bar, talking in multiple languages to the maroons and other runaways and ingesting all the information they possessed. The third legend of Toussaint was that he was simply monstrous.

All of them were legends about a person who was ignored, or unknown, by what was assumed to be the world. So that it might be possible, thinking about Celine and Toussaint together, to say that a legend is a story a world tells itself, but the real meaning of this story is unknown to the people who invent it. A legend is a story about the way no world ever realises that it's surrounded by another world, until it is too late.

15

Celine no longer thought about language in a happy way, a careful way. In her messages she let her grammar do whatever it wanted, she didn't care. Every day she wanted to be something she could admire but now the route towards living right seemed blocked or different, as if she had approached a road and found it barricaded or dug up. The route that was there when she was young was no longer there now she was older, now time had continued. But in the absence of language she wasn't sure what else she would be able to trust. All she knew was that she felt in some way out of place, with no other method available.

And this was creating little differences between her and her friends. After Julia's kidnapping and Yves's pamphlets, they had developed a series of late-night emergency set-ups, where Celine and Marta and Julia tried to figure out what moves they could make. Marta wanted them all to be *furious*, she said. The problem was, said Celine, that since Yves's hatred of women was entangled with this passion for reform and even revolution, it was difficult to resist with the right precision. She understood this, replied Marta, but still, she always loved how angry they had been. And now she couldn't feel it. It was very hurtful, said Julia, that this person who didn't know them at all could suddenly attack them, just because it was useful. Because they were famous, said Marta. She wasn't sure, said Julia, if they were in any way still famous. What she really wanted, said Celine, was not to be public at all. The problem with this point of view, Marta replied, was that you had very little choice about being public or not. Either you were public or you weren't, and they seemed very much to have been made public forever.

Always, said Celine, and this was the aspect of the affair she hated, it was the woman who was evil. The kind of story these writers turned lives into! It was always the boring woman, not loving or giving or lively enough for some resplendent man. But also: the woman who was too giving, too lively – so desperate with desire that she terrified the man in front of her. The woman was hated for doing something which men wanted her to do: to pursue them desperately and ardently. Whereas, continued Celine, it was surely obvious that many men in fact wanted their wives to be seduced. Much more common than a woman who was all desire, was a man wanting in some way to invent a distance between him and his current partner.

It was true, said Julia, agreeing with Celine, that it was Dolan who encouraged her to spend time with Lorenzo, so that she wouldn't be lonely. She in no way chased after Lorenzo. Why would she? If anything, Dolan had ordered her to hang out with him. It was all his idea. Whenever he was away on business, and he was away on business a lot, he used to send her messages, telling her to spend time with Lorenzo if she was unhappy or bored.

– And you have these messages? said Marta.

– I mean, of course, said Julia. – So does Lorenzo. He sent him messages too.

– And so, said Marta, we're back in business.

Because you should always keep an archive, not only of the messages you send but the messages you receive. You never know when you'll need attack material and evidence.

It was certainly a move, and every move was something to celebrate. But still, that night, as they went to bed feeling filled with the energy of action, Celine couldn't stop thinking about the rubble of the barricaded route. Not, of course, that Celine's thinking happened often or even ever in this way, in sentences. Her thoughts emerged as voices from outside her, then dissolved. And perhaps, she more and more thought, these voices did not belong to her at all.

Something inside her was alarming. Something inside her was vibrating.

16

They passed the messages to Beaumarchais for him to publish as soon as possible. Because in a world made of writing, malevolent writing could only be erased by more writing. But weeks went by, and nothing appeared.

All Celine was left to think about, therefore, was her ongoing problem with money. It was becoming difficult to see how she could financially survive in this situation – of living with no one. What would be wonderful would be if her friendship with Marta could become a kind of marriage, as if it were possible to live in a completely new way, something wayward and improvised, but this seemed impossible. More and more, whenever she talked about her thinking with

Marta, they somehow misunderstood each other, as if Celine was changing in one way and Marta in another.

Maybe she wasn't the only person trying to calculate a route out. Everyone seemed stressed. It was becoming more fashionable to gamble. In the streets you sometimes saw people wearing what looked like all their clothes, nomads dressed in many shirts and sweaters and coats, and whereas a few years earlier these people would have been dismissed as crazy it was now rumoured that they had access to higher truths and people wrote about them with awe and respect. It was as if while everyone went into the little tunnel of the ter-rifying future there was always the choice of becoming harder, more inward, embarked on some secret mission of self-improvement and purification.

Eventually she ran into Beaumarchais. They were by the vodka factories near his house. She asked him what was up and he replied that he had just damaged his new vehicle and the repair costs, he said, were pure melancholy. She felt claus-trophobic, even here in the open air. It was as if he had forgotten what he was meant to be doing.

– I'm very anxious, she said. – *What are you doing with the messages?*

– I'm on it, said Beaumarchais, – don't worry.

– But I am worried, she said.

– I just need to work out how to publish them.

– This means nothing to me.

It was as if for Beaumarchais any act of writing, even mes-saging to the chop shop or the pharmacy for pickup, had to be considered and authored and intent.

– I'm just thinking, said Beaumarchais. – Trust me. Also are you eating? You look tired. When did you last eat a croissant?

– I have money troubles, said Celine.

– Don't we all? said Beaumarchais.

– No, said Celine.

Celine was trying to think about whatever it was her body seemed to be thinking about, this sense of being to one side or blocked or displaced. It upset her, to be thinking so fuzzily. She was trying to understand the rules of time! It was very exhausting, this spirit labour, the work she was doing on time.

Sometimes she wished she was a man, not really or not always, but sometimes, just for the freedom and the lightness. She couldn't be casual, not in the way they could exist so casually in the world, like how Beaumarchais seemed to feel. It was as if the kidnappings and the money dependency and the libel that women had to spend their days avoiding or dealing with never occurred to them at all.

A man was everywhere thwarted, Yves had written. But try being someone who wears a dress every day, thought Celine, then see what *thwarted* means.

17

Most of all she missed Saratoga.

In her last message Saratoga had described her current problem of pets. She now had many cats, wrote Saratoga, which she had been given because she once liked cats or just said she liked cats, and these cats kept on producing other cats. And it was a problem because every time she left the house they would watch her go, sitting at the windows,

The way the forest was developing was partly its own invention and partly, explained Saratoga, because Julia had planted some seedlings which she had been given by Jacob, which he had brought back from America. She had planted them among her surviving trees and very quickly, very slowly, they had started to set up little communication systems that were new and overlapping. Everything was dry but inside the saplings it was milky, thick liquors held inside the woven tubes of each stalk. They were trying to understand the alien earth and air. Everything was rustling, was curious. They had found themselves in burnt-out soil, and the effect on them was very exciting. Little ferns emerged and reproduced in mid-air, among the branches. The look was almost comical. It was a forest where the size was miniature, a forest that was also sparse, which meant that in a way it was the opposite of a true forest, the kind of forest which seemed to be defined by density. It allowed the trees new kinds of information.

What then happened was that new interpreters emerged, to communicate between the soil and the trees. Little mushrooms appeared at the base of each tree trunk. First there were chanterelles everywhere, yellow among the black earth. Underground, the threads from these fungi grew into the hairs of the roots, so that they couldn't be separated. Everything was a blur and tangle. The threads gathered little messages from the soil and the rock. These mushrooms were new in the forest. No one had seen them before. The trees fed the fungi their sugary drinks and in exchange the fungi diverted away from the trees anything they thought might be harmful to them, the toxins or metals, and when they had gathered enough of these elements they transformed into ever crazier varieties of mushroom: porcini, cepes, boletes. Everything was a form of thinking and comparison. If water fell in one area, too far for the trees to reach, it could be transported back to the trees through the filaments of the fungi. It was an education, a little process of apparent self-assembly – the way a group of people might take over a disused gas station and somehow transform it into a cinema for the benefit of the whole community.

She walked with Saratoga among the trees, and it was very beautiful, thought Celine, because it finally seemed possible that she would not need to speak.

18

Back in the city, with this image of Saratoga inside her, Celine continued to spend most nights with Marta. They lived frazzled. They got into new wines. The wines were very curious: sometimes tasting of prunes or flowers, sometimes of stone walls and cumin. They wanted to be bold, to be future-oriented. It seemed impossible. Everything was slow. Something was happening to them that couldn't be disentangled from the economic situation, and the general masculine atmosphere, and the impending court case, but that was also its own pure thing. Their friendship was becoming scarred and tortured by time. The way this was obvious was the way conversation between them was just a little heavier. It tended to become about themselves, and until now they had never felt any need to talk about themselves, and the language they were using for each other was very brittle, a dry surface. Celine was starting to look like a thin man, said Marta. A very tiny thin old man. Had she noticed this? Had she stopped eating? Celine felt herself about to argue, decided that she couldn't.

Now, these conversations were of course fleeting and unimportant, but they ended up accumulating dusty spores and traces, and it was painful how a kind of atmosphere could seep into the places you most loved. A new pamphlet came out – signed anonymously but absolutely by the people – accusing Beaumarchais of being on the side of the current regime. The sign for this collaboration was the ambiguity of his writing, the way sincere and noble sentiments emerged from a structure of wild farce. And it turned out that Celine was on one side of this argument and Marta was on another, whereas earlier that kind of gap between them would have been impossible.

Maybe what was happening was a slight slippage in the things they each valued, or the way they expressed these values. Marta was becoming wild in the way she imagined a future world. She liked to talk about the little revolutions that were beginning or maybe beginning on the edges of things, all over the oceans. Whereas Celine felt more restrained but also more savage or ambitious. The point was, she thought, that you couldn't think about the future using the methods you use in the present moment. You had to think about the future using future methods. Otherwise any new society would be too similar to the old societies. So they needed more original thinking.

It was becoming obvious that to be in a couple with a woman was very different to being in a couple with a man. With Marta she had only private rituals, they were allowed nothing public or communal, and this was difficult to continue forever. The total strangeness of what they were attempting was becoming some kind of burden too. Perhaps whatever it meant to be with another person also required other people's public and calm attention. A secrecy was always too unreal.

To try to ignore this anxiety Celine continued to read the novels or go to the theatre, but it was suddenly a drag, the way a person can suddenly become a drag, because none of these representations seemed to be able to describe her particular state: where power was so absolutely absent.

And meanwhile all conversation was becoming more and more tense. At one party a plantation owner from Hispaniola argued with Jacob about his mania for the protection of slaves, and when Jacob said that maybe it would be interesting to reverse things, and for the whites to lose everything and the slaves to take over, the plantation owner knifed him in the arm, shouting that he should see what the British businessmen were doing in Calcutta, then he'd see what real psychopaths looked like. While in another room, high on some new spirit, Lorenzo challenged Julia's husband to a duel, then disappeared before he could reply. Instead he holed up in the countryside with Beaumarchais, working on their adaptation. And Marta did not talk to Celine for three days because Celine had gone with Izabela to watch a horse race out in the suburbs without telling her.

Everything was high gesture and emotion and there seemed no time to think.

And then one morning Celine was interrupted by Cato, who gave her a message from her ex-husband, Sasha. The message was to inform her that their house in town was going to be sold. Or more precisely that he had sold it. In two weeks, Celine would be homeless. It was an ambush, his super-suave but violent revenge. He had sold the house, wrote Sasha, to an international billionaire, who'd decided to move cities for a while.

She had two weeks to find money or a house or both. She lowered every blind, lay down and closed her eyes.

19

Nothing in the way she had been brought up by her parents had allowed her to think this brutally. It was true that in the last few years she had become more used to thinking about money and dealing with money, but she had never needed to think about it so directly and so quickly. She wondered if perhaps she could make money herself, like if she sold off everything she owned. She soon realised that she owned far too little. She needed a larger connection.

That evening, she began writing messages. She messaged Marta. In the middle of this she messaged her parents without mentioning what was happening. Then she did the same with Saratoga. Then finally she thought of Hernandez, the richest person she knew, however much she hated him, who messaged back charmingly, telling her to come the next day.

Hernandez seemed indestructible, like plastic. Everyone disliked him and yet he always survived, however many people were being knifed or poisoned or disgraced or just slowly going crazy around him. His face was still the face of a lovely boy, and his hair was still outsized. When she found him, he was dressed in some new denim couture outfit.

There was a window open to a garden. A child was playing listlessly in a corner. It was unclear if this was Hernandez's child or not. All the objects in the room presented themselves with a very still clarity. It was as if his house had the luxury of the inside and outside being delicately entwined, like a pool pavilion. They sat down opposite each other. Everything was expansive, was precious, but also the one true subject of the conversation was continuously absent. Hernandez was concerned about her, he said. He seemed to be enjoying this situation very much, of having this woman who had rejected him beg him for his help. And she felt very sick, that this man who she found so disgusting had a power over her – which was the absolute but withheld power of money.

She needed someone to give her some money, she said, to buy off Sasha. Absolutely, he said. Did she know of anyone? Then he passed across a plate of candied oranges. He asked her what her plans were, as if this meeting itself were not her major plan. What she needed, she said, was someone to stop Sasha. If only, said Hernandez, someone *could* stop Sasha. It had been something everyone had been always thinking about.

Celine hated that she had come here. She could forgive herself in some way because she was only here out of desperation, but still, she wondered if this reflected an inner lack of resources.

An assistant walked in, and Hernandez introduced them. The assistant was called Josef and he wanted to be an actor. He had a weird charisma. She asked Josef a few questions. He said that for him the only thing that mattered was theatre. Was he sure? she asked. Like totally, he said. She had a sense that in another version of the universe she would have liked to talk to him more but everything was clouded by her financial desperation. He was incredibly small, with very delicate hands. Then she realised that Josef was delicately escorting her to the door.

Celine felt too upset to resist him. The present moment was being revealed as something deeply banal, just something very oppressive and impossible. It was all about money and money was everywhere available and yet completely absent. It was everywhere available to men and completely absent for women.

The only place she had left was Marta's. So she moved in to Marta's house, without unpacking anything from two trunks. Everything else was put in storage in a suburb warehouse off the northern freeway. It made her uncomfortable, as if suddenly they were living together like a couple – even though of course Marta's husband was also there. He was always very gentle to her. He either didn't notice the closeness between Marta and Celine or did not mind. It was impossible to tell. He spent a lot of time corresponding internationally with other scientific collectors, or organising his collection, of which the most prized item was still the bones that Washington had sent him from the American wilderness. It seemed absolutely useless work, and Celine couldn't work out if this made her admire or despise him.

She couldn't concentrate on anything.

– I just, said Celine to Marta, – want people to care. And I know that obviously I am talking about money, I am talking about how worried I am about money, but not just money. I want someone to understand that it might be necessary to pay more attention.

It was suddenly obvious to Celine that mostly when you talked nothing major was said but then something was said that was absolutely and incontrovertibly true. And when that happened it was almost frightening.

The next day, the billionaire arrived in town, and took her house away. And then Marta and Celine had one final argument that felt too truthful not to be irrevocable.

20

One day Marta and Celine decided to go back to the countryside to see Julia and Saratoga, in the forest. Lorenzo and Beaumarchais were also there, on their writing spree. It seemed like an ideal shift of landscape.

Everything began very peacefully – just sitting outside with dogs, and people getting up sleepily to go inside and make coffee and write little letters or notes in their journals, or Saratoga complaining about the terrible books she was given to read, as if her teachers thought she was stupid, while Lorenzo and Beaumarchais talked business. Celine listened to them talk like background music, just enjoying something corrupted and superficial, the way Lorenzo complained how wherever you went as a writer, you found the same problems: envy, jealousy, irritation and ingratitude. It was all the problem of producers, said Beaumarchais, of people like Hernandez. Nothing could be done without a client, without a commission, and you had no way of controlling which clients or commissions might come your way. It was like, continued Beaumarchais, the way your entire love life, the entire course of desire through your life, would have to be incarnated in whichever people you happened to meet, whichever people happened to be available. Had he talked to Hernandez about the finale? said Lorenzo. He couldn't bear it, said Beaumarchais. In his entire lifetime, said Lorenzo, he had never found a producer who understood what to do with a finale.

– Talk to me, said Celine sleepily. – Tell me about it.

A finale, said Lorenzo, obviously had to remain connected very closely to the opera as a whole, no one was arguing with that. But it should also be its own little comedy, with a totally new and seemingly impossible plot. This is what Hernandez, like everyone, failed to understand. A finale should have everything, with all the characters back onstage. But what if some characters had died? asked Celine, who had been kind of listening and kind of looking at the little shadow of the forest. But no one died in their script, said Lorenzo. Couldn't she remember?

It was at about this moment that a message came from Dolan, Julia's husband, saying that he had accepted Lorenzo's offer of a duel. He had found out where Lorenzo was, and was now travelling down from the city. He would be there in an hour. It was unexpected, they had kind of forgotten it, and it might have been amusing if it hadn't also been potentially fatal. All the laziness of the vacation disappeared. Beaumarchais would have to help him, said Lorenzo. Celine wondered if maybe there was an alternative to Beaumarchais. What alternative? said both Lorenzo and Beaumarchais. Who else was there out here, in the countryside? Lorenzo thought he should maybe go out to practise, like aiming at a tree. Beaumarchais, thought Beaumarchais, would change into something different.

She was getting so bored of this, said Celine. Of what? said Julia. Of this madness of men, said Celine.

Julia got up to go and lie down. She was feeling tired, she said. She hated being pregnant. She hated everything about it. Saratoga went upstairs too, to do some writing assignments from her teachers. Celine went upstairs with her, to go to the bathroom. She went into Marta's bag to get a book. In the bag, she found a package of medicines, prescribed by some wildcat analyst – which Marta had promised her she'd stopped taking months ago. She came back downstairs, holding them.

– The fuck is this? she said.

– It's a difficult time, said Marta.

– For me it's a difficult time.

– For everyone it's difficult, said Marta.

– But you promised me, said Celine.

– What is this? said Marta. – What right do you have?

It was so precise that it was devastating. All the terms between them had lost their meaning, and this is always a kind of premonition.

Then Julia's husband, Dolan, interrupted them with his high-speed entrance. He was making little jokes and not looking at anyone.

– Where's Julia? he said.

– In bed with Lorenzo, said Celine.

And he was maybe, she observed, amazed, about to hit her when Lorenzo and Beaumarchais came downstairs, dressed in painters' overalls and holding rifles. They nodded at everyone, silently, as if this farce were entirely rational – then all the men went outside, into the subtle twilight. Around them the forest brooded and joked with bird noise.

Celine and Marta continued to sit in the living room. For a while there was a silence.

– We keep on arguing, said Marta, – I really hate it.

– We weren't arguing, said Celine.

– You see? said Marta.

– It's the situation, said Celine. – It's the atmosphere. It's infecting us. All these men.

– You can't keep blaming what's happening on men, said Marta. – Or I mean, not just blame the people who –

It was as if their conversation was now dark with holes and canyons. Gaps appeared, sudden pauses. Each conversation was hampered by miniature problems: self-fulfilling prophecies, vicious circles, inconsistent causes . . .

– Don't you ever wonder, said Marta, – why they feel the need to write so much about us?

– Writers?

– Well, yes but no, said Marta.

– Their empty interiors, their mangled hearts? said Celine.

– It isn't that, said Marta. – Or I mean. It isn't just that. You never think about what's happening. You don't see it.

– Oh but you do? said Celine.

It was as if there was no more conversation possible. There had been so much conversation and now it was all gone.

– Look at Cato, said Marta. – Look how much he's listening.

– He's listening because he lives with me.

– He's listening because something is *up*, said Marta.

Suddenly Celine found that she couldn't speak. It was as if Marta was accusing her of thinking too much as a girl, of not thinking about power itself, and it upset Celine very much because in thinking as a girl she felt that she was thinking in the most acute way about power.

– I'm unhappy, said Celine, after a long pause.

– That isn't my problem, said Marta.

The statement was so absolutely hurtful because it was very clear and also very cruel – but Celine had no time to think about it because at that moment Lorenzo came back into the house, bleeding from the arm. The duel, said Beaumarchais, had been very exciting and amusing. They had all forgotten to bring anything to mark out the distances, so they had to use two notebooks that he happened to have in his pocket. Also, Lorenzo's movements were incredibly funny because he was wearing his new pair of very expensive boots which he couldn't really walk in, but which of course at that point were impossible to remove.

The blood looked like paint on his overalls. He was pretty sure Lorenzo's arm was OK, said Beaumarchais, kind of hurrying up the stairs, knocking over a fragile fern, as he went up to the bathroom, looking for alcohol and bandages. The atmosphere was doom-laden but exhilarated. Saratoga came downstairs, furious that she had missed an entire dramatic episode. No one was mentioning Julia's husband, Dolan. It was unclear if he was still there, somewhere in the forest, or had disappeared into the black night. And as always Celine thought how amazing it was, that nothing was ever resolved in a duel, even when the duel was meant to be the absolute resolution – the same way nothing was ever resolved, it suddenly occurred to her, by conversation.

That evening Celine went outside into the forest. She felt very alone. She couldn't stop thinking about Marta, and their last conversation. Maybe every conversation left a person sullied, thought Celine, just by not telling the truth or exaggerating or realising only later that the other person was lying or exaggerating to you too. And perhaps that's why a conversation so often is an event, something that installs itself inside you. But also it was possible that some conversations wounded you because what was said in them was true.

So much effort to think about other people! The yearning for them, the disappointment in them! It was always so very difficult to make a connection to someone else. It really wouldn't seem very surprising if in the future people tried to fly off this planet forever, to disappear into the dark and encrusted sky.

She began to wonder if perhaps it was time for Saratoga to come and live with her in the city, then she thought about the way people talked in the city and she wanted Saratoga to stay away forever.

Celine wanted to grow towards the world, the way algae will grow towards whatever it encounters. She wanted the invisible to be able to circulate among the visible. It was something she had felt forever.

She went out into the American saplings.

– Keep thinking about other things, said a voice.

There were always many voices in her head, but this voice seemed to be different to any voice inside her head. She didn't know what to do. She looked back towards the windows of the house, glowing in the green twilight.

– Like, think about this, said the voice.

– This what? said Celine.

– The forest, said the voice. – The world.

– Were you listening? said Celine.

– It isn't difficult, said the voice.

For a moment Celine stood there, because she understood that this experience if she tried to talk about it would seem extreme or even crazy, but she did not feel crazy.

– I disagree, she said.

– You do? said the voice.

What she meant, said Celine, was that it was sometimes very difficult to understand something else.

She understood that she was talking either to a spirit or to herself or possibly both, but in all of these cases she liked the conversation so she decided to continue.

For instance, when she read the new translations, the ones from Eastern languages about the beginning of things, she said, she was not sure she understood them.

– Go on, said the voice.

Like how there was nothing and then there was something, she said. This was what they were saying. There was nothing and then there was dust. Then this dust began to coalesce, it began to *take*, the way mayonnaise begins to thicken. Maybe *emulsion* might be more precise, a kind of thickening into density. Or another way they had of putting this, said Celine, was that suddenly something breathed: its own impulse. It arose through the power of heat. And it was very small – like a chinchilla, or the way the smell of a cigarette that fumes in someone's fingers while she writes a message with her other hand is very small.

– What are you trying to say? said the voice.

– Just, said Celine, – that I find it difficult to think like that.

– Think in the same way you would want someone to think as you, said the voice. – With sympathy and acrobatic agility.

– But is that really possible? said Celine. – Maybe it's not even right, to try to think as other people.

– It's not about you, said the voice, – it's about everything outside you. If you remember that, you'll find a way to do it.

– But what if everything just gets flattened out?

The sun was trying to set now.

– Remember tenderness, said the voice.

For a long time Celine said nothing. She was alone but she didn't feel alone, she felt surrounded, and it was a delicate feeling. It was as if an entire world were able to talk with her. She was thinking about something she had heard from Claude, her scientist sailor. He had recently given a series of lectures about the ocean. He had talked about the death of Titere. Titere had been murdered in the war he had hoped to win, after years of fighting, so that now the islands were being run by his enemies, led by a king called Tu – and Titere's story, said Claude, had caused him to come to upsetting conclusions. He had now been to these islands in the ocean more than once. And what had struck him most forcefully was not just the beauty and the strangeness of these places but also the differences he had noticed between his first and subsequent voyages. When he had first seen them he had thought that they were paradise, but now he was not sure. Of course, he continued, they made beautiful objects, wonderful things, like the feathered gods, the god Ku with his many teeth who was the god of war, or the costumes of those who mourned, with their tropicbird feathers, their pearl shells and barkcloth stamped with blood, naturally they created all these things that were evidence of an intelligence and refinement that in many ways surpassed their own, but what he wanted to talk about was the way these things were part of a society that was also just as violent and upsetting. He had thought that they existed outside history, said Claude, but he was wrong. These islands, like the hundred states of Europe, represented a maximum of diversity in a minimum of space. It led to beauty but it also led to history, and history always won.

– Try to think in a way that's neutral, interrupted the voice. – Just something that gently speaks.

Celine stood inside the forest.

– Are you still there? she asked the voice.

It seemed perhaps that it wasn't.

Titere could sing very wonderfully, remembered Celine. She had never known anyone so concerned with gentleness and politeness. He had once come back from an evening walk in the park where he had heard, he said with amazement, at least seven couples together – and as she remembered this she also remembered with a kind of shame how much Sasha had liked to fuck her in front of windows, to push her up against a window, fucking her from behind, pretending they were looking at a view.

22

Then the summer ended. The government collapsed and because it had collapsed the order to shut down the law courts also disappeared. All the lawyers came back from the country-side, rested and tanned and treacherous. It was a moment of manic activity, inside which was Yves, loud as a machine, making sure his depositions were read in the right offices. A week later, a judge decided that Yves's double filing would be heard as a single case, in a single trial. The decision seemed ominous.

The city was a vast interior. Every room stank of mould and old food. After the duel, Lorenzo's arm had stopped working. He lay inside, complaining. Julia was feeling sick again, now that she was about to give birth. In the streets there were people selling unknown liquors and mashed-up pills. To get high was the only way of coping. No one was talking to anyone else except very lightly and full of menace. Celine wanted to move out of Marta's house but she had nowhere else to go.

– Are you hiring a lawyer? Celine asked Beaumarchais. – Please tell me we have a lawyer.

– We don't need a lawyer.

– Please tell me you're not representing yourself, said Celine.

– I'm representing all of us, said Beaumarchais.

Then he paused.

– Can you smell shit? Do I stink of shit? he said.

He lifted his shoe to his face like a contortionist.

– Dogshit, said Beaumarchais.

23

The trial was a major social event. The story of Julia's infidelity then kidnapping and release operated on the culture like an algorithm, as if it might be the solution that could interpret everything people were feeling: the hunger and the mania and the fear. As much as she was used to this publicity Celine hated it. The way people talked about the case with such abstraction and amused distance made her feel even more exposed, and this exposure only seemed more absolute because after their argument in the countryside Marta wasn't there with her. Celine had gone through everything with Marta and now suddenly Marta was missing.

The deep reason for all this public interest was it seemed hard to define, and in fact the horror of this entire story, thought Celine, was that it was impossible to analyse its meaning precisely. You couldn't know and in fact no one would ever know which hatred was the absolute, the basic thing. Was it hatred of the rich? Or of Celine and Julia? Or the police? Or of all women, their delightful and therefore enraging and humiliating bodies? And maybe in fact it was none of these and something else that Celine could never imagine was what gave the story its energy.

In the hot box of the courtroom Yves opened the trial, outlining the case against them. On the desk in front of him were his pamphlets, rustling with colourful tabs. He spoke for seven hours. When he finished he sat down, wildly trembling. Ideally, thought Yves, he would have left the scene entirely, like an actor enveloped by the velvet curtain. His speech used the word *sentiment* eleven times, and *shame* fourteen times. Twenty-three people began crying, including Yves himself.

It was very possible that the true subject, the way it always was the true subject, thought Celine, was language. Because all reality was an illusion and could only be produced in words. And therefore what needed to disappear were the words.

24

There was one night during the trial when Celine had gone to some party – entering through the fern colonnades and the water features – and in the crowd a little man introduced himself to Celine. He was a writer, he said. He had written that novel *Messages*? Then he stopped talking. He was inflated with silence. His eyebrows nearly joined in the middle.

Celine was thinking very much and also thinking that the horror of being a human was that so few conversations could be had because the amount of detail necessary to have the conversation – not even to have the conversation itself but to give the context necessary for the conversation to begin, like dates and places and names – was too wearying to be rehearsed. She wanted to talk about the way she felt when listening to Yves talk about her and her world, or when the pamphlets about her were recirculated or mentioned – because it turned out that to be accompanied by this eternal double who was produced by the words of other people was still uncanny and disturbing – but she had no way of discussing the feeling with this writer without so much preparation and information that the prospect made her feel too tired. So instead she said that she'd read that novel of his and liked it. It was very brilliant, the way he multiplied perspective. He didn't seem disturbed by this leap into appreciation and in fact found praise so natural that he replied with an immediate disagreement. That wasn't how he saw it, he said to her. His novel was a weapon. It wasn't decoration. Was that how he saw all writing? said Celine. He didn't reply. It seemed he had stopped talking forever. You should talk to Beaumarchais, she said. Beaumarchais couldn't be considered any more after his latest play, he said. His first one was good, but he didn't follow it.

It was very scary. She couldn't believe how cruel he was but then understood that he too was a true writer, he had been consumed by the spirit of literature and so he couldn't really be judged for the violence of his thinking.

She looked around for help. Young assistants everywhere were handing out drinks and listening.

25

It was as if the problem was how to tell a story, and no one knew any more how to tell a story that didn't exclude or hurt other people. There were many stories overlapping and it was perhaps this, thought Celine, that was both exciting but also dangerous. There was always a movement between backgrounds and foregrounds so that you couldn't be sure exactly where you were in the picture.

She wondered if she should tell Beaumarchais this. He seemed to need the information. It was of course so difficult to keep up with all the information! It wasn't his fault, in a way, but still, he was behind the times.

The problem Beaumarchais was having, thought Celine, as she watched him perform the next day, was that the accusations against them were so abstract and even sociological, and it was not a scale at which he could imagine humans thinking. It made him harassed and even irritated, and in the vast courthouse with its bad acoustics he was also finding it difficult to make himself heard. But he did have something beautiful about him, after all, it seemed to her, which was the calmness with which he could describe things people did not usually want described.

It was very important, said Beaumarchais, to remember how abjectly and strangely people behaved in private. And one form of sexual behaviour which seemed difficult to understand was the way a man might want to be humiliated by another man, or by a woman in the disguise of a man. But in fact this wasn't so strange. Just as it wasn't so strange if a person couldn't bear this desire they had, if they wanted to punish the object of their desire for having provoked this love of humiliation. Desire was very surreal. As for himself, said Beaumarchais, he judged no one. But what he did judge was any attempt to bring desire into the public realm of censorship. The lawyers here were attempting something terrible and deadly. They wanted everything to be transparent. But this was a perversion of a vaster order. If they were allowed to win, said Beaumarchais, then a new era would begin which would be devastating and barbaric, where opinion would decide everything. He understood that he himself had been one of the people who had done most to institute this world, with the scripts he had put out. But this was only art, he said. A world of total transparency, concluded Beaumarchais, would be not just appalling but perhaps uninhabitable.

Celine found this beautiful but also not enough for the situation. He was growing old without giving up on his past opinions, the ones he had invented in his youth. He was living as if time did not exist. Whereas she was there on a high plateau, looking at time. And to age truly, thought Celine, was to give up on all the theories you had worked so hard to invent. Large processes were always occurring, many stories were overlapping, and it was only in this way, by letting your ideas fall away, that you could remain equal to these processes and not be damaged or even killed.

26

Still, it is such a shock, to discover how much time has passed, and how much novelty has therefore entered the universe. It can happen very abruptly, this knowledge, and this was something that was happening very often across the ocean, in America and other continents – like when Washington sent a diplomat out into the Mohawk Valley to talk with Louis Cook.

Louis had lost weight but still had the same hairstyle – the shaved head and the gleaming scalplock on top. He apologised if the conversation felt slow. He had recently caught a virus and was feeling unwell, he said. However, he still had Montour, his interpreter. Montour was always his voice, after all. He hoped it would be OK if Montour did most of the talking.

So Montour asked Washington's diplomat what he'd brought. The diplomat showed them the wampum belt, some guns. It used to be that there were cabins filled with gifts, said Montour, speaking as Louis. That's what people offered. Otherwise how would anyone know if they spoke from the heart? He understood this, replied the diplomat, but Louis and his people were subjects now. So things were different. He didn't understand, said Montour. He honestly had no idea what he just meant.

When the diplomat didn't reply, Louis heavily picked up the wampum belt and gave it back to him, then nodded at Montour. He didn't want to use wampum any more, said Montour. In that case, said the diplomat, what did they want? Montour paused. They would write to the chief instead, said Montour. They didn't want anyone to misinterpret what they were saying. Even if what they were saying was very simple: they were not a foreign nation.

It was always the same lesson in power everywhere. Everything overlaps and there is always another element to a world you will have missed.

Then Louis began to rummage in a bag and removed a silver oval plate, one of Washington's peace medals – stamped with a design of a man in feathers and warpaint greeting a man with a rifle and suit. He handed this over too.

The diplomat nodded, then began to go back to his team, who were waiting down by the river.

It was so abrupt and so without politeness or respect that Montour shouted to him to come back.

In fact, added Montour, maybe they could relay one particular extra message. The problem with the Americans and in particular with their boss, said Montour, was that they wanted to steal from other people, while pretending that it wasn't stealing. They wanted to steal from people with the consent of those from whom they were stealing.

So they could go fuck themselves, said Montour.

27

What Celine meant, she thought, was this. She had made the mistake of confusing intensity or pure living with the contemporary – and this had meant constantly inhabiting a space of prediction, a mania for little predictions about the future, and not only did she not want to be in this space any more, but it would be anyway impossible to inhabit this place forever. So that it could not be the way she wanted, of living as intensely as possible. It had to be somewhere else.

So that it didn't matter that Yves lost his case against her and her friends, that the judge ruled that there was no case to answer. There were some successes which were intimations of a larger fragility. It was very obvious, thought Celine, that there was a system, and this system allowed certain options to certain people and refused them to others. So people were right to be exhausted and appalled – even if not in this single instance, when a woman was being persecuted by her ex-husband.

But it seemed that no one else would understand this as largely as she did. It was as if she had exotic knowledge but no way to communicate this to anyone – the way an alhaja might feel on her return to her family.

After their victory Lorenzo insisted that they should all celebrate at one of the latest gambling resorts. The place was a miasma of sweat. At the door a girl was throwing up behind a palmetto. Hernandez came up to Celine to tell her with an amused lightness that he was suddenly bankrupt, it turned out, so he was now playing one final game, to try to win everything back. He was talking very rapidly, like there was some narcotic in his system.

People were drinking a punch that was plant-like and sour, something resembling pulque, domestic and dangerous. It made the focus on the gambling difficult. She was finding herself transfixed by little things, like a green wasp that had settled on the plate she was using as an ashtray then disappeared into a black tunnel of its own crawling. In the kitchen behind the bar, a woman was laying out dough on a table, flattening it until it draped over the edges, then moving around it, adjusting it, like a billiards player contemplating a trick shot.

Maybe this was because the presence of money and the need for money was too distressing. She felt it too acutely. Celine stood up and moved away, to look in silence out the window, down into a courtyard, where there was a fountain and an improvised wooden statue of what might have been a goddess, imperfectly draped, its base covered in fresh bunches of forget-me-nots and rosemary. In her anxiety this idol touched her very much, even as it also confused her, the way she was always perplexed by other people's feelings or beliefs whose provenance she couldn't understand.

Celine wanted another world, but it seemed impossible for anyone to ever get another world.

– Do you remember what you once said? – Julia said to her, suddenly beside her, licking ice cream from a spoon. – When we first met?

– Me? Celine said. – No.

– You said, said Julia, – *Do you want to know what will happen to us? You will do this, and I will do the opposite. And both of us will lose.*

Three

I

One afternoon Celine heard that Hernandez had died, after his long illness. The news gave her a surprising delight, as if the death of the famous producer was her own private victory over someone who had only ever harmed her, but she didn't talk about this delight with anyone else – partly because she felt ashamed of the violence of this feeling but also because it was now a time when no one talked about events openly. Instead the rumour of his death just gradually stained the whole town.

All of this secrecy was because there was a revolution everywhere. In this new atmosphere people wanted to know who was *virtuous* and who was *disgraced* – and while disgrace is a universal category it turned out that the reasons why a person might find themselves disgraced were very mobile, like speaking in a foreign language or taking a taxi. It was never obvious which new group was about to become accused. You might stay loyal to the cabinetmakers or the party planners until suddenly all party planners were imprisoned and you had to think about your possible escape.

This was why no one wanted to talk openly about Hernandez. The final aura of Hernandez and his projects was luxury, Yves pronounced in an interview, and luxury was outdated. The revolution had been beautiful for Yves. He had transformed himself from a radical lawyer into the minister for interior security. His gruesome face was pitiless. So no one praised Hernandez at all. And while Celine in no way wanted to defend Hernandez it was still amazing to her to see how nothing specific remained from any of his shows. He had been so powerful, he had been such a major presence on the scene with his large hair and scandalous habits of kissing assistants in bathrooms and leaving dresses out for them to wear. And now he was so absent. It somehow made Celine afraid, as if however much she herself had always doubted his value it was still disturbing to discover that this value had been created by being passed from person to person and could dissolve as soon as it remained in any stable position or at the moment where someone publicly refused the value at all – like the way Yves could now say: *Hernandez? Why did everyone get so excited by Hernandez?* And all the glamour Hernandez once had just disappeared in the fearful atmosphere.

She found it very troubling, thinking about Hernandez now that he was dead. The downfall of an enemy wasn't something she could enjoy if it was happening for reasons that were not the reasons why she hated him, and in fact it was very obvious that the same machinery that allowed him to be so eliminated could also eliminate her. So when Beaumarchais asked if she would go with him to the funeral it both amazed her that Beaumarchais could be so attached to Hernandez to want to be at this funeral, but also that she wanted to go too.

The funeral was held in the eastern suburbs. It was unusually warm. In the trees pomegranates slashed with eczema sores oozed among their branches. Inside the hall there was a little soporific noise of distant metal beaters in the thick air. It was always moving, to see how everyone was cared for by someone, thought Celine, however terrible they might have been. Hernandez's last assistant, Josef, was there.

He still loved theatre but was now a copy clerk in one of the government committees, he told Celine. He didn't like it. What he most loved were shows – but he found modern shows disappointing, compared to the shows he loved before. Then he went and sat down beside a single old woman, who was wrapping and unwrapping string in her upset hands. It was apparently Hernandez's mother. No one had ever met his mother or even knew that she was alive.

When the funeral began Beaumarchais stood up to speak, and it surprised Celine how apparently sincere and personal his words were – like how he kept imagining Hernandez, as he felt himself dying, saying *fuck I'm going to die*, as Hernandez would have told it afterwards in one of his stories, said Beaumarchais, if it hadn't been him who died. Then he was interrupted by the arrival of Jacob, very late, busily mentioning the traffic or his schedule.

Jacob had also become super powerful in the crisis era. He had finally made up for his unremarkable appearance with a major position in the revolutionary government, as minister for lands conquered from the enemy. All the effort he had put into writing had finally achieved this single flower: the flower of influence. And it was therefore a moment of total amazement for everyone there, his appearance at Hernandez's funeral. It was unclear if Jacob had come out of sentimental nostalgia or delight at Hernandez's death or in order to note the names of the refuseniks who were present. It added a larger frisson to Beaumarchais's speech which, like so many speeches in the black box of literature, was about the end of literature, the death of value – because it's always agreeable to believe in the death of writing, especially if you also believe that society is dying around you. If an entire art form is dead then no one needs to worry that someone, somewhere, might be in the process of creating a work of new and exorbitant value, but instead you are personally absolved of all responsibility for the art form's absent existence.

In the square outside, as everyone waited for their taxis, Jacob came over and hovered near Celine. Her ongoing friendship with him was complicated.

– The new list's published in forty-eight hours, he said. – Get out of town. Get out of here.

– But why? she said.

– Or get yourself off the list if you want to stay, said Jacob. – The fuck do I care. Just get yourself *erased*.

Jacob's life had become a series of meetings, with agendas and files, and he loved this power very much. It seemed miraculous to Jacob, the urgency of conversation that his new power allowed him. Everywhere he went there was this power of paper: the power to permit or to condemn. It felt like the future.

– Get out where? she said.

– I have no idea, he said.

She realised very clearly that although he had always been kind to her, in fact he didn't care for her at all.

– But I can't leave, said Celine.

2

The current scene was bleak. It seemed to Celine that the world had become a series of before and after sequences, all of which depended on the most drastic foundational change – which was that this revolution had given certain intellectuals vast indiscriminate power and this was amazing and also terrifying. They were so articulate and also so violent!

You could see this in the public feud between Jacob and Yves. They had once been friends, but power had separated them from each other forever. Yves had been given the job of interior security because of his total devotion to system. His eyebrows were still dark but the hair on his head was now white. It gave his froglike face an even more disturbing effect. He was famous for his legal coldness and the extravagance of his surveillance network and the purity of his belief in revolution, and it was this purity which had caused his rupture with Jacob, who could never quite abandon his past as a writer, an aesthete who had once hung out at parties, long ago, and whose own ministry of lands conquered from the enemy was famous for being more hesitant and careful when it came to absolute terror. Their feud was a theme that somehow infected everyone's lives. It infected every position. In the official paper Yves wrote that before the revolution Jacob had worked as a police spy – having signed a contract with the chief of police, the traitor Lenoir, in a suburban gas station for a fifty-dollar payment. Lenoir himself had disappeared from the city entirely. There was a thousand-dollar reward for information on him. Then Yves wrote that Beaumarchais had been a police goon too. He was high on denunciation. In response, Beaumarchais wildly challenged Yves to a duel. No one knew if a duel was still hip or not.

It didn't really matter because everyone agreed that Beaumarchais was finished. He was bankrupt, still chasing the money the Americans owed him from years ago. He had a letter from Washington's assistant which said that the case was closed. In the city no one would publish him. He continued writing in secret, in his journal: angry letters he never sent, entries where he maliciously recorded the conversations he overheard. He spent long hours on this writing, the way he never could any more on a script. The new men and women in power, he wrote, had given people everything and taken away just one privilege – that of writing badly. But of course, he added, without that right, which was also a luxury, it was impossible to write anything worthwhile at all. So fearful was he of enraging his audience, he concluded, he had therefore become the master of a new medium: the medium of silence.

A young scriptwriter had come up to him the other day, he told Celine, saying that he worshipped what he did. It was incredibly poignant, said Beaumarchais, how pleased this would once have made him. But also it was too late.

– I don't want worship, he'd told this little hotshot, said Beaumarchais. – I just want a show on.

She understood the feeling. She had almost no money left. She depended on random gifts and handouts. She was renting a two-room apartment for herself and Saratoga on the east side and felt hungry every day, with no money to give Cato, her assistant. For the moment he was staying because he had nowhere else to go.

Celine missed trattorias, elegance, drinking. Her porcelain collection was now seven mismatched plates and a water basin. So many things felt out of date: like people offering massages on the sidewalk, or the croissant sellers. And then she felt this sense of something very close to her, almost something with a texture, to be touched rather than known by thinking or by talking. The way something might brush past a person and touch her cheek. She had no name for this sensation. In the chaos she'd become increasingly superstitious. She had an old dress, something very gentle and natural, and she wore it every time she had to go to a government office.

And meanwhile people kept on disappearing. Every week a new list of suspected enemies of the people was circulated. It had been amusing when the fascists had to flee or were murdered, like Lenoir, or her ex-husband Sasha disappearing across the border to Rotterdam, even Antoinette holed up in prison on her own had a kind of justice – but more and more the situation was too unstable to be funny.

And the largest gap was Marta. Marta had gone to Milan, after her husband had disappeared. Before being erased he had founded an Academy of Sciences and then donated his major collection to the state, including its animal fossils. It turned out the state didn't think this was enough. Sometimes Celine thought about Marta every day. There was no one whose tastes and opinions she liked more than she liked Marta's. Then sometimes she didn't think about her for a month because everything was so busy and scattered and undone.

Claude was gone travelling, or had never come back from travelling. Izabela was back in Warsaw where she was inside another revolution and it seemed she would stay there forever. Of Celine's friends only Julia was left. She seemed to have a better sense for worldly connection. After the trial Lorenzo had left town to work on a new script in Vienna, and he and Julia had gradually decided they were over. Then the revolution began and Julia's husband fled back to his estates across the ocean, so she took the opportunity to divorce him and then married a radical, a commissar for Reason. The commissar was very sweet, a very caring stepfather to the son she'd had with Lorenzo and they were very happy together. Meanwhile Lorenzo talked shit about them and their domestic happiness furiously at the exile parties and show openings, even as he himself got married too and was apparently very contented.

And finally Cato came in one morning to say that he was leaving. He was going to join the movement. He'd been offered a position on one of the committees.

– But you don't need to leave, she said. – This is your place too. You can still stay here.

– This is your place, he corrected her.

– But you live here, she said.

– Your houses were never my houses, he said. – Don't make things so convenient. You need to think things through more clearly. I always had different ideas.

– Ideas about what? she said.

– Freedom, said Cato.

He suddenly seemed sincere, she realised, in a way that perhaps he had not been sincere before.

– Was it you who denounced me? she said.

– What kind of racist bullshit is that? he said. – Of course it wasn't. Anyway what do you mean: who denounced you?

It was impossible to know whether to believe him or not. He paused at the door.

– You need an exit strategy, he said.

3

When the revolution began no one had threatened Celine because she was a radical herself, with radical friends. She founded committees to examine and defend the rights of women. She assisted street campaigns. Jacob publicly named her as an ally of the people. But now there was this split between Jacob and Yves, there were some people who believed they were more radical than others and it turned out that these purists wanted to end her form of being radical entirely – her liberal thinking and its entourage.

Every day she found it puzzling that the same kind of pamphlets were being published about her, written by the same hack writers, the same indefinite murmur of writing, except now the writers were special advisers and government insiders. They used the same techniques to produce a new effect. The quotes they now made up were about her political views, like how she apparently laughed with Jacob when he mentioned the problems of farming shortages and labour laws. *These were short-term problems,* she said, *why was he so concerned with short-term problems? He should be worrying about the universe.* It seemed that what they disliked was friendship, or the way of being that was how Celine existed – very soft and linked to other tendrils, her gift for forming accomplices.

Which was why there were now little militias who sat bored outside her house, groups of children with guns, sitting on mismatched garden chairs. The atmosphere was intense. It was very confusing because in many ways Celine was more radical than those who were officially radical, in her understanding of where power was, and how it was distributed. She had known this since she was eighteen, and the writing about her began. But the problem was that she had spent too much time among the rich, she had once been rich herself, and in the end it was that kind of history which was being judged – and perhaps the radicals were right, thought Celine, at least in theory.

She was beginning to get little pains in her lower back, her upper back. Her parents were going crazy in the countryside because her father was dying of some boring and terminal illness. Her mother sent new messages every day, because she knew, she wrote, how Celine would want to be updated.

In the city wrecked people were wandering in the avenues. If you approached someone they crossed the street or pretended not to see you. It was a time when no one had any idea how to send a message to someone else because to send a message required knowledge of where you were sending it and also where you were yourself and neither of these seemed stable so that maybe, thought Celine, she would never send a message again.

For a while she kept a list in a notebook of who was missing and who was not. She did this even if she made a new friend – but then almost immediately that friend would disappear, so she stopped writing down names entirely.

4

Saratoga was seventeen, almost the same age as Celine had been when she had come to town. It meant that Celine experienced a large anxiety of comparison. Having a child destroyed so much of you, it seemed. It destroyed so much but it also reconstituted you in so many ways you could not have predicted. Saratoga had long blonde hair and seemed innocent but in fact was deadly and mysterious. She knew maths and geometry and Latin and political theory, along with a giant selection of European poets. Her clothes combined into a permanent look, like harem pants with guillotine earrings, and the confidence or indifference of this look made Celine feel old in a way that was almost restful.

But did she never just feel incredibly afraid? Celine said to Saratoga, as they sat across a desolate room drinking a fourth espresso. Was she the only one to think like this?

– Mama, said Saratoga.

They inhabited a world of talk that was unlike any other conversation she had experienced, thought Celine. Not even with Marta had she felt so silent but so fluent with communication, while at the same time having to acknowledge that the way Saratoga thought or talked was so different from her own that it would be impossible for her to ever learn it. And in fact the feeling she experienced was very close to desire or, Celine corrected herself, it might turn out that the feeling you thought was natural to feel for your lover was really a copy of the true feeling, which was the feeling you felt for your daughter, since it was so natural for her to hold Saratoga in her arms, on a bed, on a couch, and gently whisper to her that she would love her forever.

Saratoga took the world for granted as a little backdrop through which she could freely move, just as Celine had wanted when she sent her out among the forests and their plants, and it had given her a kind of general freedom and wildness. So Celine always loved this, the way it seemed to be part of the way she had brought her up without a father, but at the same time it gave Saratoga this confidence that Celine found unsettling and even disturbing. Saratoga disliked the writers who still surrounded Celine. In their books, said Saratoga, they were always writing about the education of girls, without understanding or knowing a girl at all. While whenever writers hung out together they were always talking so obsessively about the future, about who would be read in the future or what the future would look like – but they never saw how limited they always were in the way they thought about it. The true future wasn't what was about to happen in a month or even a year but the future future, said Saratoga: alien and incommunicable. But they never saw it, because they couldn't think that wildly.

It was impossible, thought Celine, to know if the worry she was feeling was really about Saratoga or in fact was about herself.

– We have to leave, said Celine.

– You have to leave, said Saratoga.

– But if I leave then where do you go?

– You know that Hugo wants me to go away with him? said Saratoga. – I mean he wants me to marry him.

Hugo was charming and atrocious. He came from London. He had a minor fame as the author of a whistleblowing report on the atrocities the British were committing in India, and was now due to go back out East, to oversee an investigation. But before that job was due to start he had travelled over illegally to go to the auctions. The government was selling off whatever had survived from the wreckage of people's houses. Hugo had come over because he loved both porcelain and tales of horror. And then he had met Saratoga.

– I mean, said Celine, – I guess it's one way out.

It was difficult to tell what Hugo really meant when he spoke. Saratoga liked him because he was from a different world entirely. He understood none of her references and this was liberating. But he was also such a jasoos, she said.

– Jasoos? asked Celine.

– It's a word Hugo learned, said Saratoga. – It means I don't trust him.

– Do you ever trust any of them?

– I mean –

– Because handing over one's soul to a man, I wouldn't recommend it, said Celine.

– You always say that, said Saratoga. – And I never have. Then Saratoga downed her coffee.

– This coffee tastes blue, she said. – Do you know what I mean? It just tastes blue.

– No, said Celine.

– But why are you afraid? said Saratoga. – I mean, no: forget that. I understand why you're afraid. What I'm saying is: *what are you going to do?*

– I have no clue, said Celine. – Your grandparents are going crazy. My father keeps attacking his nurses. Or something. According to my mother. So how do I go anywhere?

– But you have to try, said Saratoga.

Celine felt that the words she was using were more and more not wrapping themselves around a situation. They were little scraps that might have been pretty and alluring but they couldn't do whatever it was she wanted them to do.

The only person Celine could think of who might help her was Jacob.

5

In the last few weeks this general war between the radicals and the purer radicals had reduced itself to a particular argument. Some, like Jacob, wanted to abolish slavery in the Atlantic islands, and therefore supported the revolution there in its many forms, while putting out flyers and pamphlets and posters in defence of the rights of black people. Other radicals, the purists, like Yves, cared only about economics and refused to recognise the rights of other people as important, if this might reduce the nation's systems of production. They had already been fucking generous to the Jews, they said. So maybe everyone could now stop arguing and be more pragmatic. They had no time for people sitting around, imagining ideal futures.

Their problem was that the future was arriving at uneven speeds and it was starting to confuse the stories they were telling. In Hispaniola the ex-slave Toussaint, as he worked on revolution, had now given himself an extra name, Louverture: a name which meant a breach or illumination or opening. It was a new addition to his legend, and it seemed to imply that the powerless might be capable of doing anything, that they would fight forever – because if you have ever once worked on a plantation, knee-deep in stinking indigo shit, then you are going to be OK with the smell of the white man's kidneys as you hack at his fleshy body, you are going to prefer the smell of that person's kidneys to the swamp and the psycho owner. And right now there was a new story of his legend – of how Toussaint Louverture had just betrayed the Spanish.

The story was that a diplomat called Ulises – the diplomat who had once been posted to Paris, many years before – had been sent from Madrid to do business with Louverture. The Spanish wanted to set up a network of American colonies, and they wanted Louverture's help. But meanwhile Louverture also met with a businessman who proposed for a fee that he could travel on the Spanish ships incognito and on Louverture's behalf begin to foment revolutions among the black people against their common enemies. Louverture's plan, of course, was to persuade the Spanish of their perfect intentions while also earning themselves some money, not to mention creating revolution for the slaves, and because the diplomat Ulises was a delicate creature with no guile in him he agreed to this plan at once. But what Ulises did not know was that on that very same evening, with all the Spanish money transferred into his accounts, and the businessman off on his revolutionary travels, Toussaint Louverture rode through the night for another meeting, with his red handkerchief tied around his head in delicate knots, like a very elegant spirit of terror, this time with the French consul, where he promised to fight for them against both the British and the Spanish if they would guarantee the freedom of the slaves. But first, he said, and he said this very quietly, in Kreyòl, there was something the consul had to know, in case he was thinking of screwing him over. None of them could ever win against the blacks. Not a single fucking fat white.

It was this kind of story that was confusing Jacob and his enemies very much and therefore in its turn making the atmosphere in town very violent and difficult for Celine to read. To understand Toussaint Louverture's loyalty seemed very difficult for them, as if his idea of revolution was more comprehensive than the ideal they all shared. So that he could outwit them at any moment – he could zoom in or out of the picture, with some kind of higher technique.

6

The morning Celine went to see Jacob she woke up with a cold sore on one lip and a patch of eczema in her armpit. He'd told her that as minister for lands conquered from the enemy he had to oversee a refugee camp that had been set up outside the city, so he offered to meet her down by one of the river docks after he was finished.

She found him in the morning air, as if everything was beautifully normal and without any menace.

They walked together along the riverbank, watching people set up the botillerías with their arrangements of glassware and painted signs. He was her friend, she said, this was why she wanted to speak with him. In response Jacob's face was as neutral as possible. He possibly nodded, it was very unclear.

Jacob asked if she wanted a drink. It was eleven in the morning, she said. Absolutely, said Jacob.

She was used to being hated, she said to Jacob. She had lived with death threats, pamphlets, slogans, everyone talking about her with malice and delight. Surely he remembered this. So why, she said, would she now be on the list? It made no sense. She was a radical. All her friends were radicals. Ah, said Jacob. Now, he really wished he could help. But she had been denounced. It put him in a very difficult position. The list was basically untouchable. Celine asked who precisely had denounced her, because if she knew then she could possibly defend herself. Jacob replied in fragments that were so elliptical she could not understand him. All of politics, it suddenly seemed to her, maybe consisted in never finishing one's sentences. True power was always in allowing other people to interpret someone in the way they wished to be interpreted, without saying anything at all. Celine looked at him, then began again. Once, she said, she had seen him at one of her parties and he was weeping in a corner – did he remember? – he was crying because of something someone had written about him. And if that was just how he felt about a *review* . . . Jacob shrugged. He refused the insinuation. It was true, he said, he'd really thought he had a vocation. He really thought that writing was the way to invent a better society. And in a way they had. Books did it all. Books created opinion, books brought enlightenment down into all classes of society, books destroyed fanaticism and overthrew the prejudices that had subjugated everyone. But now books were over.

She realised she was feeling very constrained, almost crowded by the way he was speaking – and she looked around for some kind of comfort or recognition of her pain, but the landscape just continued, the willows and the boatmen calling and the squirrels.

But somehow she didn't understand this, continued Jacob, apparently irritated, as if it was Jacob who had been wronged and not Celine. She kept on forming committees for female education, or commissioning reports on the rights of women. It was as if, he said, she didn't believe in the revolution. She seemed to think that what was needed was *more books*.

– I just thought, she said, – the meaning of the constitution was that it was a constitution for everyone, for the whole community.

– I don't think, said Jacob, – it's for you to say what the constitution means.

He stopped at a salami stall and bought himself a panini.

– I'm trying to help you, said Jacob. – I really like you. I'm trying to explain. Why can't you see that?

It was all the more horrifying because she realised that Jacob believed all this sincerely and she suddenly felt she was going to cry and did not want him to see her cry.

So Celine said that she had to get to another meeting, and walked up the embankment steps to the street. For some minutes she stood there, while something happened to her body that seemed to be a series of palpitations. Then gradually they faded and she got in a passing taxi, back into the city. She watched the city process past her, all the offices and the theatres and the street corners, the temporary shrines to the dead set up in windows and on railings or the pavement – little portraits on paper, or wax madonnas shrouded in the kind of cloth used to wrap dumplings. She felt very weird and very wired.

It was possible, she thought, that she had only days to live.

7

For twenty-four hours, Celine was frantically thinking of just killing herself and Saratoga, of dosing Saratoga with poison and then slashing herself in the bath. Then Julia messaged her: *where there's women, there's hope.* Two hours later she came to see her. She had a new look that was neoclassical severe: a bleakly shapeless monochrome shift dress. She had also cropped her hair and bleached it. It made her seem even more vulnerable, however much she had found a way to a definite power. Her husband had told her the news, she said.

– I'm trying to think what we can do, said Julia.

– I just saw Jacob, said Celine.

– That's not a useful move for us, said Julia.

This was partly, Julia explained, because he had already done her a favour – helping her to preserve her forest in the countryside. It had become hers when her ex-husband disappeared over the ocean on his speedboat. But there were also some industrialists who were friends with the radicals who wanted to buy the forest to burn it down and build factories. And Jacob had been really amazing, she said, the way he argued that her forest was a space that was shared by everyone and therefore should be protected, but this also meant that now she couldn't go back to Jacob. She couldn't ask him for a new favour.

And more importantly, she added, she kept hearing that Jacob was finished.

– What do you mean finished? said Celine. – I just saw him, like yesterday. He's everywhere.

– No, I think he's over, said Julia. – Or nearly. That's what I'm hearing. He's about to be arrested.

– But why? said Celine.

– The business with the slaves, said Julia.

It seemed amazing to Celine that these conversations were happening with Julia – she had a new edge and heft and snappy manner. Or maybe it wasn't really new and had always been there but somehow the events she lived had never given her the opportunity to display it, and one aspect of the universe's constant unfairness was the way that once you had known a person in one context or in one era it required an almost impossible act of imagination to give them new forms of attention.

– So OK, said Celine. – But then if not Jacob then –

– We need to see Yves, said Julia.

– Yves? said Celine. – The one who tried to destroy us already?

– He's minister for the interior, said Julia. – We can't care about his *past*.

Celine realised that she was feeling sick. Inside her lower lip there was now an entire cluster of ulcers, like dried chillies. She wondered if she would ever see her parents again. That morning her mother had messaged to say that her father had almost died that morning. He had fallen and cut his head on the stairs. She was glad he no longer understood what was happening around him. It would upset him too much, wrote her mother. She couldn't understand why her mother was writing to her like this, thought Celine. She felt nothing at all, just total detachment.

Maybe, thought Celine, this was because there was a sensation inside her that was something like *exitlessness*. In every diagram of entrapment she had been forced to make since she was young, she always thought, she also always believed she could find an escape route. And yet now here she was, in this future epoch, and it turned out that perhaps all the escape routes were gone. It was like a story where the hero is trying to leave some villain's crazed laboratory, while all the metal doors are sliding shut around them. They had gone before she could even recognise her need for escape.

8

Yves was now installed in Lenoir's old offices. All the rooms were little cubes, with dirty light, and the office was a severe arrangement of squares and rectangles: drawers and shelves and cabinets in neat symmetrical rows, each filled with files.

It was typical of Yves to be so into the supermodern methods.

When Celine and Julia arrived he was in another meeting, they were told. So they had a few moments to appreciate the novel beauty of this office: clean and angular, like a space-ship. On his bureau was a pile of magazines printed on beautiful paper. Celine picked one up. Books were over, people said this all the time, but still magazines were every-where, and maybe this was logical. The magazines were the opposite of literature – they were sceptical of nothing, the universe they described was completely unreal, and it was the same here in this office, thought Celine: a world brought to an unnatural surface of abstraction.

Then Yves came in and as soon as he saw Celine the whole effect unravelled. He was suddenly a dishevelled thing inside a precise interior. It was very wrong to dislike someone for the way they looked, thought Celine, with his spasming hand and froglike features, but it was also impossible to disentan-gle the way he looked from the way he thought, like some kind of medieval allegory.

This untidiness had recently got worse because Yves's girl-friend had recently abandoned him. One night in the blood-soaked carnival atmosphere he got drunk in an under-ground bar and left with another woman – even though, Yves insisted, they had only slightly kissed in an alleyway before she told him she was married and thought that maybe she anyway didn't like sex at all. He thought about his lost girlfriend every day. Every night he tried to stay out as long as possible to ignore the exhausting business of getting undressed and into his bed on his own. It was making him look appalling.

Yves nodded at them and then gestured proudly at the files arranged around them. It was the most advanced system for information gathering that had so far been invented, he said. Inside every file were memos and forms and registers containing reports on spy networks, dissident factory workers, farm estimates, as well as people's sexual lives. After all, he continued, ignoring Celine's agitation, this was the era of information. They were even writing slogans on the banknotes: the law punished the counterfeiter, the nation rewarded the informer. If anyone had a grievance then they reported this grievance to the authorities. Because as soon as something was written down then it became real, and could be addressed. The only problem was that all this paper needed organisation.

Outside in the square kids were hanging out with glazed eyes and long hair. It was a macabre contrast with the grids of this room and perhaps impossible to think about. Did they want him to order something in? said Yves. They were kind of living here on takeout from Balthazar. They were working twenty-hour days. Celine shrugged. He called out to one of his assistants to bring something up. Then he turned back to Celine and Julia. He seemed in no hurry to ask why they there, presumably because he knew why they were there and didn't want to talk about it.

Julia began to explain but Yves interrupted her. He

wouldn't help, he said. He of course admired Julia's husband, but no. He couldn't do anything.

It must be a wonderful sensation for Yves, thought Celine, to be able to talk to them with this kind of savage authority – or maybe even disconcerting, something addictively sweet but also sickening.

It was very clear, he said, how people were thinking. Any enemy must be removed. And it was obvious that Celine was an enemy from the way she was always attacking the regime in public, the way her name was being used by women writing insane prophecies against the committees for their mistakes and limitations.

So there wasn't, said Julia, any possibility of doing something noble in secret?

Yves looked at her grandly. He despised secrets, he said. Soon there would be no such thing as privacy and he was glad about that. Like when Jacob published his pamphlet on the ethical life and the new society – did they hear what happened next? One of his girlfriends sent messages to the four women who thought they were his only other girlfriend, and also to his wife. And when he saw her at the dog races, and said to her *well, that was kind of an unexpectedly aggressive thing to do*, she smiled and said: *But surely you wouldn't want to live a life of secrecy? If the new society is to be born from the ashes of the old life, surely we must burn the old life to the ground?*

– And you admire that bitchass craziness? said Celine.

She understood that in her position it was stupid to be so direct but she also felt very angry, because it was obvious that, as she had expected, Yves would never help her and that therefore they had made themselves vulnerable for nothing.

An assistant interrupted with the food from the downstairs

restaurant. Yves let the assistant leave, then he replied with total savagery.

He knew that people like her thought it was important to know shit, said Yves. But what they needed to understand was that no one needed to know anything at all. They didn't need to read the classical texts, or the history of art. They could spend their entire leisure time at peep shows if they wanted. The classics were over, he said.

He picked up a package of pelmeni in hot sauce and started to eat.

– What you need, said Yves, – is to be vigilant in your soul at every moment. Do you love your child more than the regime? Do you love your husband more than the regime? *Do you love wine and chocolate marzipan more than the regime?* Because if you do, you won't be entering the promised land.

No one spoke for a while. This often happened now, the sudden stoppages when people talked to each other. You began a conversation and then it became impossible and you stopped.

9

Why hadn't Celine predicted this? It was a question she used to shout at herself in the monologues she kept up through the night, but it was also possible that all prediction was impossible. Everyone had network diagrams of the world in their head and these network diagrams were having to be rewritten every day. Everyone believed that they were living in the world centre. But in fact centres were proliferating everywhere and were infinite. Some people knew this already and they were the most modern, and one of these was continuing to be Celine and another one was a trader who had long ago met with Louis Cook and done business with him in Mohawk country. Over the years this trader had made his way south, and was now somewhere in Louisiana, in swampland, among the alligators and the lost roads. Originally he was French, but in fact he really had no idea of nationality any more. He was savage and flabby and large. His face was beginning to resemble more and more, he thought, a cock and balls. He tried to forget this. And the reason he was becoming more contemporary than other people who were younger or hipper was the intuition which he was now trying to explain in a report to his bosses back across the ocean.

It was as if, he wrote, there was this pressure on the map. It looked empty, but it wasn't empty. There was some kind of invisible force. It meant that while it was possible that they could do great things out here, that they could divert trade from the Iroquois in the North, it also needed great thought.

For a few minutes he stopped writing. A battered kettle steamed beside him. He made himself a new cup of old tea.

He wanted to tell them a story, he wrote. Recently he had tried to go north, upriver, with a party of three other businessmen. And then he had been stopped. The people who stopped him spoke in Sioux, asking who they were, where they came from, where they were going. He was obviously trapped, he wrote. But he replied in the Dakota language and when the Sioux listed the traders they knew, luckily his name was one of them. This seemed to help. Apparently he had met with them years before. Three of these people then swam into his pirogue, and they all continued upriver. A short while later they got caught in a shallow, and dragged the pirogue to a camp. The camp was Lakota. Then followed a long conversation with their chief, Black Buffalo, after which the Lakota took all of the goods he was planning on selling – his cloth, tobacco, axes, vermillion, powder and bullets. He was very distressed, he wrote, and wanted to continue upriver, but he could not. Black Buffalo ruled this territory, he said. With luck they had managed to escape from the camp, and had spent a night hidden inside the rotten trunk of some dead tree. Then they had made it back to town. One of his associates seemed to have acquired a spider bite which might turn out to be fatal.

What he wanted to say, he wrote, was that there was this pressure on the map, and it was probably important to think about this. The relationship they most needed to form was with these Lakota. If they could make a relationship with them then they could cut off the flow of money to the north or even, best of all, they could somehow take over this country. If they could bring goods in via Florida and get them to the Pacific then they would have an entire continent, he said. The problem was the Spanish. And the British and the Americans. But his conclusion was the same. They needed to get hold of Louisiana, but first they needed to start some kind of diplomatic mission with the Lakota.

He stopped, then he began again, this time in a new notebook. He had started keeping a private notebook, for his own therapeutic needs.

He was having trouble sleeping, he wrote. He was currently somewhere upstream on the Missouri/Mníšoše River. It would help him very much to know exactly what was happening back home. He wanted to know that there was still some kind of supply chain. It was all very disastrous, what he was hearing. It was no way to run a business. He was really scared, he wrote.

10

It's so difficult to think, if you are trapped in a deadly situation! If Celine stayed she would be killed. But she didn't want to leave because it was her city, with her friends and daughter in it. More practically she didn't know how to leave. All the routes out were being closed off. So that while the city was deadly for the moment she still had to inhabit it. And now the landscape she had known forever provoked terror and nostalgia and pity and love, where before there was boredom or irritation.

It was the day after her interview with Yves that Beaumarchais told her he was due that evening to have a conversation with Yves himself, not in the privacy of his office but onstage, as part of a writers' congress Yves had commissioned. He thought it might be the last time he was ever onstage, said Beaumarchais. He would like very much her support. Celine had been thinking that she would never go out in public again until she had made her escape but also she loved Beaumarchais, she thought that friendship was a value more important than any other, so that even if she was about to be killed this seemed no reason not to live in the way you always wanted to live. And so Celine went with him.

It was her last glimpse of language, thought Celine.

For some weeks Yves had been publishing a series of articles in the official newspapers, arguing that it was time for all signs to say what they meant. There was nothing more important, he wrote, than this question of representation. It was a very abstract problem but it seemed that it was precisely this abstractness which made it seem so dangerous and so alive, and why so many people therefore felt they had to be there at the congress Yves set up. It was held in a repurposed sports arena, with the audience sitting upstairs, looking down on the arena's old lines and scuffmarks on the floor. Around everyone was the smell of terrible meat – pork skin, hot sauce – combined with the sweeter aromas of doughnuts and roasting nuts.

He thought that everyone agreed, began Yves, that the usual mirror was too small for the central hero of their time. The usual mirror? said Beaumarchais. A novel, said Yves, a script, whatever. It was too small to contain the reflection of the kind of heroes seated there among them, the future geometers of this planet. He absolutely agreed, said Beaumarchais, not knowing how else to reply. To describe the era's new hero, added Yves, ignoring Beaumarchais, would require a new kind of writing, something that allowed readers to understand the historical force of the new truths. Whereas would he not agree that in his plots, Yves continued, there was no sense of the revolutionary army as an entire mass, there was no attempt to represent thousands of armed soldiers advancing like lava? There were just individual people, with their own neuroses.

It was very obvious that Beaumarchais was doomed, that people were separating from him as they watched and Celine felt very warmly and desperately towards him, even as she felt herself separate from him too. Her reasons, however, were different to the reasons why the audience was now hating him. Even though language was now turning against him Beaumarchais would never give it up, and this was why he and Celine were disappearing from each other. Because Celine was going away, not just from a place but from language, whereas Beaumarchais could not remove himself from his medium.

Instead of the old realism, said Yves, he wanted a new form of representation: a work that would depict the most general and universal features of an epoch, representing them through unique characters that were both specific and abstract, characters that combined the greatest possible generalisability with enormous inner richness. He was very sorry, said Beaumarchais, but he didn't understand this word *generalisablilty*?

Life changed so very fast, continued Yves, that by the time a writer finished a work, he realised that his hero had already changed. That was why the classic forms, transferred to this epoch, this extraordinary epoch, created false assumptions and, most importantly, false endings.

– We need a hero, said Yves. – Someone to place among that constellation of Robinson Crusoe, Don Quixote, Hamlet, Oedipus . . .

– And Figaro? said Beaumarchais.

– Figaro? said Yves. – You mean the Figaro in your script?

– I think it was Hernandez, said Beaumarchais, – who said that it was Figaro who killed the system.

– Who the fuck cares about Hernandez? said Yves with sudden savagery. – If I wanted Hernandez's opinion, I'd fucking ask him. Except of course I can't, because he's dead.

Beaumarchais looked very shaken and upset by this violence. He felt that it was important to remember, said Beaumarchais, how radical he was. Under the old regime, for instance, he had famously been censored.

Yves said that he couldn't remember any censorship. What he remembered, said Yves, was Antoinette had been one of Beaumarchais's personal friends. He had been friends, in fact, with *many women*. And what was more, he added, there was now a crucial difference between what had happened then and what was happening now. Before the revolution, bad taste was only a personal defect. Now, however, it was something worse, said Yves. It was a counter-revolutionary crime.

Absolutely, continued Beaumarchais, but still, it was important not to consider him as in any way *successful*. He had only ever been himself, lazy as a donkey, not part of any group. But that wasn't true, said Yves. *Deeply* unsuccessful, continued Beaumarchais.

– You had an opera made, said Yves. – *They made an opera of your play.*

– Everyone gets an opera made, said Beaumarchais, – that doesn't make you successful! They didn't even mention my name in the credits, that's how unimportant I was.

Beaumarchais was breathing very fast. His body was so vast and sensitive on that stage, beside Yves. It was obvious to him too that he was finished, and this was an enigmatic feeling, an exposed feeling, something almost similar to the feeling of being desired, it was so intense. Nostalgia overwhelmed him. He had always loved this city. Back home, in the provinces, they were still spooning tea into their mouths, a cube of sugar wedged behind a molar. Such pettiness, such swamp-like existence was not for him. He wanted the nighttime and the terrible hangovers. He found it impossible to believe that the city was no longer his. He always wanted the room, and he had got into the room, but now the room was being taken away from him and this was a prospect he had never imagined.

In the bleachers, Celine looked down at him and felt a keening pity, like the real was something too sharp and dangerous for anyone to touch it.

– The more we talk, said Beaumarchais, – the more I understand the revolution.

– It isn't, said Yves, – something that can be understood.

– Of course, said Beaumarchais, trying to continue. – But if I were ever to understand it, it would be through these conversations.

It was true, replied Yves, that it was very difficult to analyse the depth of one's own complicity. To match the government's system of mutual surveillance a person had to always spy on themselves. Of course, he added, he admitted that from a certain perspective, a very limited perspective, what was happening seemed very regrettable – but from a vaster perspective it was very different. It might take lifetimes to discover the revolution's true meaning.

Celine felt sick, like an astronaut. She was leaving all language behind, the way an astronaut leaves behind the earth. And at least she understood her mission, thought Celine, even if she was about to be dead.

II

She walked the streets for some hours and then went home late in the dark, feeling deeply alone, and dreading the silence of the apartment if Saratoga was asleep or out with Hugo. Instead she found that in fact very disturbingly she was not alone – because Yves was inside her apartment.

– The lock was broken, he said.

It seemed to Yves to be a rational explanation.

– Where's Saratoga? she said.

– Who? said Yves.

It made her feel at least a little calmer to think that

Saratoga was not here and that therefore he could not harm her if he was here to harm someone, but also Celine was now realising that since she was alone perhaps it was more likely that she would be harmed.

It was very late, she said. If he could maybe come back tomorrow because she was super tired. Oh but he was so tired too, he said. He worked all night, every night. And in fact tonight as usual he'd been working, after the congress, and as he was working he was thinking about her, about their conversation, and it occurred to him that he should come and see her.

Then he stopped, as if he expected her to continue, then began speaking again before she could find a way of talking to him.

He hadn't expected this kind of place, he said, as he looked around the bare apartment. Her security arrangements were terrible. Like, the *lock*, for instance. Did she realise how dangerous it was, to live in a place that was so fragile?

There was very little light in the room, just the light that was coming from the moon outside, which was basically too faint for Celine to see. Nevertheless she tried to look at Yves and keep on looking because she felt that it was important to hold him in her mind and not let him become more monstrous or abstractly terrifying than he was, so that if she could concentrate on him sweating or the way his hair was hanging down into his eyes it would keep him in the right proportion.

She was thinking that she didn't know where Saratoga was. This might have usually concerned her, but right now she didn't want her to come back until Yves had gone. But it seemed very difficult to know how Yves might leave.

He wished someone would give him some medicine, said

Yves. Sometimes he worried that he was too energetic, that there was too much of him and he was spilling over, he was overflowing – did she understand him? – he felt this right now, he said, and he really wished that there was someone who could help him.

It must be terrible, said Celine, and she said this as gently as she could without it being obvious that her voice was not entirely her own, it was also vibrating with fear and she refused to let him hear this fear out loud. But it was important to talk because meanwhile she was trying to calculate how violent he might be.

It was just, he said. Why didn't she like him? He was really very sweet to people who liked him. But she never wanted to be his friend.

– But it was you who hated me, she said.

It was surprising to discover that however much she understood this to be some kind of psychotic incident her thinking always wanted to find out what a person meant.

– Well, it was a big fucking mistake, said Yves. – Because now look at you.

It was of course very possible that Yves didn't intend to hurt her, that all he wanted to do was terrify her and demonstrate his power in a way he felt he had not demonstrated enough to her, but it was also possible that he was deadly.

At least, thought Celine, trying to calm herself, he was still sitting down. He was sitting down and she was standing up and this meant that she had some kind of self-protection.

– You look so scared, said Yves.

The meaning was maybe kind but the tone was murderous.

But then Saratoga entered the room at high speed and with grand noise, inside some private drama of her own, and suddenly stopped, confused, as she saw a man she did not know inside their apartment. Yves stopped too. He looked at her, and something inside him seemed to dissolve. It was as if it was incredible to him that someone could have entered this room in which he finally had all the power – as if something had now altered in the balance of the room which he wasn't strong enough to resist.

– Who are you? said Saratoga.

He got up, slowly. Compared to her he suddenly seemed old and had no more power in him.

– I'm the minister for interior security, he said.

He seemed to be trying to be proud of this title, like it was a title with glory attached. But Saratoga just stood there. And so instead of waiting to see what further impression he might be able to make Yves finally nodded to himself, then moved past her and shut the door.

And Saratoga remained there, looking at Celine, the way any person looks at someone when they think there is a confusion that needs an answer. It took Celine a while to find a way of answering – only after the street door slammed and she could hear Yves's footsteps in the drowsy street.

Then finally Celine replied to Saratoga's question, by holding her very tight and not letting go.

12

The next afternoon, an improbably pink afternoon, Celine went to see Julia. She was feeling so fearful and unhappy all the time that she was beginning to be almost fond of her terror, like it was at least hers and something she could look after. She found Julia with a piece of paper in her hand. Celine looked at her closely. At this time a piece of paper was either very good or very bad.

Julia said she was excited. She had spoken to her husband. And her husband had got Celine a place, under a pseudonym, on a transport to Boston. It was leaving in a week's time.

– But I don't have a week, said Celine.

– So hide, said Julia.

– So like what? said Celine. – I never see you again?

– I mean no, said Julia.

They stared at each other.

– We have no idea, said Julia.

– But what about Saratoga? said Celine.

– It's whatever she wants, said Julia. – If she wants a place too, there's a place.

– There's a place?

– There's a place.

It was almost impossible to think about. Who would need to escape? It was insane that she was even thinking about it. Everything she loved and hated was right here, it had always been that way, and so to be told that she might never see this city again felt fantastical.

– What's new with you? said Celine. – Tell me everything. How's your husband?

If this was the last conversation she ever had in civilisation she wanted it to go on forever, and also be the kind of conversation she had always had, without their urgent and terrified tone. And it seemed that Julia understood this and made a movement towards her.

– I mean, I caught him reading porn the other day, said Julia. – It's really terrible.

– Because you don't like it?

– Because he wants to talk about it, to explain himself. It's like when he's super jealous, just the other way round. I don't want to talk about it.

– Because you don't like it?

– *Because it doesn't matter.* There's nothing to say. But he needs to talk about it. It's destroying my head.

– What kind of porn?

– American porn. With tribal violence and shit. And now every time we're in bed together, he says, he can't stop thinking about it.

– But you don't care?

– Why would I care about his imagination? I didn't marry his imagination. I married him because of his *face*.

To leave, thought Celine, was so heavy because it was equivalent to the weight of everything you left behind, the infinite detail of your friendships. There was so much living and it was strange to think it would go on happening in the middle of so much dying, and that also she would go on living even without this backdrop. And in fact it turned out that a city was not so much a backdrop as a little network and it seemed impossible to think that she could live in the same way somewhere else, but then of course people do and so would she.

– But where do I hide? said Celine. – I can't hide in this city for a week.

– Stay out in the countryside, said Julia. – Use one of the little cabanas in the forest.

– In your forest?

– It's not really my forest, Julia corrected her. – No one owns a forest.

And it suddenly seemed ideal to Celine, to become something invisible inside a green forest. It seemed the most natural progression in the world.

13

Celine went home to speak to Saratoga urgently. She wanted her to come with her very much but more than that she wanted her to be happy and it was possible that these were contradictory wishes. She found Saratoga reading a book of science fiction. She nudged her gently on the shoulder, she pushed the book away. It was a page describing a trip to the moon. It looked very beautiful, the idea of a trip to the moon. There were engravings under tissue paper, like a film of water. Someone was floating in a basket among some stars.

– This is maybe going to have to be resolved quicker than we thought, she said.

– What do you mean? said Saratoga.

– I mean what you are going to do, she said. – What we are going to do. I'm going to America. Julia set it up.

– Like when? said Saratoga.

– Like now, said Celine.

Saratoga looked at her for a much longer time than Celine was expecting.

– But so I think I might go away with Hugo to India, said Saratoga eventually. – I mean I have no idea. I haven't really thought about it. I love you. I just really don't want America.

– You don't think America could be wild? said Celine.

– I mean sure, said Saratoga. – But not with them.

– What them?

– I mean, the fascists, said Saratoga. – The ones who got out.

– I'm not a fascist, said Celine.

– I know but still, said Saratoga.

Celine felt desperate. She understood that everything she had wanted for Saratoga, all the future she had imagined, was now outdated and irrelevant, and that in fact everything she felt she was losing wasn't important at all and the true thing was this fact of Saratoga's personhood, solid and impermeable, with its own wishes and decisions. But at the same time she couldn't help being furious at this general urgency that seemed to be separating them forever.

– Hugo wants to marry me, said Saratoga.

– I know, said Celine.

She tried again.

– I don't want you marrying someone because you feel like you have no other option, said Celine.

– Because you did that.

– Because I did that.

– But it's not my only option, said Saratoga. – Or that's not how I see it.

Celine was looking at Saratoga's book and she felt suddenly as precarious as language, just precarious the way the words were floating there, little smudges of ink on a colourless surface.

– So you won't come with me? she said. – First I'm going to Julia's place in the countryside. Then I'm going to America.

– Mama, I love you so much, said Saratoga. – But I won't come with you.

There was a long hiatus.

– Do you remember her place in the countryside? said Celine.

Saratoga looked at her like she was crazy.

– Of course I remember, said Saratoga.

14

The next morning Celine left town without Saratoga but with an assistant called Yvette, both of them concealed behind the tinted windows of an official vehicle. The vehicle and the assistant were provided by Julia. The assistant had been accused of sabotage and treason, and Julia wanted to save her too. She hadn't even said goodbye to Beaumarchais, thought Celine, and this worried her because it was possible if you did not say goodbye to someone that this would mean you would never see them again, and for this to happen with her and Beaumarchais troubled her very much, as if it always needed to be true that they could talk to each other goofily and irritate each other with their wild opinions. But now perhaps this would never happen.

When they reached Julia's place in the countryside they drifted down a path away from it, so that instead of going towards the house they continued into the forest. Celine for a moment was about to look back, to look at the house, but then she realised that in fact she wanted to let it disappear and the reason was that it reminded her too much of Saratoga. And so the vehicle carried on, into the forest, down a catastrophic track, then stopped at a little house. It was dark and kind of boarded up. It stank of old meat. The driver left them with a can of milk and a sack of dried beans.

She felt such desolation! There was this fear in her that she had moved in some permanent way from Saratoga – as if there was a wall of time between them, that there would be some things Celine would want to do with Saratoga or for her but she could only prepare for them. Whereas it would be Saratoga who would carry them out, on the other side of the wall.

Her dreams were hectic, with many chase scenarios and many times where she was losing Saratoga and could not find her, and she woke up with her heart beating very fast.

But still Celine lived in this forest, waiting for their transit. All the causes around her were continuing their intricate living – the near causes and the distant causes. Every morning she went out into the exotic forest and it was almost amusing to realise that since she had never lived inside a forest the exotic nature of certain trees that had come from another continent wasn't exotic to her at all, because she knew nothing and therefore had no expectations. She liked learning the shapes of the leaves, and began to discover that she was learning a little list of groves, entangled patches of brambles. Every day as she went outside there were times when she didn't know where she was exactly, but then she found herself back in a place she remembered. It was like learning a language, the way you read a text you hardly understood and then suddenly you found a word you cherished, and from that word began to understand other words too.

One day she happened on a group of trees, among which people from the villages were mooching around, looking on the ground, as if they had lost something. The way they moved was very gentle and considered, like some kind of choreography. She went closer and asked a woman what was happening. They were looking for mushrooms, she said. Celine tried to follow their gaze. All she could see was surface. You could tell their presence because of minute signs, explained the woman, trying to help Celine. There were little movements in the ground as they grew, she said, or also certain plants that grew at the base of the trees, together with the mushrooms. Sometimes, she said, it was also possible to tell their presence because of moisture on a log, or a line of animal droppings. Celine stood there, letting herself steep in the scene. The air smelled wet and vegetal, like it was something you could eat.

Each time Celine turned round inside the forest, she felt disoriented. It was as if there was no one else in the world, even though people everywhere might already be looking for her – groups of soldiers, drunk people who could kill her if they found her. It was very confusing to feel so endangered and so isolated.

She went walking into deep bramble and gorse bushes, and reread all the messages she had ever kept from Saratoga, while Yvette went looking for someone to sell them eggs or little herbs.

A week, it seemed, lasted forever if you were scared.

15

The day before they were due to leave Celine heard movements as soon as she left the cabin. She looked among the trees. There were some soldiers walking towards the cabin, from across a field. They were little stains in the air. She turned and went behind the cabin, then ran deeper into the forest. It had been raining and the leaves were dripping gently. There was a whole little hydropneumatics system happening and she entered the system herself. The depth of her fear surprised her, even if she had been in a state of permanent anxiety for weeks and maybe even years – so that for this anxiety to transform itself into something so much more concrete and specific was confusing.

A detailed vocabulary from stories of escapes – footprints, noises, marks – came back to her, and she tried to think in this way but it was difficult. She was leaving dark footprints on the wet grass. She went further into the woods, where the ground was more matted. She was trying to move lightly but fast. She could see the colourful blurs of the soldiers in their outfits coming nearer through the trees.

Finally, she reached a kind of hidden area and lay down flat and very still, under a canopy of ferns. She lay there, looking at the soil's surface. She could smell the ground swelling and rotting and enjoying itself. A little procession of minute insects was living inside it. The soil was something rustling and communicating. She waited like this for a long time, horizontal, against the earth. It was as if the ferns were reaching over her, like she and the ferns were coming to an understanding, however crazy that might seem.

Then she felt a voice again.

– Don't be scared, said the voice. – But history is just a question of scale. And right now your sense of scale is *appalling*.

It was of course not the first time that she heard voices in this way, but still, it was frightening. She was frightened by the soldiers and now she was frightened by this voice, the way she had been scared of the voice she had heard in the forest many years earlier, before Saratoga was born, and also after Lorenzo's duel. And perhaps precisely it emerged whenever she was most afraid.

– Who are you? she said.

– I'm trying to talk with you, said the voice. – I'm trying to console you.

– Go on, she said.

– Just: remember where everything came from, said the voice. – Think back that far.

– But how? she said.

– Imagine an explosion, said the voice, – that happened everywhere at once. There was no atmosphere at all and so there was also no smell, no sound. There was only heat. Think of an afternoon when it's so hot that no one's even moving in the swimming pools, and to walk across to the pool pavilion is too giant an endeavour because the air feels thick and burning – and then increase such heat: maybe that's how you'll be able to comprehend the heat at this moment.

It was very strange because although the experience she was having was an experience of language, it was also very definite that there was no language or any other noise audible at all: just little breezes in and out of leaves.

– I'm sorry but *who are you*? said Celine.

– Now, in this heat, continued the voice, – all that could exist is a minestrone of particles, like the thickest minestrone you can ever imagine. But everything always cools eventually and at some point, maybe after a few hundred thousand years, things became different. The gas settled down with gravity. What happened next was galaxies and stars and planets, like your earth. Then one day lightning struck the boiling fluid on the earth and something new began to happen. Something began living.

– I'm sorry, she said to the voice. – But I have no time right now for ancient history. Look at me. I only want the super contemporary.

There was a silence.

– Don't take this personally, sighed the voice. – It's not just you. But you need a better theory of the *perverse*. All of you seem to think that the perverse is when someone misapplies a category, like falling in love with a foot instead of a person, but if you could see the way we think –

– Who's *we*? she said –

– then you'd understand that the mind of the universe is the height of perversity, a structure striped with comparisons and similarities that would seem only incongruous if perceived according to your categories. You realise, for instance, that it was very difficult finding you in this forest, you seem so similar to a tree.

– I think, said Celine –

– There have been humans for, what, just 30,000 years? And the planet on which you live is something like 4.5 billion years old. *Do the math*, honey.

– But I don't live at that perspective, said Celine.

– But you can try, the voice replied.

The light was beginning to fade.

– And then you must go away, it added.

– But I'm *trying* to go away, said Celine.

– You must go further, said the voice.

It seemed like many hours had passed, and Celine realised that the noises of the soldiers had disappeared. The voice seemed to have disappeared too. Then it was night.

Celine went back to the cabin. She felt deeply heavy, as if something had happened inside her, the way a narcotic or virus feels. The next day, she woke up late. For a long time, she lay there, thinking. None of these thoughts had words. It was a series of incredible pictures, that extended and extended – and it wasn't obvious to her how this series would end.

16

Then Celine and Yvette were travelling across the ocean in hurricane season, making for America. She was in suspension, between two states, and in this suspension it seemed very natural to think about all the history which had come before.

Because one effect of getting older was that you accumulated more living, this was only natural, but it also diminished the importance of many events in her youth, events which she had assumed would always define her. Suddenly the conspiracy to install Rosen in power or her efforts to defend Julia seemed incidents that might not be the only stories about her that could happen, and while it was melancholy it was also, however fearful she felt, almost exhilarating.

Perhaps this, she thought, was what the voice in the forest was saying.

What she thought about most of all was Marta, and what Marta was doing in Milan. She wished she knew. It was as if Marta was at the end of a very long tunnel, and her figure was diminishing every hour. It occurred to her more and more that it was Marta who had first seduced her, and then Marta had gone. Of course, this was not the whole story, but it felt like the story right now. She did not know exactly why this seemed important. Then one night she thought she had found an answer or an approach to an answer, which was the very simple fact that Marta was a woman and she was too. If Marta were a man, or at least this is how it seemed to her, she would have looked at this person who had seduced her and the story they had suffered together as something ordinary and even disgusting – like she was just another heroine, abandoned on her blue island. But because Marta wasn't a man, because their own possibilities of freedom were equal, it allowed a different kind of feeling to emerge. She wanted lightness, thought Celine, it was what she always wanted, and this was the only true lightness – when everyone's power was the same. So that it also followed that it was utopian precisely because they had hurt each other. The total ordinariness of hurting each other was what was so beautiful and so free.

Meanwhile the hurricanes continued. And everything kept on coming back to her, in the violent noise – minute things, like Julia once saying to her that maybe she wouldn't agree, but she only liked carp when it had been soaked for three days in grappa. Or, very old and no longer able to see clearly, there was her father serving himself chicken. He kept dropping the pieces beside his plate, and when this was pointed out to him he replied, not at all disconcerted, *but that's how we used to eat in the countryside when I was a child.*

Until finally the light came and a thin grey shore was visible. The ship moved unevenly towards it. The sea at dawn was sludge: morbid, mournful, garbage. They came to a garish harbour. She hoped very much that this was finally America and she could think of herself as safe.

It occurred to her that for a long time, maybe forever, men had wanted her to be surprised if she ever felt solidarity or freedom with women, if they ever desired each other or created power together – whereas her experience of this desire and of this power was that it was entirely natural and therefore almost unremarkable. She refused to belittle it by being surprised. Of course, she wasn't naive or innocent. She understood the giant structures that she was meant to submit to and which constituted a vast feral violence in the atmosphere, candy-coloured and poisonous, but she still didn't see this as a reason to be surprised when she felt softness and freedom with another woman. To be surprised would be to say it was rare. Whereas in fact there were many moments in all history, thought Celine, or at least surely there must have been, when little glimpses of utopia were possible.

17

No wonder Celine thought about the voices she heard in the forest, or felt so confused. It was so frightening to be chosen! She wanted to talk to someone about what she heard but had no one. She missed Marta, it would have been good to talk with Marta, she thought. And then gradually she found that the other person she missed was Claude.

It seemed to her that Claude might know how to think about these voices. He had some kind of aura of the chosen too. What she meant was: only a very few people could think about voices, because in fact it was an era of writing. Whereas Claude was open and porous, like a piece of fabric.

The stories Claude told himself were becoming more and more transparent. He was now on his way home from his last trip into the ocean, he had recently written to her, and had stopped at the island where he had once met Titere, and which now belonged to Tu. Here he had agreed to bring back a sailor who was returning to Europe after living on the islands learning their languages, understanding their plants. This sailor's plan was to carry with him a little box of seedlings, that he would plant in a nursery. He had bread-fruit, palmettos, vanilla pods, bananas. They were packed into a barrel, ready to be transported.

Before the ship set off, they went for a last audience with the king. Tu offered the sailor gifts: a necklace with tiny fish and a paddle, scored and zigzagged like an armadillo hide. In reply the sailor began to address the king and tell him that, now he was leaving, he wanted to give him some advice. He felt society here needed to become more open. He said this very much for the king's benefit, he added, because it would surely not be long before a natural resistance to this oppression would emerge among the people. He wondered if it was because of their terrible isolation. All around, he said, there was just sea. It might be this isolation that kept a society so ancient. But they could not rely on this isolation for much longer. There would be many future invasions.

And Tu replied, wrote Claude, that of course to the white people the sea was absence and terror, because they didn't understand. If they had been born here, they might have understood things differently. The sea and the islands weren't in opposition. Everything that happened here could happen on either land or water, it didn't matter which. For instance, the little atoll over there, said Tu, that was where the sea god threw his javelin one morning, and threw it so hard that it disappeared from sight. Then that night, when the sun had gone down, it was seen burning in the sky, disappearing across the face of the moon.

– But that's a myth, said the sailor.
– Must I explain everything? said Tu.

Then he dismissed the sailor with his barrel of seeds, said Claude, and allowed him to prostrate himself in farewell.

This was one of Celine's favourite stories, now that she was moving away from everything.

18

It turned out that Celine's ship had docked not in America but instead on one of the islands scattered in the archipelagos beside it. They were in a rundown harbour city on Hispaniola – among the plantain boats and the riggers and the warships and the vegetable importers. They had to stay for at least a week, she was told, while the boat was repaired.

From the boat she was escorted along a street that was stinking of animal slaughter and cocoa. The air was very heavy on her body. There was scaffolding everywhere and also burnt-out buildings, and with difficulty she tried to match these images with the image she already had of this place from articles and conversations, this place whose money so many families she knew had stolen. There were cabarets and billiard halls and rum bodegas and a barbershop, outside which four wax heads advertised four wigs. Around her she could hear people talking in Kreyòl, and while it sometimes sounded like Celine's language at the same time she could not entirely understand it, and it made her feel ashamed to be so limited.

Of course, she had applauded when Jacob made his speech against the plantation owners – when they wanted to claim their votes in parliament but would not allow the vote to be extended to their slaves. She had applauded him very much, the way he made them look so incoherent and so evil. But to have a beautiful interior, she understood, with its sympathetic moral thinking, was not enough. Much more effort was needed, if you wanted to pay attention to other people.

She was taken to a cheap hotel, owned by a former European. That afternoon, he took her for a walk into the city. He began telling her stories of how he had once travelled at sea. He spoke her language with surprising fluency. She asked him about this and his reply was unexpected. He had been a sailor, he shrugged. Or basically a pirate. For a long time, he told her, he hated the sea. But then he discovered he kind of liked this life because he loved learning new languages. Wherever they stopped, he talked to people. He kept a notebook. Like what kind of notebook? asked Celine. What kind of words? For instance, said the pirate/hotelier, on one island a man made a sound while gesturing a kind of stabbing action, and the sound sounded something like *ma-te*, like the espagnol for kill. So he presumed that this too was the word for kill. Or a bird of paradise twisted round a palm tree and then the man pointed to it, making a new sound that seemed closer to *manoo*, and so he wrote this down as well.

But how, said Celine, would you know what it meant? He looked at her. How would you know, she continued, if this sound meant bird, rather than flying, or the killing of a bird, or something else entirely? He looked at her. It was maybe true, he said. It was a conundrum.

He seemed suddenly unnerved. He had liked that life very much, he said. The life of a sailor. They made their way back to the hotel. It was maybe why he also admired the guerrilla revolutionaries here, he added – and he stared at her as if expecting her to be uneasy or disagree with this statement of admiration.

Instead Celine held his smiling gaze – but at the same time

in this mess of language she couldn't deny that she was feeling a little disturbed, not by any fear of revolution or guerrillas but by something she was suddenly thinking about names. She was remembering Cato, and she felt ashamed how she had no idea what Cato's real name was. Now it seemed very important and very wrong, this erasure of his name. But at the same time she herself was enjoying her distance from her own name, from the image that had accompanied her since she was eighteen, her little hologram or double. In Europe she had always been known, or thought to be known. People thought they knew who she liked to sleep with or what kinds of chocolate she liked to drink, they thought they knew how she liked to fuck or be fucked and this assumed knowledge of other's opinions about her was a weight she had to carry every day. Whereas here in this state of suspension she felt the possibility of other states, like lightness, or proliferation. She was troubled by any image of herself, and suffered when she was named. She wanted friendships where all images were vacant: to abolish the horror of the adjective. If you had to use adjectives, she thought, whether about a person or a piece of music or any other sensation, you were on the side of the image, and therefore of domination, and therefore of death.

But still, she also missed Cato. She had wronged Cato very much, and now it was too late.

– So how much did you pay for your transit visa? said the pirate/hotelier.

Celine stared at him, in the dirty hallway of the hotel.

– What transit visa? said Celine.

19

It turned out that no one could continue to America from this war zone without an exit visa or transit visa, it wasn't clear if these were two different documents or the same document, and there was a lot of confusion and anxiety, the basic sorrow of existing inside a bureaucratic system. Many people had dreamed of living in a supermodern society and now they were discovering to their horror one aspect of the supermodern – which was that radical power was always dependent on the frictions of its paperwork, and therefore the ideal of total power was only matched by the experience of its failure. It meant that whereas this town had seemed like a place of activity, most of this activity was in fact useless or a form of procrastination. Many people wanted to leave the island but it was difficult to get out and perhaps impossible. It depended on your connections.

It always seemed amazing, how much influence words could have on a solid world.

Anxiety swarmed everywhere. From the hotel there was a window looking down to the sea, its little thin horizon. It felt increasingly very important to cross that horizon. People tried the consulates and embassies. Then they went to travel bureaux to see if they could fix things. Many people who promised they had influence turned out to operate in studios up tiny staircases, or along dark corridors in empty warehouses. Meanwhile the newspapers were everywhere, with their columns of ships that were meant to be arriving or leaving, except that every day the lists changed and the only boats leaving weren't leaving for the right destination, or required more paperwork than anyone could organise.

And meanwhile everything continued, warm and grey and tropical.

20

One night a businessman asked Celine if she wanted to come out to see a show. The gore effects were apparently spectacular, he said. It seemed like an opportunity to discuss her exit visa and maybe even effect something, because this man's appearance was elegant and efficient and even kind, or at least certainly not appalling. She therefore said yes, and on the way to the theatre mentioned her visa problem immediately, but he just said that there would be time to discuss that later, and immediately the suspicion that she was conditioned to feel for any man returned – where everything was always put off, not discussed, kept secret – a suspicion that a man's motives were always salacious or dirtied or incoherent.

The play was very violent, the special effects were unsubtle. As it finished, Celine's new friend said that he'd told a friend of his to meet them here, someone who'd recently arrived on the island too. He looked among the seething crowd. Finally he began excitedly waving at a man who stopped a little way off, looked at her, then bowed to her with a smile that seemed to indicate he knew her.

– Ulises, said the businessman, introducing them to each other.

– But we know each other, said Ulises.

He seemed definite, but for a moment Celine had no idea who he was – and, she thought, there was surely no reason why she should have remembered, she was ageing at high speed, and when a person is ageing many names will be lost. Ulises tried to clarify. He had known her many years ago, he said, when he was the ambassador for his government in her city. He had always attended her parties. But now, he said, he was here.

Very gradually Celine began to recognise a person she remembered, inside what had become his body. She had last seen Ulises maybe twenty years ago, when she was beginning her attempt to live more freely and needed men like him for all the plots and counterplots, and she had used him to hand over Sasha's lost note to Antoinette. He had aged operatically and at the same time hadn't aged at all.

Ulises said that he was trying to negotiate with Toussaint Louverture and his troops, on behalf of the Spanish government. There was talk that Louverture was now being paid by the French. It was very confusing. Then he leaned towards her and said, as if confiding something very disappointing, that he was here with his wife. It was very odd, the way he said this – as if it might be necessary to alert her to this fact, like he was living in some kitsch script.

21

At dinner the windows were open onto a stinking canal. The most popular word being used was *transit*. There was a manic listlessness everywhere. A government associate of Toussaint Louverture was also there, not talking about politics but writing. He quoted a poem that had just come out in a magazine, a poem that had moved him very much – about how sometimes it seemed that they were at the centre of a fiesta, but at the centre of the fiesta there was no one. At the centre of the fiesta was the void, he said, or nothingness, or emptiness. It was difficult to translate. But at the centre of this void was another party.

Celine felt that she liked him. She wanted to talk to him, but she was hemmed in by Ulises, who was sitting next to her. Ulises mentioned visas, then hinted at his large power. He was looking at her in a very disgusting way, as if she was suddenly vulnerable in this city, far away from the other city she had once called home, and therefore open to total attack. But perhaps it was also possible that this was an important lesson, that it was a way of showing her that she was the one who must go away, far away from her city, from the culture she had once known.

Celine turned to her other side to speak to Ulises's wife, who was only drinking water and not eating anything. It was too hot here, she said, as if that explained everything. She told Celine her name but it was very difficult to hear since she spoke so quietly. Celine asked her to repeat the name, but then still couldn't exactly hear the reply. She felt she couldn't ask again. It seemed impossible to talk to her but there was no one else she could speak to because Ulises's wife was the only person to talk to who could protect her from Ulises himself. Celine's loneliness sat beside her, or on her shoulder, heavily, a little dense refugee. Celine asked her about reading. Ulises's wife replied that she never read books. Reading was boring, she said. What she liked were shows.

It seemed so uncanny, thought Celine, that here she was, and so was Ulises, this little scrap of the past. It was as if suddenly it might be possible that as she made her movement away many other forces were converging on her route. Then Louverture's associate got up, excused himself, and dropped a scribbled note beside her plate as he left the room.

22

When she woke up she felt hungover. She lay there looking at the ceiling. She looked at the note beside her from Louverture's connection. It said that he would come to see her very early in the morning. She lay back down, staring at a damp stain on the ceiling. Then abruptly she got up and went to find Yvette.

Together they went into the countryside. The countryside was a dictionary of plants they had never seen before – all of which, it seemed, were fond of dissimulation, confusion, camouflage. They examined alpine plants, caper berries, tiny chilli plants, lianas which extended their roots among the stones, plants with velvety leaves which apparently breathed at night, sensitive plants that retracted at the merest sound of a human voice. Seed capsules burst, in the heat, with a dry noise, like someone's nails crushing a flea. She began making little drawings for herself in a broken notebook, scribbled over with lists for packing and emergency addresses. They began as flowers and ended up as monsters.

But still it seemed the eye was not satisfied with seeing, it wanted more, it wanted to listen too.

In the afternoon they went back into the city. In her room Celine lay down in the heat. After a few moments Yvette came in to tell her that there was someone waiting to see her. Celine felt sick. She assumed it must be Ulises. Instead in came Louverture's associate. He had come to see her twice already, he said. Celine wasn't sure if this was some kind of rebuke but she had no time to wonder more about this because he continued very fast. He had come to give her and her assistant a visa. He of course wanted nothing for it, he added hastily. He had just felt sympathy for her. It was not appropriate, the way the men were treating her.

It seemed very difficult to know how sincere he really was, or what he in fact wanted. She liked him but also found his way of thinking kind of laughable. He was like some little dentist or accountant, in his idea of women and protection. It wasn't that Ulises had wanted to fuck her that was the problem, she wanted to say. The problem was how absurd the idea should have seemed. But at the same time she needed and wanted these visas very much.

– Thank you, said Celine.

She stood and stared at him. She didn't invite him to stay. He seemed upset at this, but still, she stared.

It was necessary, if you were a woman on your own, to be this graceless, she thought, because otherwise there was so much misinterpretation. However you behaved, you could be hated.

– But really, thank you, she said.

Two days later, she continued her escape to America.

23

Something was coming adrift for Celine, and it was maybe her sense of parts and wholes. It seemed increasingly difficult to relate all the parts to a whole, in some problem of topology. What if the whole of something could never be expressed? she was wondering. Everything was raggedness, interdependency, looseness, casual and expendable like a shopping list, something to be expanded and subtracted and scribbled over. It was like she was gathering up new information in her headlong procession away from what she had imagined to be a centre, so that where she had once had around her in an orbit the names of Marta and Jacob and Beaumarchais and Yves and Julia, now new names entered the space she was understanding. And it felt important to her to try to interpret these new stories, like the story people were reporting about a recent visit to Washington of a delegation of American chiefs. This delegation was led by Louis Cook, the Mohawk colonel. Celine had never heard this name before. He had come, the news stations were saying, to demand that something should be done about the illegal American settlements.

Louis Cook was a hero. His hair was white but he still did fifty push-ups every day.

As for Washington, everyone said this was a bad period for him. He spent days in bed, complaining about his paunch. For two weeks there were lavish dinners in honour of the delegation in the banqueting suites of grand hotels but still no one could get Washington to leave his room at all. Finally, on the day when Louis Cook said he would leave town and fix this problem with more violence and blood, Washington made contact to set a meeting up. It was very obvious to the commentators why he had been so reluctant. People were arguing in the newspapers that the highest value in this land was freedom, and the highest freedom an American could possess was the freedom to settle anywhere you liked. It placed Washington in a very difficult position, and he disliked arguing from difficult positions.

Celine felt very interested in this story, the way she always felt interested in any story about power, and how it was exercised. But of course it is always difficult to know all of a story. She knew the sentence Louis transmitted to Washington, although she did not know that Montour, his interpreter, was now too old and ill to be there, so Louis had only himself to speak with. Washington spoke about American freedom, said Louis, but this was only the freedom to dispossess.

Louis's thinking, however, was less philosophical. He was all grief. It was impossible, Louis thought, to make Washington understand the way the banditti and the Yazoo brokers were not just stealing the land but leaving it depleted – burnt out, overgrown with grasses. Their pigs and cows trampled down the plants. The deer were migrating. And at the same time he had this problem of the Lakota out West. They were getting richer, while his people in the North were living in settlements that were more and more reduced. He understood that to some extent all people were imaginary to everyone else, but still, he felt disappointed.

He refused to show this grief, however. He was the oldest person present, and he knew that it was important never to show your grief in a room. So all the reporters saw was Washington spreading a large map on a table, then drawing lines on it in extravagant red pencil – a pot of which were now always beside him on his desk.

24

Celine arrived in Boston and immediately realised that whatever journey she was on was still stained with the problem of money. Obviously this wasn't a surprise, many people found themselves in a desert, or in a cloud, trying to flee, but still in every case large talent was required to continue on this journey and one part of this talent was money – either having money already or being able to get hold of money, the same way you needed as much language as possible.

In Boston Celine sold everything she had that she didn't immediately need. She was introduced to various families who found her exotic and very difficult to talk with, but she sold them her clothes, fabrics, lace, along with her last pieces of porcelain left over from the first set she bought, and it was very difficult to watch the porcelain disappear – the various plates, the water dish. But then one of the women to whom she was selling the porcelain must have seen how distressed she was, and they sat down together and this woman told her how years earlier their house had been burnt down, in the war against the British, and they had lost everything. Of course, continued this woman, it wasn't a catastrophe, they were all safe, herself and her husband and their daughter – but what still upset her was that they had lost two boxes of old baby clothes, along with the first drawings their daughter had made. She was their only child, the only child they would ever have, said this woman to Celine, and to think of those drawings now gone, she said. To think of those drawings now gone.

It was as if however exciting this era was it was also notable for how much people were losing every day, thought

Celine, so that while in the newspapers people tried to imagine modern life as something stern and clean, without fairies or witches but with new beliefs in class purity and the nobility of revolution, the real thing was this private sense of everything erased.

Meanwhile she tried to improve her English by reading newspapers. There were many words she didn't know so she tried to understand the sentences from little particles and link words, or sudden overlaps with her own language. She kept a notebook where she wrote down words she felt she knew, and whenever she was waiting for something or found herself bored, she took out this notebook and read it, like her pirate/hotelier in Hispaniola. To only have a small vocabulary had a strange effect on reading, as if these articles or reports she was reading were hinting at a mystery that those who spoke the language more fluently might never notice. It was apparent that people here feared many things, they feared people from the North and East and West and South, they feared the black population, the people from the islands or those who had escaped from slavery in the South, they feared the Mohawks and the Sioux, and in reaction to this fear they seemed to propose a total violence against the people who made them afraid, which didn't seem rational to Celine or in any way likeable, even though the people who thought these things could also, as she knew, be very caring and attentive in different ways.

It was a contradiction, and more and more Celine no longer enjoyed a state of contradiction.

With the money she had saved, as well as the extra amount she had made from selling off her things, she looked for somewhere to live. At the back of a newspaper she read about a farmhouse for sale in the countryside upstate, near a town called Albany. She had no idea where Albany was and had to find it on a map. She messaged that she would take it. She hired a driver to take her out upstate as far as a station. From there she set out with Yvette and a guide, a Mohawk man, along a path hacked through a forest – surrounded by parasitical plants and wild vines. It made her think of Claude, of the way Claude must have felt, when he was out in the islands and the sea, having to understand a world he had never thought he needed to understand. There were clumps of rhododendrons, violet, pale lily, all kinds of roses, then creeks with aquatic plants. Eventually they reached a village. The noises were unimaginable too. There were heath hens and other birds whose names she had read but never seen.

And then they found the house, with a little group of maple trees beside it, and a large barn. There was a door in the wall of her bedroom which opened out onto a field.

It was all completely alien but somehow familiar, and she finally realised the reason for this about a week later, when she was out walking in the woods. The trees here, she suddenly noticed, were the same as the trees in the forest around Julia's old house – the American trees that had been planted in their exotic new countryside, many years ago.

25

For a few weeks, Celine and Yvette organised how to grow vegetables and fruit. Yvette showed her how to sow seeds, how to find weeds, how to water, and she found that to be taught like this, to gather new information, was a reassuring state. Otherwise Yvette spent a lot of her time away in the nearby town, setting up sale networks for what they grew, and so in this absence Celine started doing something she had never done before, which was writing. It was so beautiful to be alone! When she finished working in their garden, she came inside and began writing. She liked how messy it made her the same way she loved the gardening – because the pens here were different to the pens she was used to and so her hands were often blackened and smudged with ink. At first she tried to write just little sentences describing how she was feeling. Her lack of confidence in the future, she wrote, obliged her to limit her aspirations only to the everyday sphere. She sketched this kind of sentence then stopped, then started again. It was impossible to know the kinds of sentences that might be useful in this era, or if not useful then at least possessing a certain kind of gravity.

Everything she wrote, she destroyed the same day. She liked making language but had no wish to preserve it. Nothing good could come of sentences that were allowed to exist on their own.

She began to write very short stories, each made from two or three paragraphs. She found it easier to write indirectly. Her stories were fantasias, cartoons. They were set in some kind of future, featuring her and an array of fantastical creatures, and for a while she busied herself with these stories, as if they could teach her something important. Then she felt unsure.

In this new house, she felt cleansed because she was alone. The windows were full of ladybirds. There were nine spots on their wings. They gathered at the windowsills, or in the crevices beside the stair treads. She liked to lie in the sunshine and listen to the blurry vibration of their wings at the window frames. When they died they left little dry casings that tumbled down the stairs.

Then one morning Yvette came to her to ask about leaving. She had met someone in town, she said. She thought that perhaps she would like to leave, and start a family. But she would be very sorry to leave Celine, she said.

The morning Yvette left, Celine sat in the house and realised that for the first time in perhaps her whole life she had no people around her, not only no friends or enemies but no assistants or diary managers. This condition lengthened and deepened over the next few weeks. Sometimes, a girl came over to help her but usually there was no one. She liked this emptiness. It was of course often restful to have someone do things for you like clean a house or dig a vegetable bed but also assistants, she realised, had always made her anxious. She didn't like the burden of being responsible for someone's time. To see them stand there, waiting for your orders! Also, their presence in a home made a home both more and less homelike, as if a home were being staged in a small theatre, and she finally realised what it was that Cato had been expressing, in his final exit from her life, when he had told her that her houses were never his houses. It was never a home, if someone was employed there. The money corrupted everything.

In the dead time of the afternoons, after caring for her vegetable garden and a few animals, she tried to read old novels, the ones she used to love, but she now found them boring and full of little tricks and inaccuracies. She put them away, in a stack on a windowsill. In the late summer, they turned to dust and talcum and jasmine in the heat.

When the weather began to turn colder, she went into town to buy some warm clothes. She bought moccasins from some of the Mohawks. She had never seen this kind of shoe before. These people were some of the last survivors, they told her, of the Iroquois – after the American wars. They lived up in the valley. She found them very easy to talk to. She stood there, and they talked.

They had very little money, they said. Everything was very hard. First there was the problem of the Americans, who had been taking everything they owned. And now there were the problems of the southern ports, like New Orleans. Everything was passing that way. There was very little they could do.

She offered them some money of her own and they looked at her, amazed. The next time she was in town, she brought them a kettle instead. It was very funny, talking to them in her accent, which they replied to in their own accent – all of them communicating in an adopted language. It was as if this language became something new and exciting to speak, and a second language could be something much more elastic than a first language, so that in fact the people who thought they spoke this language fluently because it was the only language they knew didn't use it with the same exuberance or flair.

In this way, they told her stories about the land they were living on. It had been formed, they said, from the moment when a woman fell from the sky, the way a maple seed falls to the ground, onto the water beneath. The animals tried to help her survive, in this terrible water. They tried diving to the bottom of the water, where some mud might be found. Eventually a musk rat emerged with some mud packed into its paw. Then a turtle came forward and told the woman to spread the mud on its back, so that land could form. The woman was so delighted with this that she began to dance on the surface of this land, and the more she danced, they said, the more the mud spread and spread, until her turtle island became a world. In return, Celine told them the stories she most loved too, which weren't about the beginning of the world but about trying to think about whatever might be real: like the story of a man who always thought he was living in a romance, or about a man who one day travelled to the moon.

There was one woman she became friends with in particular. Her name was Catherine. She worked as an interpreter, she said. She came from a family of interpreters. Her father, a man called Montour, was now dying. So she was now the family interpreter. In fact, she added, he always liked speaking her language. She was sure that he would find it very interesting, to meet Celine out here.

They all met the following day, at their little camp just out of town. Montour was sitting among a large pile of blankets. Some dogs were wandering around beside him. He spoke her language very beautifully, with the kind of elegance that can often happen when someone speaks another language, with more care than someone who uses it every day.

She understood that he was an interpreter, said Celine. It was a very difficult job, said Catherine. Of course not always, not when people wanted to understand each other, but most of the time they did not want to understand each other and this made their task much harder. He didn't want her to think that it was impossible, however, added Montour. It was just, he said, you had to be very strong, to be an interpreter. You had to have a lot of strength to carry something across from one person to another.

– What kind of strength? asked Celine.

It seemed that Montour needed to think about what to say next because for some moments he was silent.

– Not to insist, he said eventually. – Not to insist on being a single thing.

She was not sure if she had understood correctly, if this enigmatic sentence were deliberate or caused by problems of translation, but before she could keep talking he began talking to his daughter in their own language. It seemed that he needed to rest, said Catherine to Celine. But he wanted to say that he was happy that his daughter had such a friend. Montour smiled at her translation. It obviously had pleased Catherine very much, and the love between them was very clear – and Celine was relieved to discover that this vision made her happy rather than only desperate for her own world with Saratoga.

The year began to end, and it seemed so strange to Celine that something as momentous as her previous life was ending – but at the same time the horror she had experienced was also continuing, elsewhere, so that in fact nothing had ended at all. Whenever she was in town she asked at the post office if anyone had sent letters to her. By anyone she meant Saratoga, but for months there had been no messages at all.

When the spring began, just ever so slightly, Catherine taught her how to make sugar from the maples, tapping spiles into the tree trunks then placing a bucket underneath. In the fragile nights they spread the sap into low troughs and the next morning broke the ice. Underneath was a kind of concentrate, which they then evaporated on hot stones over a fire.

Something was ending, thought Celine, and it was very possibly her story.

And then one afternoon she was outside her house, hacking into a gigot of lamb which she was going to roast for dinner. Suddenly, behind her, a deep voice made itself heard, speaking her language with a terrible accent.

– I've never seen butchery done so gorgeously, said the voice.

She turned round immediately in the American forest and amazingly saw the elegant figure of Lorenzo. He had come, he said, to take her back into the world.

27

Celine had assumed that she had come to the end of her story. It was in no way the finale she imagined, but it seemed to be the one she would have to accept. But now it also seemed the story couldn't end, not even out here in the American forest, but would extend itself in extra loops and tassels and extensions.

The next morning, Lorenzo transported her to his house in Philadelphia. He was newly funny and expansive and it seemed amazing to connect this Lorenzo with the Lorenzo who had been with Julia, years before. It was like she had acquired, against this alien backdrop, a new friend out of the shadow of the old one. He had given up scriptwriting, he said. The atmosphere in Europe was too intense. With his new wife he had come out here, and was now writing a text-book about Italian literature. As a hustle he was also trying to make plans for land speculation. His obsession was Louisiana. He thought it represented a large possibility for doing deals.

As soon as they arrived in town he took her to a bookstore on South Street – which was where everyone, he said, hung out. All of them were exiles, like Celine, but exile, it turned out, was a vastly ambiguous category, because no one became an exile at the same time, and this delay in arrival was a symptom of the way each person was in exile for asymmetrical or even contradictory reasons. Here they all were, therefore, the reds and the whites, the reactionaries and the radicals, but from the perspective of America these differences tended to cloud or even be deleted entirely. It made friendships confusing, the way they all lived together, tangled and matted, because in the end it seemed to them that just to speak the same language was very important and perhaps more important than whether you agreed with someone politically or had at some point wanted them dead.

At first it was very depressing for Celine, this world into which Lorenzo introduced her. Everyone seemed as obsessed with writing as usual. The only difference was that whereas the writers she used to know thought of writing as something utopian and hopeful, the young writers in exile tended to see literature as haloed with doom. They argued in anonymous reviews for expressionism, garishness, codes, hysterical enjoyment of horror. Death, it seemed, had invaded the picture and made them radiant.

All of them crowded round a writer called André – the latest writer to be praised as original. There was always a new writer! thought Celine. There was always a new element in an infinite series! André was fluent in many ancient and distant languages but was perhaps most remarkable for being unusually beautiful for a writer, being tall and sleek with high cheekbones and pleasing stubble and precisely flowing hair, and it made him surprising and difficult to judge because no one really trusted that someone so beautiful could also be a talented writer. But it was true. André believed in an international project. If he were ever back in the city they had once called home, he said, he would dedicate himself to researching the history of every language, because every language was equal, with no higher value at all. He had nearly been killed by the radicals but had managed to escape on a boat out, via Lisbon then New York. Somehow on this journey he had become a friend of Washington, which gave him a radical glamour.

Celine found the hustle out here in this bookstore and the apartment conversations very confusing. It was like they had all come across the ocean, a little diagram of high-speed arrows, only to be trapped in a spiral, infinite and boring. People were continuing conversations as if they still had influence over events thousands of miles away, when in fact they were dazed and removed from that history entirely. Every day someone began talking about the lists – the list of people forbidden to return, the list of people who had been killed. Of course, they were trying to understand a logic in these lists, to assert a power over events they used to enjoy. But what made this even more surreal was that it took so long for newspapers to arrive that the events the newspapers were so frantically predicting or reporting had always already happened, or turned out to be impossible.

One day Celine read that Julia and her husband had been arrested and were being kept in prison indefinitely. For some time she could not continue reading anything, because she was thinking all the time about Julia and what she might be feeling. Weeks later, when she found herself able to read again, she immediately read that Jacob had been executed. Then, in an older newspaper that had arrived much later, she read that Sasha – who had tried to clandestinely come back home for reasons no one understood – had also been arrested and then killed. This upset her more than she would have expected. Then she read that after the recent period of savage unrest Yves had disappeared. Everything was movement and uncertainty and it was amazing how even for Yves she felt this blurry kind of melancholy.

For many years, perhaps, a person can go through life not thinking about dying – but at a certain point they start thinking about dying all the time, and even if it was very sudden, this list of the dying, it was no more dramatic, thought Celine, than most people's experience, whether inside a war or not. Suddenly for everyone there is a moment where many people they know are dying, or beginning to die. So that maybe it wasn't odd that she thought with affection even about people she had hated, because she had known them living, they had accompanied her in her own living, too, and there was always something tender about living, even in Yves and Jacob and Sasha, with their ambitions and their violence.

One day Lorenzo came to tell her that there was a message for her at the bookstore, and for the moments it took her to walk through the sodden streets she bore with her the warm light of Saratoga. But instead it was from Izabela in Poland – forwarded across the ocean – written in the kind of style they used to message each other before, with intriguing vocabulary and futuristic sentiment, but Celine now felt oddly distant from this kind of writing. The situation, wrote

Izabela, was pure anxiety. Their little intelligent revolution seemed to be finished. But what she'd wanted to say, wrote Izabela, was that Celine had appeared to her in a dream! Somehow they were driving together. Then it suddenly occurred to Izabela that she didn't really know anything about Celine's parents. And Celine had said: *Oh, you must mean things like the contested will and all of that.* And that was the end of the dream, wrote Izabela. On another page she then added an extra paragraph. All she had been able to think about had been revolution, money, parliaments. She spent her time waiting to see which friends would be killed, and when. She would give anything to join Celine again in that restaurant where they went once, wrote Izabela, the one near Celine's house. And they would surely have the onion soup.

Celine read this in the noisy bookstore. She missed Izabela, because Izabela was the sign of a way of living, but felt guilty because this letter didn't interest her at all. It was overwhelmed by the absence of Saratoga. All she had of Saratoga was the last picture that had been done before she left town, where Saratoga was dressed very simply, in white muslin, like everyone else, and it confused Celine very much, this picture, because in it she looked exactly like Claude, and she had become so used to forgetting this fact of Saratoga's father, as if she had been born out of nowhere, that the resemblance disconcerted and even upset her.

She wanted to leave this strange version of society and go back to her house in the country, but also felt that this would disappoint Lorenzo. So she made herself stay. One night Lorenzo had a dinner for some of Washington's assistants. Celine hated the basic tone. All the men here seemed to be bored by their wives, but instead of this disturbing them and making them think about how to change such a situation they seemed to like it or at least assume that it was normal, and therefore also assume that no woman should ever speak. So Celine spoke mostly to Lorenzo. He thought that Europe was finished, he said, but at the same time he could not speak the language here with any elegance and it was humiliating to have to be in this world, where no one got his jokes. Opposite them André, the young writer, was describing an unknown writer who was in his opinion the greatest writer alive, who published nothing and did not write novels or poems or even essays, he wrote in no form at all but just a journal which he showed in fragments to friends, and these fragments, said André, were little sentences describing weather, both the outside weather and the inside movements of his mind. It was possible, she heard André add, that the journal was the most important contemporary form, because it was a form of blankness, of gaps.

It was from inside this surface of conversation that Celine realised that Lorenzo was holding out some porcelain to her. At first she didn't understand. He wanted to give her this, he said. She stared at it. There was one water bowl, and one side plate. They were each painted with blue stripes. He had seen two pieces of her porcelain in a house in Boston, he said, when he was out there to teach at the university. He recognised it immediately, from the particular shade of international blue she always liked. And so he had bought it, to give to her.

Amazed at herself, bewildered, Celine burst into tears.

The next day, she decided to finally leave, and go back on her own to the American landscape. In her house she tried to think about this little moment of society created by Lorenzo, and why she felt so unhappy. Certain feelings seemed to be rearranged inside her. And in fact maybe everything she cared about had been reconfigured, but it was requiring a lot of energy to accept that and understand it. Maybe it was somehow connected to how to exist at the furthest edge of the present moment. It wasn't anything to do with the future, she knew this, the future wasn't a concept to think with, and maybe in fact much more importantly you had to enlarge the scale more than she might ever have expected. It was difficult, she thought, to be more precise about this right now. It was as far as she thought she could go.

She loved the plants in her new garden, the giant trees. She might have liked to become a tree, she thought, as in some fantastical story.

She began to reply to Izabela, then realised that she couldn't. All letters were impossible, the same way she hadn't wanted Lorenzo to bring her back into this world. Everything she had lived had been about her friendships and their interactions. And now they were fading away.

28

As she escaped out of Europe across the ocean Celine had seen herself as moving inside a cloud, something necessary but therefore without meaning. She was in transit, and there was no meaning in transit. But maybe there was something much larger going on, she was thinking, if only she could see it. Perhaps Lorenzo was right in a way, that the ending she had imagined here in America was only an apparent ending, a little trick of perspective, and there might turn out to be more than one ending: or a series of false endings before the true finale. He was just wrong that this would mean re-entering the world of conversation.

As though in answer, one morning Catherine, her Mohawk friend, came up to her house with a gift of food, to celebrate Celine's return. She brought cheap clay dishes filled with pumpkin stew, black bean chilli, fried pumpkin blossoms. They were new tastes that Celine had never known before. Also little baskets woven from black ash, little strips of black ash woven together.

This began a period of education and delight.

Catherine had a daughter who sometimes came and sat with them by the beech tree or looking at the old maples, and the more Celine talked to them the more she thought about Saratoga. It suddenly seemed terrible to her that she was not with Saratoga, or near her. She missed her in a way that was almost impossible for her to define. It wasn't more fierce than the way she had once missed a lover, like Marta, in the full desolation of wanting to taste someone who wasn't there. It was at once more bodily and more abstract, a kind of absence that accompanied you always.

She began writing messages to Saratoga every week, even though she had no idea if they could or would ever reach her. And meanwhile she spent the summer talking with Catherine. She began to learn her language, in the slowest way possible. They named things together, and she wrote them down.

One day Celine went out walking in the woods. She found little white flowers, entirely white. They were the strangest plants she had ever seen, just white from their stalks to their leaves to their petals. She touched one and the plant felt fleshy. It was in dense shade, among leaf litter. That evening she brought Catherine to look at it, to ask her what it was. It was a ghost pipe, said Catherine. Celine had never seen any plant like it: this albino thing. It seemed impossible that such a thing should keep itself alive, with no sunlight at all.

Gradually, it began to seem to Celine that she was travelling not so much in a cloud, or across a desert, but along a bridge in the fog. She was on some kind of rickety wooden bridge, hung high in a mountain. If she could keep crossing over, then she would come to somewhere amazing. But every time she stepped on the bridge, someone came to tug her away because they needed her or wanted to talk to her. They never noticed that she was on this bridge, however. The bridge was her secret.

Was this, thought Celine, a greater meaning?

In her lessons with Catherine it began to seem that if she were going to understand the words then she would have to think in a different way. There was a nut called a *pigan* or *pegan* or *pican*. There was no way, she felt, of her spelling any of these words correctly – the words seemed too intricate and slippery for her usual system of sounds. There was a word to describe the force that moved a mushroom to flower overnight through the soil. There was a word for the way the sweetgrass looked when it was ripe. What she found most difficult was the way the world was divided into the animate and the inanimate. There was a way of speaking to a person that was not the same as speaking to a notebook. It was a different verb. She had never needed to learn this before, the way Izabela once described how Russian had its little words for repeated motion and single motion, for motion on foot or motion in a vehicle, but whereas such differences had seemed maddening to Izabela, Celine found the unusual forms out here delightful.

Some words seemed untranslatable, or could only be paraphrased in sentences so extended that a word no longer felt the same as a word in her own language, as if in this language a word could contain so many more implications. Or there were some words she could not understand at all, like the word Catherine kept using, something like *dodem* or *dodet*, to describe the way there was a bear that cared for her and oversaw her world. Celine had no idea if this bear was real or immaterial. It seemed difficult to explain the distinction to Catherine, and perhaps there wasn't one.

If she had to define the kind of bridge she was on, thought Celine, it would be something to do with the new knowledge that Catherine was bringing her, or the new vastness she was entertaining, out here in the forests. It no longer seemed eccentric to think of a forest as a place that was peopled – or to believe that you could speak with the sun or animals or plants, the way she had heard voices before. It was like the world was a backdrop for voices, and there was no reason why a single voice should always be produced by a single visible thing.

And it occurred to Celine very simply that the reason why this rupture or enlargement didn't alarm her was because she had invented new versions of herself already on at least two or even three occasions. The men around her talked about change – but always with this vast bedding of security around them. In any crisis it was always possible for a man to separate from his wife or begin a new job or move to a new country, and therefore never to know the true terror of ruin. And whereas this masculine security had sometimes appealed to her so much that she was even jealous of them for this extra power, she realised that to have these reinventions forced on her maybe allowed her access to a larger wisdom, however disturbing it might be.

29

Sometimes you need a new element to confirm you have changed and one day this happened to Celine. In her newly cosmic mood André, the young writer, came out to see her in the countryside. She looked at him, astonished. She was sitting out on a bench with Catherine. He seemed completely exotic and unnatural, out here in the countryside.

– Why are you here? she said.

What made André specifically unusual, much more than his looks and his gentle hair, was his idea that any future depended on understanding India and America, the frontiers and peripheries. You had to think South and West and East, he thought. His passion was anthropological, and it made him lovable, in his way.

He thought they had arranged this, he began to stammer. Wherever he went, he tried to take as many notes as possible, he said, and in particular he wanted to understand what the people here thought about the spirits. And Celine had said that she could maybe introduce him to some people who were living here. They had arranged this visit weeks ago, he said, at one of Lorenzo's dinners. She looked at him: he was burdened with materials – sketch pads and paints and brushes, and many notebooks and pens. He had also brought her post from Philadelphia, he said, and Celine felt a great hope surge inside her but also felt she had to first work out what was happening here.

– But what did we arrange? she said.

– That I would come out here, he said, – to talk with the Americans.

– I never said that, she said.

– We were with Lorenzo, he said.

He was sincere and insistent and he was also here. It seemed impossible to send him away.

Celine turned to Catherine and first translated into her uncomfortable English everything André had just said to her. It seemed, said Catherine, not so easy to explain to someone like him. There were spirits, of course, but they were also animals, and she was not sure that he would know how to think in this way. But what, asked André, did that mean? Well, said Celine, translating for Catherine, who was starting to talk much faster than she was used to, as she lost herself in thinking, it meant that animals also had a social life, the way people did. The reason this conversation was so difficult to explain, she added, trying to help André, was that Catherine didn't see any distinction between the world of nature and the world of people, or the world of people and the world of spirits. All these worlds were peopled by souls, and souls could always communicate with other souls. Even if, she added, still translating, the only truly perfect communication would be between souls from the same community. As soon as forms moved among other forms – whether a human talking to a plant or a mushroom talking to a jaguar – you still needed diplomacy and translation.

André said he didn't exactly understand how this movement between different levels worked. But of course not, said Celine. The way of seeing the world that he liked, where he observed a world outside him, everything ordered and in categories, made it impossible to do the kinds of things that Catherine could do when she was thinking or talking. Catherine had metamorphosis. Whereas they just had *literature*.

He seemed disconsolate – as if the information he was being given was unsatisfactory, or so alien it was also untrustworthy. Still, he wrote it down. It was like they had reached some kind of limit of his understanding, and while it troubled André it somehow made Celine feel vibrant and even powerful. She felt sorry for this boy who had come out so far to see her, with his sincerity, and who was too pretty for other people to take seriously. She kind of liked him.

Celine tried to calm the tone.

– What did you say about post? said Celine.

– Oh but yeah, said André.

Then he handed her a message from his pocket, without looking up from his notes.

30

The letter was at last from Saratoga. Sometimes letters seemed incredible in their persistence in reaching people. They were such determined animals! The address was scribbled over and marked with little cryptic postal stamps and courier codes and strangers' handwriting. At some point it seemed to have been folded in quarters.

She was leaving her husband, said Saratoga. She was divorcing him. She had found the situation out here very disturbing, she wrote. There was total European anarchy and savagery. It was very obvious that at a certain distance – like an ocean – a person could not be represented by another person. So there could not be any justice in such a system. But most of all she realised that she disliked Hugo. She had thought that he was witty, she wrote, but she was wrong. So she was coming back to Europe. Then she added that she missed her mother very much, and thought about her all the time. She wished that she had more messages from her.

Celine reread Saratoga's sentences many times. It was like when the Tarot cards confirmed you in some vast change of living. It seemed obvious and even overwhelming to her that it would be very wrong to continue living separated from Saratoga. This was surely part of the new meaning that she was approaching, in her cloud. Of course, it was possible that, since this letter had already taken four months to reach her, by the time she herself reached Europe some new change might have taken place in Saratoga's projects or the projects of the universe. But this was, surely, the kind of risk that the message demanded.

She looked at the battered piece of paper. It was like a little scrap of Saratoga that she could feel in her hand.

31

The next day, Celine travelled back to Philadelphia to plan her exit from America. In the bookstore she found Lorenzo eating sandwiches with saucisson and mustard, rereading one of his old scripts.

– I'm going back to Europe, said Celine.

– But you just got here, said Lorenzo.

– I've been here six months, said Celine. – Or in fact no, more than that. I can't remember.

– But that's nothing, said Lorenzo.

Anyway, added Lorenzo, he thought that it was a very dangerous scheme. There was so much disappointment possible, in going back. He himself had been thinking about the people he used to know. Everyone was so different now, he said, so untrustworthy. It was difficult to know what would be left of the world you knew, if you went back.

– You know Julia was arrested? said Celine.

Lorenzo paused for a long while.

– The thing is, said Lorenzo eventually, – everyone knows that Julia will do anything. I'm not worried about Julia.

– Why does everyone think they know everyone else? said Celine.

– I mean, said Lorenzo –

Lorenzo put a scrap of sandwich down, using the cover of his script as a plate, as if to begin a major speech.

– I wasn't *asking*, said Celine.

She felt suddenly inspired with fury, as if fury was the missing element that would allow her to enter her true finale.

– How does anyone think they know anything about another person? said Celine.

– I used to sleep with her, said Lorenzo.

– So fucking what? said Celine. – You think that means Julia knows you too, just because she knows how much you like to lick her asshole?

Again Lorenzo didn't speak, this time with a different kind of heaviness.

– You see? said Celine. – People hate being talked about by other people. It's an absolute terror.

And they were right, continued Celine more gently, sitting down opposite Lorenzo, they were absolutely right to fear it, because to be talked about by other people was the first lesson a person ever received in death, their first lesson in being turned into an object, into something that was you but also not you, at the same time. And yet when people talked about other people the conversation seemed to them so precise, so absolutely precise and pertinent, like the way, she finished, he thought he understood Julia totally.

– I'm sorry, he said. – Maybe you're right. In fact I'm sure you're right.

Celine felt high. It was another of those moments where a voice emerges from a conversation that you had not expected and which you could not entirely think was yours, something emerging in some way from a state between two people, when a conversation was a real thing containing sincere statements and not just an exercise in indirection or subterfuge, and this was very rare.

– The point is, she finished, – you have no right to talk about Julia.

A week later, Celine began to zigzag back across the ocean from America – while the trend forecasters and analysts continued to describe what would happen next. The monarchy would return, they said. Or there would be war communism. Maybe first there would be a military dictatorship. All of this was obvious. Because it was always possible, with careful and patient analysis, to predict what would happen in the future.

Four

I

How a person changes is a mystery, the way how any form changes into another form is a mystery. Some people, however, do not change at all and perhaps this is the greater mystery, and certainly the greater sadness. To be changed into another form is to experience true happiness.

For some time after her return to Europe Celine had the impression that she was changing into something mute and also fantastical, because to leave language behind in the way she was leaving it is certainly to enter a realm of the fantastical. Around her many people were believing in gods or in politics and it seemed to bring them a lot of comfort, but Celine didn't find comfort in this way. Her instincts were stranger. When people talked about a new order of things she just found it difficult to understand what they were saying, and more and more she tended to think that if she did not understand something that seemed obvious to other people it was because there was a logical step missing inside what seemed to the world so coherent and unbreakable.

You'd think that if something major changes inside you then it would be obvious to you and also obvious to other people. But in fact perhaps it takes a long time for these changes to be obvious – to yourself or to the world. The world is very busy and cannot be noticing everyone's changes! So that really it is always down to you to notice how you are changing, if you are changing, and this can take a long time because you are in fact part of the world's frenetic business.

For Celine, however, an experience that was so extraordinary happened that it was finally very easy for her to notice that everything was different inside her, and inside the world too.

2

One evening, on a moonlit night after the revolutions, Celine, Izabela and Julia were returning to the city from a trip out into the countryside. It was a dark hot summer, and Celine and Julia had come to stay at Izabela's place somewhere in the middle of the European forest, which was now a large blur around them. As they travelled, they were talking about the moon, this enormous blotched disc in the sky, and the life that might be all around them in the universe, unknown.

– There are only two possibilities, said Izabela. – Either we're alone in this universe or we're not. And both terrify me equally. Because if we are alone then that is super terrifying. But if there *are* other beings then what are they doing? Are they watching us? Are they listening to us now? Are we in fact a zoo for their private amusement and edification?

They looked up at the desolate moon and the large black spaces around it. It was impossible to see what was happening on the moon, the way presumably it must be impossible from the moon to observe the activities on earth.

When they reached the house they dragged out some sofas to the garden and ate chocolate and biscuits chased down with spirits. At one point in the night Julia toasted the plant inside them that was alcohol. And in fact they drank so much that they all fell asleep outside, in their clothes, lit by the giant stars.

3

The next morning, as dawn slid down, Celine woke early. It seemed to her that there were small but definite changes to the way the world was looking: like different flowers in the garden, and fungi. It was possible that this was simply one terrible effect of drinking too much and so she went into the house to find some water. To her terror, the calendar on the wall in the kitchen was saying that the year was now 2251. She went back outside to tell her friends but was interrupted by something she found in the courtyard: a construction resembling a boat, decorated with thousands of minute silver balloons. The material these balloons were made of looked soft, but when she touched it she discovered it was oddly solid, a sort of highly flexible metal that she had never seen before. She opened up the vehicle and sat inside. Its interior was multicoloured and very cute.

Then, as she was about to get out, it began to float steadily up into the air.

At first she was almost delighted by the new sensation. She looked out the window at the approaching sky. Then she looked down, and in the streets were only people or just emptiness. The city had become endless – little buildings, factories, stadiums for slaloms and races – until finally she saw the fields outside the city, and the vehicle swung over many minuscule horses.

She began to leave the lower atmosphere. She saw in succession the Mediterranean, then the Black Sea, followed by Iran and India until Japan passed across the window of her rocket, and some hours later the whole Pacific Ocean emerged, but it too disappeared and was replaced by the continent of America. She could clearly distinguish all these revolutions of the earth, and eventually saw the Atlantic Ocean and then Europe reappearing in the window but now could not distinguish the different countries, because she was too high.

All this happened very leisurely, like perhaps the time it might take to stay in bed all day reading, after finishing a long project. And meanwhile she continued to surge upwards into the glistening dark sky. But then abruptly, when it seemed that this drifting could continue indefinitely, the rocket was upturned – the way any vehicle might be upturned on a road if it went over some abandoned roadworks in the dark – and she felt herself plunging downwards. Her ears were popping and she was screaming without exactly realising that she was screaming. Everything was incredibly strange – but the strangest was when she looked out the window and saw the moon suddenly in front of her: its white surface, now she saw it close up, colourful and intricate. Then she looked away again because she thought that this must be impossible. At a point when the pressure and speed seemed too intense to bear she heard a sound of a great rushing, a sudden inflation, and saw around her the silver balloons expand to a giant density – so that the airship, which had been rushing downwards in headlong confusion, now started to slow, and finally landed gently in an expanse of sand.

She got out, and looked up into the air. For a moment she felt safe because this was surely at least her world and therefore she could somehow find her way home, until she looked up into the sky. A little planet was a faint mark in the sky, like an enlarged star. Then she realised this star was the earth and Celine vomited.

4

The moon was pretty but also weird and dense with foliage and ferns, like a matted surface of lights. She walked through meadows made of wild flowers. It seemed like she was walking for hours but it was difficult to understand time here on the moon, because all the lighting effects were different. There was a flower that looked like gorse but smelled more like daffodils or manure. She bent down to examine it closer but then hesitated, out of anxiety, maybe, or carefulness.

– Go ahead, you can touch me, a voice said.

She stood there, silent. Everywhere she went, she thought, even on the moon, voices echoed around her. She waited for whoever had spoken to show themselves. Nothing appeared. After a few minutes, she decided to keep on walking. She needed to return to her spaceship, she thought. She didn't want to see the sights of the moon. She wanted to go home.

Then what seemed like a person approached her. She couldn't tell if this person was a man or a woman, and perhaps, she thought, it did not matter. They were very tall, with darkly colourful skin, dressed in a sober white suit, something very precisely tailored. Although you could have assumed this person was human, it was also impossible, noticed Celine, to understand how this person moved.

– Please, they said. – We have been watching you.

– Who are you? said Celine. – Also what do you mean *watching*?

– My name's Harper, said Harper. – We can see whatever we want on this planet.

– I'm lost, said Celine. – I came from the earth. I don't know how I arrived here.

– We call this planet the earth, said Harper, – but you call it the moon. The moon is a world like yours. And your world is our moon.

There was a silence while Celine tried to be calm.

– Hang out with us, said Harper. – Come and see.

5

Celine felt very scared, but fear is a very confused sensation and can be interpreted in many ways. Her fear was close to excitement. It was seeming possible to Celine that up here on this planet something inside her was stirring, something was alive. It was as if there was a new way of living or thinking that she had been trying to achieve on earth and what was happening to her here, however unbelievable or hallucinatory, was a way of telling her to be true to this vision and not to let it go.

So Celine said yes to Harper.

6

Harper beckoned her into a floating vehicle that was waiting nearby. As soon as they got in it began to move but in some apparently motionless way. It was as if the landscape moved but not the vehicle, as it hovered over meadows or jungles or valleys, then at a certain point the vehicle just dissolved around them into the fragile purple air and revealed a collection of tents and little pavilions and other playful structures, a luna park that Harper called a city. It was all made out of a material that gleamed in the sunlight – a light which seemed purer than on earth, presumably because the air was not contaminated with so much human dust and exhalation.

Celine asked Harper how it was possible that she could speak to them in her language.

– We can speak all the languages that humans have used, shrugged Harper. – Between ourselves we prefer to use the language we've perfected, with colours and perfumes as well as sounds. Anything can speak with anything.

– Like a plant? said Celine.

– Naturally, replied Harper, – the plants talk to each other. Also the mountains talk to foxes. Everything is talking to everything else: algae to tomatoes, lizards to clouds. They have to take care, of course. Everything is a diplomat that talks to other diplomats.

– I find languages very hard, said Celine. – I mean I find it very hard to learn a new language: I feel the shame of my bad accent all the time.

– Accent? said Harper.

– Don't different nations here have different accents?

– I mean, said Harper.

– Or different cities then?

– No one here lives in a single city, said Harper. – Everything is portable.

Then they beckoned Celine inside a neon pavilion.

7

The pavilion turned out to be the largest house Celine had ever seen. It seemed that Harper shared this space with many other aliens, as if a house were always a party. The vibe was very friendly, even if the relations between these aliens were hard for Celine to understand, which perhaps shouldn't have been surprising, she thought, because it's always difficult to enter a party, when people seem to resist you or at least maintain a secluded composure. At first Celine thought that the beings here came in a variety of colours: from dark black to cream, via red and green and blue. Then she realised that she had no way of knowing what colour their skin was because these aliens didn't wear clothes in any way she understood, but instead a kind of semi-transparent veil that fitted tightly around them, on which they could project whatever colour or illusion of clothing they wanted, so that it was in fact possible they had no skin at all.

It was a world, it seemed, based on extravagant colours. For dinner, they served little pills that contained, explained Harper, all the nutrients they needed. The pills were mauve and pink and russet. Around Celine the walls were a variety of deep dense colours: a pale sea blue, crisp green, the darkest purple that was somehow also iridescent. They were like tapestries if tapestries had been pressed and moulded into little waves, abstract squares of thick colour. They were made of velvet, jacquard, nylon, bouclé wool, fake fur, or something that seemed like all these things.

– But what do you all do here? she asked. – How do you live?

Everyone began to laugh.

– This is the happiest place in the universe, said Harper. – We don't need to do anything. I understand this might seem weird. Humans always have to make things. Whereas here all production and reproduction is done without any effort – through mediums, in code.

– I don't understand, said Celine.

– Think of a book, said Harper. – Or a portrait. A medium is something that allows another thing to extend its life beyond its usual boundaries. A medium is a place where life multiplies.

– Sure, said Celine, – but those are just images, just words.

– Maybe think about it like this, said Harper. – Ever since the universe began, it has been trying to find the best way of providing itself with information about itself. The more the universe thinks, the more it gradually organises itself, in more and more extravagant mediums. The first mediums were molecules, and cells, until gradually they assumed the form of minute organisms, then animals and fungi and plants until soon the code assumed the form of little communities. Then it became language, like books and magazines and gossip. Then language became images. And then we arrived here.

Celine was staring crazily and fearfully.

– Come with me, said Harper.

Harper took her out of the pavilion, along an avenue that was made of some kind of sparkling glass, to a structure like an optical illusion, as if a skyscraper were bent over into a semicircle. Enclosed inside it there was a selection of other buildings. From the windows there were little views to clouds and galaxies, just appearing occasionally beside them as they walked.

– You see? Harper said.

And they entered the factory buildings.

8

In some buildings there were rows of objects or machines. But in other buildings there was nothing, or almost nothing – just screens in which numbers appeared and disappeared at high speed. After walking through a rocket hangar Celine saw what seemed to be an elaborate writing system housed inside some kind of botanical museum. There was a humid dense perfumed air, and palmettos and savagely colourful insects, and inside this dense foliage was a series of hands that were made of polished mineral, maybe zinc or granite, attached in rows to rods, all writing at high speed on plants that were unravelling into what looked like paper.

– But what's happening? asked Celine.

– They're making books, said Harper. – They write stories.

– But it's a machine, said Celine.

– A long time ago, said Harper, – we realised that a story didn't need an *author*. The hands are a kind of joke.

– But what are they writing? said Celine, who was trying to read the books as they were printed.

– Oh, novels, said Harper. – Also descriptions of the planets, histories of sands and rocks and lichen. Whatever they want to write. This one, for instance, is writing a novel about your earth.

The writing hands seemed very delicate, with long fingers and nails painted a luminous neon orange.

– But can a machine, asked Celine, – really write a novel? Can it think of its own compositions?

– Of course, said Harper. – What did you think, that you weren't a code too?

Then Harper beckoned her into a new room that seemed lit from its own walls. There were large windows looking over desert sands with stunted cacti and other greenery. In this room various aliens were moving around tables on which were little bottles, retorts, spigots. Meanwhile there were partitions everywhere, making an arrangement of different zones, all transparent to each other.

– This is where we reproduce ourselves, said Harper.

There was a pause in which Celine failed to understand.

– We don't make new beings inside a body, said Harper. – We prefer to invent them in these colourful, open spaces.

– But why? said Celine. – There's no greater pleasure than making a child inside you, then being with it always.

– For precisely the reason you just described, said Harper. – Why arrange things in such a limited way?

Harper seemed to be shimmering with delight.

– If you want to understand the moon, Harper added, – this is what you have to study: our method of reproduction. It's what makes our happiness possible because it allows us to be free.

It was very strange, to feel that you suddenly understood what was happening, thought Celine, when you also did not understand what was happening at all.

An alien was giving a turquoise drink to a miniature alien, then showing it how to make itself glow in a series of translucent shades.

– Is this your child? said Celine to this alien.

– Oh but no, said the alien.

– All the adults look after all the children, explained Harper.

– But do you love it? said Celine. – I mean: can you love this little being?

– Of course, said the alien. – Why not?

9

That night Celine lay on a sofa, while pulsing lights drifted in the air. A fountain was deliciously trickling in a kind of interior courtyard beside her. The atmosphere was very hot. It seemed like there was silence, and at the same time there was also a kind of dense repetitive music in the background, like the noise made by cicadas in the green and black twilight.

Celine was trying to determine what she was feeling. It was as if out here in the future, on the moon, something she had been thinking was being demonstrated to her, or at least offered for her consideration.

– But how did I get from there to here? said Celine to herself, out loud. – That's what I don't understand.

– Is it really so odd? said a voice.

It seemed that it must be progress that she was no longer so afraid of these invisible voices, but at the same time it was confusing. She looked around into the planetary dark. It seemed to be coming from the fountain, she thought.

– Did you speak? she asked the fountain.

– Absolutely, said the fountain.

Celine stared at the apparently innocent miniature cascade.

– Ask me anything, it said.

– I'm sorry? said Celine.

– Ask me anything, I want to help.

– I'm just, began Celine.

Then she stopped. It was indescribable.

– I understand, said the fountain. – It seems very confusing for you. But perhaps it isn't so confusing, perhaps what's happening here isn't so different to what you know.

– It's still, said Celine, – very unnerving. For instance, talking to water, or whatever.

– I mean really? said the fountain. – After all, you have stories told by sofas, by coins, by petticoats and pockets. Why not other things as well?

– But they're in *novels*, said Celine.

There was a silence, as if the fountain felt embarrassed or rebuffed. Then the fountain was suddenly a porcelain soup tureen, with frilled and ruffled edges. It just metamorphosed, even while she was continuously staring at it, the way an animation might transform – and Celine realised as she stared at it in amazement how disturbing she always thought soup was. Perhaps, she wondered, it was the way soup has no edges, or the way the elements which are contained in it are unprovable and undefined. It's incredible, when you think about it, to consider how simultaneously inside the elegant

257

hard shape of a soup tureen is the sloshing formless soup, like also the way the blood exists inside a body or the million words inside a book.

– There's no reason, said the fountain, – why only certain beings should speak and not others.

– I guess, said Celine.

– And in fact, continued the fountain, – voices don't need to come from a certain place. I mean, I can make myself heard anywhere, even when I can't be seen. The universe is a collection of voices that can echo each other and talk.

– But how? Celine said.

– How what? said the soup.

– How that? she said. – What you said?

– I mean, said the soup, – how anything? Sometimes you're walking down the street and then you start singing. And then you stop. It's just like that.

As if to illustrate this, or perhaps simply out of caprice, the soup suddenly acquired a large number of heads, and began sipping a kitsch cocktail with great severe concentration, playing with a miniature paper parasol perched on the glass's edge.

It was a fearful thing to fall into the hands of something this supernatural, thought Celine, the way it's also fearful when you're left alone at a party with a celebrity and suddenly can't see your friends. But still, if this being starts talking to you, in whatever language you can understand, if it puts its words in front of you the way in normal life someone might offer you a plate of fettuccine, then you should certainly try to listen to those words.

– I'm still not sure that answers my question, said Celine.

– I understand, said the cocktail drinker. – Every story begins as a question of *how*. But what people really want is a story that transforms the how into *why*. Now, this kind of story is impossible. It's like the story of the universe. There was nothing, and then there was something. There was no space, and then there was space. There was space where none existed, the way a baby creates space inside a body. There wasn't any *why*.

– I'm still having trouble, said Celine.

– I mean really? it said.

And its head became a bottle of sauce, which poured itself back into the space it had vacated, and suddenly it was a fountain again, trickling in the background.

There was nothing again, where there had just been something.

IO

The next day, Celine woke up early and went for a walk along a kind of canal, through dark brown reeds, under a blue sky. She emerged into a piazza where many of the aliens were gathered, talking in what seemed like an excited kind of conversation because it was being conducted in a series of bright colours and notes, but when she stopped to ask Harper, who was talking with a friend at one side of the crowd, they told her that in fact everyone was a little anxious or on edge because of this arrival of a stranger among them.

– You mean me? asked Celine.

– I do mean you, said Harper.

Celine went up to one of the moon's inhabitants.

– Can we speak? she said.

– I mean, sure, said the alien. – Why not?

– I just thought, said Celine. – I mean, I wasn't sure if you would want to. If you think that I am dangerous.

– You look extraordinary, they said.

– Thank you? said Celine.

– Absolutely, said the alien. – I love it.

There was a gold sweat or sheen on their surface. They were very elegant, thought Celine.

– I'm Celine, said Celine.

– I'm Mica, said the alien.

This was how her friendship with an alien began.

For the rest of the day, Celine and Mica talked. When they got tired of talking Mica showed her little buildings and gardens and wild deserts made of silicon dust or diamonds. The following morning they met up and continued talking. These conversations continued for some days. It was a paradise of conversation, thought Celine. If Mica were ever late, she began to miss them. She had never talked to someone so abstract. Mica taught her how to wear clothes in the alien way, to learn the secrets of projection. Sometimes it was easy, and she wore little blouses and tweed trousers with tiny bows at the waist, or dresses printed with unicorns or in psychedelic swirls. Then there were days when nothing came out right, and she slouched around in track pants or pyjamas. But suddenly she discovered a way of giving herself taffeta violet trousers or an orange fitted T-shirt with an organza orange pleated skirt. The way they appeared each day became a common project. Together, they liked to vary what they wore, to confuse everyone on the moon, so that they projected absolute severity when they were feeling at their most frivolous, or a delicate lightness when they were talking of the darkest philosophical things. Whenever she asked Mica if they didn't want to hang out with someone else, Mica replied that there was no one they wanted to talk with more than Celine.

It would have been a friendship, if there were friendships on the moon, thought Celine, which presumably there weren't. The effect was frightening but also exciting.

She remembered Montour and what they had talked about with Catherine, in America. It was possible, thought Celine, that this was a situation he would have recognised and she wanted to be equal to his ideals – not to insist, not to be a single thing, but to let anything inhabit you. But still, he was right: it was very tiring.

– I think I'm still having problems of scale, said Celine. – I once talked with something that –

She paused. She tried again.

– I mean, I've tried to think about this problem before, she said.

– I understand, said Mica. – It's very confusing. But how long will your thoughts remain fixed on earth?

She seemed to think for a long moment.

– Let me show you something, said Mica.

Then they showed her into another building that Celine had not noticed because it was transparent, but from the inside the walls looked densely woven from a kind of opaque mesh. They altered colour depending on the angle of the sun. There was a large square cut out of one of these walls, so that you could always see the universe: tender and gigantic. While on another wall, with rows of backlit transparent seats made of a clear and puffy material, you could watch little scenes happening on the walls, moving slowly like a zoetrope. These were all scenes from the earth, said Mica. Celine could see explorers, battles, farmers asleep in orchards, many dogs. She asked Mica what this was.

Everything that happened on earth migrated here, explained Mica, the same way rumours or words could migrate, like seeds. All of human history had been projecting little images and sounds, little copies, that were floating out to reach them here.

There were long sequences of forest or wilderness or desert, just leaves moving and making a rustling kind of sound, or the wind, or buffalo mooching sedately at a far distance. But also Celine could see Marta, reading and rereading the messages she had sent her, and then Beaumarchais, dying, on his own, with a jug of old water beside his bed. Images from everywhere were appearing. In the American forest large animals were resting.

The more Celine experienced the more it seemed that she was on the edge of a major understanding, as if she would be able to see her planet very precisely and very wildly, the way perhaps a printing mechanic might understand a print machine – just thoroughly and with an affable precision. It was a vision of action at a distance which might have once seemed spooky or uncanny but in this place seemed rational and obvious – a vision of causes and effects zooming in and out of each other, all the pamphlets and ships and bacteria and words and images, everything entangled, liquid and exciting. All history, including the history of words, it turned out, was really natural history.

The next day, they came back to this kind of theatre, and in fact for many days, more than a week, Celine sat inside this chamber with Mica beside her on a soft banquette, watching the earth happen.

II

Celine thought about her conversations with Mica all the time. Her closeness to an alien now felt familiar and almost unremarkable. The house she lived in had varieties of windows and she would sit at these windows and let the breezes envelop her. Each breeze, she understood, had its own personality. There were very playful winds and sober winds and winds that thought very distinctly and philosophically. Meanwhile in the far distance the earth rose greenly, then disappeared.

There was something about living at this new perspective which Celine found totally delightful. Even if she also missed bodies, she thought. She missed the feeling of someone's solid and sweating body against her. But then perhaps this was old-fashioned of her, to miss desire so much, the way she found it old-fashioned when people so needed to know who was a woman and who was a man. All of life, it seemed, had been warped by that relation.

It was as if she were turning into an alien herself, and the idea was entertaining and seductive.

Then one morning Harper came to see her, with Mica trailing despondently behind.

– Is this true? Harper said.

– Is what true? said Celine.

– That you were looking at the earth, with Mica, said Harper.

– Um, sure, said Celine.

Anger was a cloud around Harper. For a long time no one spoke.

– Don't be mad at Mica, said Celine.

– I'm not mad at Mica. I mean, no, I'm very mad at Mica. But really I'm mad at you, said Harper.

It wasn't so much the secret visits to the theatre, said Harper. It was what these visits represented. Something terrible had been introduced to the moon by Celine, Harper continued. A trend for seclusion and enclosed friendship was everywhere, like a virus – so that duos hung out reading together or just talking about each other in a way they had never experienced before, about mutual plans and future projects and wishes. And all of this, said Harper, began when Celine seduced Mica.

– But I never seduced anyone, said Celine. – I never wanted that to happen.

Harper paused. They understood, said Harper. But nevertheless it was happening, and many inhabitants of the moon were angry and disconsolate. It was not obvious what they wanted to do. They let the unhappiness of this final sentence stain the air around them. Then Harper shrugged and disappeared.

It was terrible to find that even here there was society, thought Celine, with all its boredoms and predicaments. She understood why Harper was so angry. No one should have to think about desire, and certainly not on the moon. But also she had no interest in feeling guilty for a feeling that she had not deliberately provoked.

– Let's go somewhere, insisted Mica.

Mica took Celine's hand and walked her up to the surface of a lunar dune, where she could see the expanding sky and all its stars. It was as if a line of chandeliers were receding infinitely in every direction. Then suddenly Mica took her hand and they were diving off the edge of the moon, down into purple space.

– Please, said Celine.

It was very difficult to have the kind of conversation she wanted to have, when she was also floating and somersaulting very gently. They were in some kind of pocket or fold that was above the moon but still inside its atmosphere, and it meant that gravity was a very faint force offering a pleasurable resistance as they swam inside the ocean of air. So that even though the conversation was awkward and also melancholy there was this constant comical delight that was difficult to ignore.

– Look around you, said Mica.

It was obviously true that the view was beautiful and dazzling, said Celine. She was in no way arguing against the beauty of the universe. It was just, this was not what she wanted. She had no wish for any attachment.

– I showed you everything, said Mica.

– But I didn't ask you to! said Celine.

She felt suddenly incredibly tired, even though of course to move was this new flowing thing, requiring no effort at all. The tiredness was all in what was happening between them and that of course was invisible and also much more terrible than gravity. It was this need to be explaining yourself to other people, when all you wanted was something closer to solitude. It turned out that it was always difficult, thought Celine, when there was a person who wanted you. It didn't matter if it was an alien or a man or a woman. The task was always to try to anticipate what rules or assumptions you might have broken without you knowing, and perhaps to have accepted Mica's invitations to talk and then now to be rejecting them was in some way immoral or at least uncivilised but she could not help it. There were so many laws in the universe that could be broken invisibly and silently but also fatally.

– I don't want love, said Celine.

– What's love? asked Mica.

– This is impossible! cried Celine.

But then she also realised that to know what you want is a wonderful potency, and if this means that you will cause pain or even the end of a world, it cannot be said to be your fault or something which you should refuse.

She loved her friends but she also loved something more than this. There was a value that she found greater than desire, something to do with the voices she could hear, something that had only become clear to her here on the moon, and maybe it made her less likeable but it was true. She would not do what others wanted her to do. She was the woman who would leave.

– I don't want you, said Celine. – I like you very much but I don't want you.

– Because you don't know me, because you're afraid, said Mica.

– It's not that, said Celine. – I don't want anyone. I mean, I don't want to be together with someone. Why is this so difficult to understand?

Mica was crying and the tears were little drops of gel, sparkling in the backlights from the stars.

– You could take me with you, said Mica, then gestured into the sky, where the little earth sat in the blackened air.

Celine didn't reply. For some time they floated gently in the atmosphere, doing somersaults and mini dives, while Celine thought about the earth, its parties and its languages and its killings and its kidnappings and its money. It was suddenly obvious that there was no way she could stay here. She could never belong to the moon at all.

– You're wonderful, said Celine. – You're fantastical. I wish I could.

– So why not? said Mica.

Celine circled dolphin-like and finished beside Mica delicately in the vast air.

– Because you'd die down there, she said.

12

Celine hurriedly returned to her lunar house in the blue night. Sudden fear vibrated inside her. There were lights moving in the distance and she could feel movements around her, plants seething in the ponds. She had this sense very definitely and urgently that something was being planned against her. Quickly she found her old clothes, and for some time fumbled with them since it had been so long since she last had to dress in this way. When she emerged it seemed like she had lost important time: she could hear sounds in the atmosphere, awful vibrations that were, she assumed, the way that the inhabitants of the moon were making the planet turn against her.

In the dark she stumbled through a series of cartoon backdrops. When she finally reached her beached spaceship it was now stranded inside a kind of jungle that had grown up all around it. There were thousands of plants and lianas. And Celine stood there, motionless, because she realised that she had no idea how to make this vehicle leave. The silver balloons looked bedraggled and cold and old. In the distance the earth rotated listlessly and its clouds were beautiful swirls in the twilight. A fine rain was falling.

Then Celine had an idea, and this idea was conversation.

– Help me, she said to a greenly dripping tree.

For a terrible moment there was silence. Then at last one of the trees replied.

– Help you? said the tree.

– Please help me, repeated Celine.

– But how?

– I need to leave this planet, said Celine. – I'm begging you.

For a long while nothing spoke again and she worried that nothing was going to happen. Lights were changing in the distance like small fluorescent sticks. They seemed to be approaching in some kind of gradually increasing horde. Everything seemed frantic and unusual. Then gradually the plants began to slither away, until her spaceship was revealed in a single clearing.

– Thank you, she said.

She sat inside the ship. For some seconds, she was buffeted by the winds. The winds were immense. There was nothing but the sound of the wind. Then eventually a kind of scraping noise began, and then a sliding, and the ship began to levitate unsteadily into the atmosphere.

13

Celine kept looking forwards as the vehicle waded through the murky atmosphere. Finally, she decided to look down. She was very high. It was as if she could see the surface of the moon resolve itself into abstract whiteness, as if it was trying to recompose itself now that she was gone. But she had no time to examine this closer because with a lurch the vehicle disappeared from the moon's atmosphere, so that suddenly it was careering through the blackness.

It felt like many hours passed. Somewhere the sun illuminated the solar system. Meanwhile she was concentrating on trying to understand the direction she was flying in. Sometimes she was upside down. Then she was plummeting vertically towards the earth. Then the earth would be lost and Celine had no idea where to look for it, and it felt possible that she would miss the earth entirely and go disappearing into the endless dark. For a long while it seemed like she was static, just hanging there among the stars and the other planets, and she was beginning to think that perhaps she would stay here, just float out here somewhere between the earth and the moon, or perhaps would in fact keep floating and would disappear past the other planets, to the edge of the solar system into the infinite dark, until she felt herself steeply drop and cascade through the earth's atmosphere, in which she slowed, buoyant, the way a little object might slow on earth if it's dropped into a bowl of batter.

Then Celine began crying in relief.

She had come back to the landscape she knew. She could see Izabela's house in the countryside, and the rocket swung down and past it, then followed the road that took her back into the city.

Five

I

It was maybe a year after her journey to the moon that Celine
and Saratoga returned to their city. Their reunion had been
complicated. From America Celine had followed messages
from London to Amsterdam, and from Amsterdam to
Geneva, then from Geneva had gone back to London where
she finally found Saratoga. For a long while they had lived in
the countryside, in the green and British rain, until now at
last they returned and found that their own city was still fan-
tastically the same – even if both Celine's parents were now
dead (her father of his brain disease, her mother in a smash-
up on the roads two weeks later) and the entire system of
government had once again changed and so many people she
had argued with had vanished or been erased, like Beaumarchais and Jacob and Sasha, and in particular Marta, who was
said to have left Milan and was now living in Naples or maybe
Sicily and who featured often in Celine's most painful
dreams. But people still ate pancakes on the streets and called
these pancakes by special names, as if the pancake had been
newly invented. And meanwhile young people were arguing
about literature, the fake literature and the true literature,
and it was comforting because it was the same argument as
always, just with different characters, now talking about a
return to order and a love of the classical after the violence
and retribution of the years before.

It was almost amusing, to see how fragile a government

could be, a little machine that could be switched off and on very quickly. Of course the revolution always thought it would be permanent, that it would do amazing things to time, but to be permanent in this way it would have needed to persuade so many more people, not just each other but wives and girlfriends and especially children who were too young to be in the revolution itself. Maybe this is what makes all prophets so woebegone and upset, that you cannot do the amazing things with time you want to do, you cannot make your revolution part of the way people live their lives every day. To do that a revolution would need to become domestic – and this was a condition that the revolutionaries in this city had so drastically feared, because the domestic was where women were. And now they had no time left.

Whereas for Celine time was getting larger and larger, like she was onto a major discovery, the way she had discovered something gigantic on the moon. Celine had tried to leave and had now come back – but really she was always leaving. This was what the moon had taught her, thought Celine. She was always disappearing and it seemed like she could move away more and more.

With the money she had inherited after Sasha's death Celine had bought two properties for her and Saratoga. She had become very precise and effective with money. In the city they found a little apartment. While in the countryside they bought Julia's ruined place. The house itself had been destroyed when Julia and her husband had been sent to prison during the catastrophic season of terror. All that was left was the wild land itself. Now that Julia had emerged again into the world she had done this cheap deal with Celine. The project was partly as a present from Celine for Saratoga. Saratoga had ideas she wanted to explore about soil and meadows and plants. As well as forests she studied astronomy, and terrified men who wanted to sleep with her by talking to them about planets and gas explosions. But it was also for Celine a new form of living.

They began by planning a house with a forest attached. Then Celine realised that all they really cared about was the forest. The new house became something smaller, like a studio – a little structure of windows, surrounded by green. Saratoga had become friends with the man who ran the National Garden, and he had introduced her to a dealer who brought her plants that no one had seen in Europe before, that he had transported with Claude from the islands in the ocean. Every month this dealer came out to oversee what was happening. Saratoga mixed up seeds and plants in crazy profusion and it was very exciting, because it felt like there had never been something so ragged before.

Perhaps this felt particularly futuristic because in the city itself it seemed that time had stopped. Soon everything would just be museums and shopping. It was as if there was a whole new elongation of the present, thought Celine, as she moved around, so that while it might have been usual to divide all history into the ancient and the recent past, the same divisions now needed to be used for the present itself: the ancient present, the manic present – and then the future present, just out of reach. One night in town Celine tried to order in from Balthazar and it turned out that the joint had shut. All its staff had disappeared – even the manager, with his little notebook full of secrets. It had just shut, Celine was told, and would never reopen.

2

Some stories happen because of causes that are very visible and this was often, thought Celine, the way most stories happened to her. But other stories come out of nowhere. And Napoleon had come out of nowhere.

Napoleon was now in charge of everything, and it seemed that however surprising this was everyone was nevertheless happy with the outcome, after the madness and the blood before. He was a soldier who was also a dictator and this seemed to many people to be the best solution to the ongoing problem of power. In a famous speech he said that he wanted this kingdom to last for a thousand years and it felt possible that it might happen. Like everyone else he still liked killing, but he preferred killing people from other countries rather than his own. At this time Toussaint Louverture was expanding his revolution against the slavers and plantation owners in Hispaniola. The dictator, meanwhile, wanted to exterminate Louverture and all his associates. He was planning immediate wars in Europe and Africa and America and the Pacific. It seemed that there was nowhere he didn't want an empire, and so there was now news from everywhere too which always needed to be decoded, as if inside every brain was a little model of the globe – vast and incomprehensible.

Everyone's projects were overshadowed by Napoleon. You had to do things that might make him love you and certainly not make him dislike you, and the possibility of this happening seemed endless because it was never obvious how deep his passions would go – the people drifting to sports matches in the pink twilight, the children skating on the frozen ponds in the park . . . Anything was possibly a reason for him taking an interest, or being bored, and it made the atmosphere very anxious.

But it seemed to Celine that she could be free of this attention, however much she was still haloed with celebrity. She was in her forties, and this meant that she was no longer part of the culture, the endless having of opinions, like she had been removed from it very silently and this was very relaxing. A long time ago she might not have thought this was relaxing but instead something tragic and even disquieting, but now that she was living in it this freedom of ageing was very enticing. It was like the way she found it so difficult to write a journal or a memoir: there was nothing there, in some way, when she said *I*. She could be anyone.

She was the person who moved away. She was an arrow disappearing into the distance and she found this movement beautiful.

Of course, ordinary things still happened. She had started sleeping sometimes with André, the young writer she had met in America, but the distance she experienced between her and André was still the distance between her and whatever people meant by the world. André's conversation was all about his plotting in the world, the nights he spent in the embankment office block Napoleon had set up, writing plans for legal systems, or his project to sell the newly conquered territory of Louisiana to the Americans. Since the dictator needed dollars to finance his imperial wars, and America needed land to expand against the Mohawks and the Sioux, it seemed an obvious trade. He had lived out there, after all. He understood that the way trade worked was much more fluid and multiple than the way they imagined, the same way the rivers were multiple, but the Americans didn't understand the connections and therefore underestimated their power. André always believed in this international perspective, however much he was scared of Napoleon and his endless power. Meanwhile the dictator disapproved of his friendship with Celine. He disliked all women, or at least all clever women. And certainly a woman without a husband made Napoleon neurotic and disturbed. He admired domestic virtue.

None of this intrigue interested Celine. A city, she thought, was a space where there were too many minds thinking in the same space as she was thinking, whereas André could not leave the city for more than a day.

– What do you want? she once asked him.

– Oh, you know, said André. – I want to be happy. Life, liberty, the pursuit of – the pursuit of –

Celine's concerns were different. To be connected to the contemporary was no longer desirable for her, she was thinking, or perhaps even possible. Inside her was a vision of the moon.

3

– Why did I begin this thing with André? said Celine one night to Julia. – What was I thinking? Why did I ever sleep with him?

– You're unhappy, said Julia.

– I'm unhappy, said Celine.

– You don't like this kid?

– Of course I like him, said Celine.

– But but but, said Julia.

This was at a party near Glove Park. It was still a little light. Outside a haze sat among the foliage. The dry trees were robed in potentiality.

Julia had now remarried for a second time: her third husband was a banker. Unlike the Commissar, her second husband, he had no interest in the son he had acquired along with Julia. He had meetings with the dictator every week to discuss problems of international credit, because the dictator needed money more than anything. It seemed that by this time in their lives Julia had been everything: aristocratic, then revolutionary, then counter-revolutionary, then democratic, and now so rich that she was unique. She wore little sandals and diamond toe-rings, to draw attention to the scars from rat bites on her feet she had got when she had been imprisoned during the terror. Her dresses were super simple, little muslin robes that did not cover her breasts or arms, and in fact were the same colour as her skin so that from a distance she always looked naked for real, with slicked-back hair, as if she'd just emerged from an ocean swim. It was obviously triumphant in its savage attitude but also some-thing about this style disturbed Celine, it felt in some way inauthentic and it occurred to her that this was possibly related to the way Julia had in many ways existed throughout her life for men, but then Celine berated herself – because it was never pos-sible to judge another woman for the way she tried to survive. It was so exhausting not to see oneself through the minds of other people that it could sometimes seem to you that every woman who did not think like you was captured or seduced, and it was important to remember not to look down on other women, because who knew what secret strategies they were pursuing?

Maybe, continued Celine, it was more accurate to say she was bored. Like consider her sex life. She thought, said Julia, that André was sweet.

– Yeah but no, said Celine. – It's not that. It's more: he never has the right tone. Like one night he came back all crazy and told me to get on all fours.

– Do we need to talk about this? said Julia.

– It was like he was acting, said Celine. – And acting is so boring. Then he started trying to push my dress up but was doing it so badly so I had to do it myself.

– Santa Maria, said Julia.

– You know that feeling? said Celine. – When you're fucking and just absent, like you feel alone? And you're too aware of the outside noises?

The plants in the room were breathing in and out, they were little lungs.

– Well, what do you want? said Julia. – How do you want to live?

– I want to leave everything behind, said Celine.

Julia was about to reply but she was distracted by an argument that was happening in the line for the bathroom. It was Yves – their mortal enemy, who now worked as a ghostwriter working on politicians' memoirs – who was being assailed by a young man Celine did not know. The young man was calling Yves an executioner, a psychopath.

– I was a *lawyer*, said Yves.

It seemed like Yves's face had been ravaged by terror, or ageing, or perhaps the two were the same. He was now entirely bald and the effect on his features was drastic.

– You were in the administration! said the young man. – You were a minister.

– I had that job for less than a year, said Yves. – Really I was a lawyer. Who remembers such things so long ago?

– It's the recent fucking past, the young man shouted.

To look at Yves was to experience a long descent into

unreality, thought Celine, into elements that could never be reconciled, and yet she also found herself surprisingly but definitely sorry for Yves at that moment, at the same time as feeling a delight at his humiliation and at the possibility that justice might be possible on this planet, when she thought of all the people she loved who were now dead. And it seemed that something similar occurred to Julia, because as they turned away she began telling Celine about a benefit performance at the Comedy that was being held for Josef, a former office worker in the committee for interior efficiency. She was speaking as if she would know him, but Celine couldn't remember. He used to work for Hernandez, said Julia, who seemed suddenly hesitant in the way she was talking. The one, she continued, who was incredibly small. He had recently been found living down by the lower canals, she said. Celine asked her why there was a benefit for this office worker. Because, said Julia, he saved so many people.

– Saved who? said Celine.

Sometimes in a conversation there is a moment that is suddenly elongated and sticky and alive, and in this moment Celine and Julia looked at each other and Celine observed with amazement that Julia seemed to be trying not to cry. But before they could continue a man came up to them and interrupted, without entirely noticing who he was interrupting, since what he wanted to do was introduce himself to Julia. It meant that Celine had a moment to look at him and for a long while she could not remember why she knew him, he seemed at once so recognisable and so nondescript, until suddenly she realised that it was the former head of the censorship bureau, the man who had banned then praised Beaumarchais's play and who had been so scared of Antoinette. Somehow he had survived, and here he was. He looked distraught, with large shaving grazes on his mottled neck. Julia smiled abstractly at him in a way that was designed to demonstrate that she was busy with Celine and he backed away, apologetically, then suddenly saw who Julia had been talking to and Celine and he looked at each other, paused, absolutely still in the knowledge of how difficult it would be to have a conversation that could be adequate to the time that had passed between them, the fleetingness of their relation. And so he went away.

It made Celine feel uneasy, as if something terrible had just happened. She had not seen this man for more than a decade, maybe two, and it was very confusing, to see him here, since he represented something so minor from her previous life, but at the same time it meant that she was suddenly remembering places she had not been to for a very long time, little squares and houses or the bridges over the river. It was horrible to be so walled up in your past!

In this miasma she tried to find some kind of normality or clarity.

– You never answered my question, said Celine.

– What question? said Julia.

– Who this office worker saved?

– He saved Beaumarchais, said Julia. – He loved theatre. He used to work for Hernandez. And he also saved you.

– But what do you mean? said Celine. – I thought you saved me. Don't you remember?

It was as if history was a substance that could leak from every decor. You only had to very gently press a surface and this terrible liquid, thought Celine, would always seep out.

But she would also disappear from history, thought Celine. She was an arrow that disappeared into the dark.

4

Although it might seem that to think about power is a habit that's particular to certain moments, like when a dictator is everywhere, it's also possible that it's universal. It just presents itself differently and with more acuteness in different locations. In the ocean, while Celine was trying to understand her new situation in the city she still loved, Tu was just as perplexed as Celine. Here he was, king of all these islands, and his confidence was diminishing every day. He was finding that to maintain power in such an overcrowded space was very difficult, and certainly much harder than he had imagined, and it felt like the world he wanted to create was evaporating from his grasp.

By now Tu was in control of many islands which he had hoped would gradually understand themselves to be one territory. It turned out to his dismay that this territory was still fractured by the old thinking, as if each island was a separate place. Whereas the true thing, Tu wanted to argue, was that a place could be itself and also part of a larger whole, or maybe more precisely both things sequentially and on a loop. And while it was possible for people to think like this in the abstract, he worried, it turned out that there were too many factions and little cliques to make his ideal seem true. And at the same time there were many Europeans, absolute strangers to these discussions, who kept on returning and wanting power for themselves.

What Tu felt he should really do was write a constitution for a federation, but the writing of a constitution took consultations and committees and he wasn't sure he had the energy for so much politics. Instead, thought Tu, he would do something absolute and unique. He would build a new and gargantuan temple.

Together with advisers he developed an extraordinary construction, with many hidden levels, and very large. But then there was the problem of where to build it. People seemed to have many loyalties and it made them angry because not every loyalty could be fulfilled, which made the arguments about where to build the temple increasingly stressful for everyone. It became obvious that no one really thought of themselves as one people, or not in the single way that Tu had hoped. Finally, he ordered the temple to be built on an islet that had never been inhabited by anyone. When it was finished, it was dedicated with a ceremony of the highest secrecy. From then on, it was forbidden to visit the old temple. The old temple became overgrown.

But the problems Tu had faced in building the temple did not go away. The new temple never acquired the kind of gravity he had hoped it might achieve. It was too pristine, people said. Something was missing. The old temple seemed more interesting, and so gradually people went back in secret to place offerings there, or little fetishes. Finally, Tu died, and everyone went back to worshipping at the old temple openly, and no one visited the new temple any more, so that eventually it became overgrown and ignored.

Then there were little temples everywhere, just like before.

5

Celine broke up with André the same night as the show in honour of Josef, the office worker who had saved so many people. The night had a frantic tone, as if everyone was worried that at such an event too much information might be broadcast from the past. At the theatre Celine looked down into the audience and it was like looking at a cemetery, she thought. Everything functioned in layers. On the surface were the living but underneath were the invisible layers of the missing dead: at the very bottom, the dead of the former regime, then the dead analysts, the dead civilians, the revolutionary conspirators, and finally the most recent dead, who had tried to resist the coup. It was amazing how old the dead could get. The dead got old very quickly. And yet what was maybe more amazing than the presence of the dead was the presence of the living – these amazing rows of unpredictable survivors . . .

The dictator sat in the imperial box, which was decorated in swathes of canopied fabric and studded with gold bees. He sat beside his wife, looking bored.

Celine was trying to work out how to talk to André about them separating, but André seemed too delicate with depression. It turned out, he said, that Napoleon didn't want him in on the Louisiana deal. He was putting it together with Rosen instead.

– Rosen? said Celine. – Like my friend Rosen?

– The finance maven, nodded André.

Rosen had maintained his aura as the most successful financier in Europe.

Well, Rosen, said Celine, feeling older and older, certainly knew everybody. He felt very miserable, said André. He really thought this would be his major opportunity.

Then Julia arrived and Celine turned to her instead because there was something very heavy inside her which she needed to discuss.

– You never told me, said Celine. – What you were going to say.

– About what? said Julia.

– About Josef, said Celine.

– Told you what?

– How he saved me, said Celine.

Slowly Julia allowed herself to approach the conversation.

It was all about the list, said Julia. Before it went to the committee of final executions, the list was managed by the committee for interior efficiency, and Josef worked in this committee after Hernandez died. Very quickly he felt too guilty to be working there. At first he made deliberate mistakes in the filing, like names spelled in the wrong way, so that a lawyer could then argue that their client had been wrongly identified. The problem was that the files got larger very fast. And then one morning the papers came in condemning Celine and Beaumarchais and all the actors and the studios – and Josef loved the old studios. So Josef came up with a plan that was as fantastical as it was brave. He worked late in the office until everyone else had gone home, then crumpled up the papers of the condemned and soaked them in water to soften them and make them more compact, and then swallowed them.

– Sorry what? said Celine.

– Exactly: swallowed them, said Julia.

He took these little balls of paper fibre and cuttlefish ink, said Julia, and ate them, like croquetas. But after a few days of this he realised it would make him too sick. There was too much paper to eat. Now, every evening, said Julia, he went to the bathhouse by the river. And this gave him a new idea. The next night he repeated the exercise, soaking the pages in water, but instead of eating them he put the damp pellets into his pockets. In the twilight he walked to the bathhouse and in the steam that stank of sweat or semen or whatever he made these pellets even wetter and then pushed them out of the window of a bathroom cubicle, which was directly over the yellow river. For days, said Julia, he repeated this, until all the files disappeared before they could reach the committee for final executions.

– It was only recently, finished Julia, – that a journalist found this story out.

Before Celine could respond, Josef stood up in his seat to acknowledge the applause. Celine observed him very closely. It seemed amazing that this little man had saved her and she remembered suddenly Hernandez's house, and a garden, and a little boy.

Josef began a garish speech. During that bloody period, horrible to remember, he said, he had had the pleasure of saving many victims from the revolutionary axe, at the risk of his own life. Then he paused because he was coughing. Each morning, he continued, he came to work at the committee. Each day he stamped pieces of paper and filed them away, so that the next day a person could be killed. It was obviously not the same thing as killing a person, not the same thing at all: the stamping of a piece of paper, that had been written by someone else, authorising the killing of a person by yet another person. But at the same time it was not obviously not the same thing, either. So he had decided he needed to act.

And how happy he would have been, continued Josef, if his resistance had not also involved the cruel necessity of risking the lives, more than once, of his comrades in the committee. He had to admit that, without their courageous humanity, all of his efforts would have been useless. They unofficially closed their eyes to his thefts, continued Josef, and, through their silence, associated themselves with the glories and dangers of his enterprises. But the tigers who had drunk the blood of men, he concluded, although seized by fear and suspicion, weren't vigilant enough to suspect him. His neglected exterior and tiny frame gave him an air of simplicity that made him seem unimportant in their eyes. He had dared to be human in an era where humanity was a crime.

There was a standing ovation that lasted fourteen minutes, led by the dictator.

Very gently, Celine took her hand away from André's.

– We have to break up, she said.

6

That night there was a dinner after the show in a private room with a view over the black park. Everything in the room was in appalling grand new taste. It was sleek and gilded. A frieze of illiterate hieroglyphs had been stencilled around the walls.

There were rumours that Napoleon would come by, for a drink. He was due to pick up Julia's husband to go and discuss Rosen's latest offer – some innovative credit swap he had invented, to help finance the dictator's projected foreign takeovers. The imminent presence of the dictator made the atmosphere erratic, with very fast conversation. But Celine was finding it hard to concentrate. None of this attracted her any more. It was like she was fading out, she thought, as if the colours inside her outlines were disappearing, so that she was there and not there at the same time.

André was trying to explain his theory of writing to Claude and Lorenzo. Lorenzo had finally come back from America, bored of his intellectual life. He still had his goatee and was always handsome but what used to be muscle had now relaxed into a kind of barrel of plumpness. He was finishing a secret project which he wouldn't show to anyone. A network of fictions, André was saying to him, constituted the fundamental basis itself of society, and the story he wanted to tell would reconstruct these relations, give them form. Lorenzo stared at him. So that basically all history was the same as science fiction, said Lorenzo. No, he didn't mean that, said André.

Meanwhile Julia was complaining to Celine about a new book of memoirs Claude had written – which went into pedantic detail about his intellectual wars with long-dead scientists.

– What's the point in name-dropping, she said, *when no one knows any of the names?*

Celine understood her feeling. So many people were publishing memoirs of the life before. Hernandez's ex-wife had just put out a memoir he had written, along with a selection of his letters. He had written these letters before the revolution, and so the dead were talked about in ways which were obscene, lascivious, mocking, and obviously true. They were not rewritten, like a history might have been, out of respect for their fate.

– What are they talking about? said André to Lorenzo, looking over at Celine.

He was feeling wild with grief.

– The past, said Lorenzo.

And he very much agreed with them, said Lorenzo. The past should never be thought about with any reverence. It was like the way, Lorenzo added, he had recently picked up some old magazines from a storage box. He was writing something about the past himself, he said, his first and maybe only book, and so had remembered he had these magazines and started reading them. He felt very disturbed, he said. All the arguments they had been having with each other, or with the people they disliked, seemed so limited. He couldn't remember the books over which they were arguing, and even if he could, then he couldn't understand why they had found those books important enough to argue over. It had made him realise, said Lorenzo to André, that the most intelligent people he had ever known, all they ever produced was conversation.

– But what about works? exclaimed André.

– Atmosphere, said Lorenzo, – is worth much more than any work.

Then Celine saw Josef get up from his place to leave. It was very early and therefore unexpected but, he was saying, he felt very tired. And Celine suddenly realised that it was urgent she should thank him, however inadequate that would be, to explain how she had never known about his bravery that had allowed her to escape. She rushed up to him at the door. She wanted to do whatever she could for him, she said. They stood there, looking into each other's eyes. It seemed that there were many moments in a life when conversation was impossible and this was one of them. After a while, Josef tried to say something. He had only done what anyone else would have done, he said. He was simply pleased, he said, he was simply pleased.

A taxi driver came in to say that he had arrived – and Josef disappeared forever, into the absolute night.

Celine waited there for a long time, just looking at the absent street. Then she was interrupted by a small commotion as a group of people came into the dinner late. It was the dictator with his wife – and then behind him, very magically, Celine saw the fantastical figure of Marta.

7

Celine stared at her. She had no idea how long it had been since she had last seen her. It seemed entirely natural for her to be there and also ghostly and unnerving.

– I didn't even know you were in town, said Celine.

– Well, I'm back, said Marta.

Her eyes were wildly smiling and it was beautiful. And Celine was about to embrace her and remove her to some corner so they could talk without anyone watching but suddenly the dictator and his wife introduced themselves and Marta moved away.

Napoleon was very petite and thin, with very delicate wrists. He was so thin that when he spoke his whole face moved. He wanted to speak with her, he said, because they were going to be neighbours. In town? she said. No, of course not, he said. They were going to be neighbours in the country. He had just bought a house very close to her own. He

hoped he wouldn't regret this, he said. He'd heard from
André that anyone from anywhere came to visit her, including people who disliked him.

He seemed very uncomfortable and irritable.

It wasn't really a house, what she had in the countryside,
she said. It was more of a forest. Hardly anyone came there
at all. They knew, he said. He had heard that what she was
doing with her land was wild.

– You don't like the wild? she said.

– We don't, said Napoleon.

– *He* doesn't, said his wife.

– We have different views, said the dictator.

It seemed obvious that he wanted her to say something
more subservient. The dictator disliked women and loved
order – so to have a woman producing a space that was pure
wildness and in particular a space that was near a space he
himself owned was presumably something he disliked very
much. But as well as this there seemed some kind of malevo-
lence in his tone which she might have dwelled on more, this
neurosis about foreigners and critique, if she wasn't preoccupied by Marta's absent presence and also indifferent in some
way to whatever power wanted.

– We'll talk about this again, said the dictator.

Then Napoleon left to speak with Julia's husband and his
wife followed before Celine could say anything to her. She
looked around urgently for Marta but could not see her, so
she went to find Julia, to ask where Marta had gone. She had
just had to leave, said Julia. She'd said she'd try to come back
later. She wasn't sure.

It was suddenly like some party from the old days.

– Isn't it amazing? said Julia. – I mean amazing that we're
all still here?

And Celine agreed, even though what it meant to be *here*, she was suddenly feeling, was very difficult to define.

8

In the atmosphere of the dictator it seemed that everyone would have problems understanding how they should act, as if all actions had become fuzzy or more confusing. He could extend himself as far as he wanted, not only within the city but across continents and oceans. Everything was spookiness. In America Louis Cook was having to think about the last moves he could make while knowing that his thinking was being made fuzzy by this extra outside force that was warping everything despite also being invisible, the way a magnet or other force warps things which cannot see it.

There were new viruses spreading everywhere. Some of the camps were completely deserted, or there was just one lodge with a couple of people still in it, pale and delirious. As for Louis, he was almost unrecognisable with liver disease and also maybe throat cancer. Still, he insisted on reading his communications. The communications this morning were one letter and one newspaper. The letter was from a trader in the South, asking if he could come and visit. He had heard that Louis Cook's people had been very badly treated by the Americans, and wanted to propose a possible deal. They could maybe set up some kind of trading outpost or depot, to diminish the power of Black Buffalo and the other Lakota chiefs. It might also, he thought, interest Louis to know that the land south was about to be sold to the Americans. Or at least this was what he had been –

Louis threw the letter away.

This was the time when the dead were appearing often to Louis. Upsettingly they seemed to visit him looking the way they had looked when they were dying too. Often it was Montour, his old interpreter. But more recently it had been Washington, with his eczema and terrible paunch. There were so many connections in a life and it was amazing to discover how indifferent you could become to all of them as time consigned them to distance!

He turned to the newspaper. In the newspapers they were also talking about the possibility of this deal between the French and the Americans. It seemed that the Americans were expanding their territory wherever they liked. Or certainly that was their plan.

Everyone around Louis thought that his time for deals was over. They were making decisions without him.

Louis picked up a fresh new notebook. He was writing in a notebook more and more, given how difficult it was for him to speak. He believed in the principle of friendship, he wrote. He believed that they should all hold a vast meeting somewhere, the Mohawks and the Lakota and the many other peoples. He wanted to speak to Black Buffalo and all their allies, and come to some conclusions. They should think about the map of the lakes and the great rivers. They still owned all of this, he said. Their problem was their isolation from each other. He saw no reason why the future had to be apocalypse and darkness. It just needed a different solution.

To write this much was exhausting. He tried to remember how to spell *solution* and decided that he couldn't. Instead he went and threw up in a bucket outside.

9

All living was exhausting, but there was now a new element in the array of forces she could act with, thought Celine, which was this presence of Marta, or friendship – and it added an excited confusion to her thinking, warm and golden like the lamplight. She had often dreamed of Marta but now she started dreaming of her every night. In these dreams they talked not about themselves or what had happened in the past but little things: people they liked, people they hated. Each morning she wondered about writing to her, then hesitated. She didn't know how to write to Marta now, because she didn't want there to be any misunderstanding. She didn't want to repeat their way of being with each other when they were young. But still, she missed her. And yet at the same time she was worried about being rejected, and every morning that went by without a note from Marta felt miserable and upsetting.

It was terrible to be returned to this kind of condition, this constant interpreting of the slightest tremors in communication methods. And still, days went by and there was nothing from Marta.

Instead she received a note from Claude, a little sentence: how he was thinking of her, after seeing her at that dinner the other night, how sometimes he had such precise memories that came back to him from their friendship, memories of joy. It was so precious! he said. And he wanted to tell her that. Or one evening she went for drinks with an exiled Russian lawyer in a new place out by the pencil factory. He mentioned that his wife had no idea where he was at this moment. And she remembered how for a long time when a man said this she really had believed that she, unlike the wife, was the recipient of the truth, whereas now she knew differently. Often in fact a man's wife knew everything. And certainly that a man was lying to his wife almost always meant that he was lying to you too.

She had left desire behind. The city was a desert. But perhaps friendship was more interesting than desire and in the city there was now Marta – if Marta wanted to be found.

10

A month after Celine had seen Marta again, Lorenzo published the book he had been writing since he had come back to town, his first and only book, a kind of memoir of the recent past as a series of portraits – not of famous heroes and protagonists but of minor apparatchiks and true believers. It was all true and at the same time entirely invented. Real names were transported into unlikely situations. Invented people performed actions which really happened. It was unlike anything else he had written and was immediately translated in many European cities. Very quickly, Lorenzo became hated in the city. This was partly because of the international fame, but it was also because of his book's insistent comedy and irony. Everyone wanted power and believed that they lived in the centre of things. And yet here was Lorenzo's book that seemed to find nothing interesting in their empire or mastery at all.

It therefore wasn't surprising that a series of rumours

immediately began that many passages were lifted from other writers – until finally the president of the Association of Writers wrote a long essay listing fifty-seven of these imaginary acts of plagiarism and reproaching Lorenzo for his stylistic and intellectual errors, finishing with a definition of Lorenzo as an ethnographic rarity. The surprising thing was that Lorenzo then published a wild and therefore courageous text in reply, dedicated to attacking his accusers.

It was just when this came out that Marta wrote a message to Celine, asking if she had seen it – as if they could still make out a little golden spirit hovering above them, which was the spirit of resistance.

They had been brought together again by something as old-fashioned as Lorenzo's ego.

The accusations against him, wrote Lorenzo grandly in his defence, were an attempt to liquidate a book and a writer, and it reflected a wider decadence of taste. His critics, wrote Lorenzo, were militantly ignorant. He had been described as an *ethnographic rarity*, wrote Lorenzo. He understood that this was another way of stating that he was Jewish, or at least foreign, and he was grateful for this racist insult, because it demonstrated very simply that the real problem here was nationalism. And nationalist interpretations of anything, wrote Lorenzo, followed logically from the kind of psychological, irrational, paranoid instability that saw phantoms everywhere. Instead, added Lorenzo, he wished there could be a different model for thinking, where all zones of influence were constantly acting and reacting on each other in a kind of chemical experiment – a cloud of relationships which bore no correspondence to borders or definitions.

The following day, the president of the Association of Writers sued Lorenzo for libel for his phrase *militantly ignorant*.

The trial took place in one of the new courthouses that had been built out on the edge of the city, near the sports districts. It was expected that Lorenzo would be killed. Celine and Marta sat publicly beside him, as his last remaining friends. Instead the trial lasted only two days, because there was so little relevant evidence. The judge dismissed the case in a judgment that took him only seven minutes to read, and Lorenzo was free to leave.

What followed for Lorenzo was a month of partying, while even more articles continued to be written against him, as if many regime writers were amazed at the way an institution like a court had continued to be independent of their opinions, as well as the miraculous way Lorenzo himself continued, untroubled by their accusations.

And inside Lorenzo's long fiesta Celine and Marta began to see each other again and started to let this little golden spirit of resistance sit beside them – and they were able to do this because there was this other extra reason like a curtain over their thinking, that they were only looking after Lorenzo. So that in secret their two souls could communicate with each other without embarrassment or self-consciousness.

Lorenzo was enjoying his late notoriety. He was too old to care about other people, he said. And in fact it was really Celine who had taught him this, he said. Taught what? she said. That it was impossible to care about the opinions of other people, said Lorenzo. Because no one knew anyone. Which meant that you could never be hurt by whatever other people thought.

The world was a series of mysteries, agreed Marta.

– Like did I tell you this story before? said Lorenzo. – One night I left a casino to find a girl I was in love with. This was so long ago, when I'd moved to Venice from the provinces.

– Venice *is* a province, said Celine.

– *Everywhere's* a province, replied Lorenzo. – It was very dark, and I got into the wrong gondola. In this gondola there was a girl from Torino. Her father had remarried and her stepmother wanted to marry her off to some ancient billionaire. When the girl refused, the stepmother had her locked up. But somehow this girl managed to persuade an assistant to release her, and smuggle her to Venice. She had just arrived. And that was when she met me.

– And then what happened? said Celine.

– Oh, nothing, said Lorenzo. – I was in love with someone else. But actually it was sadder. On the journey to Venice she'd ended up losing all her money. She had nothing. She begged me to get some money to her. And that night, while I was trying to work out what to do to help her, the police took her away. I never heard from her again.

– When was this? said Celine.

– Don't ask me that, said Lorenzo. – Whenever I get involved with dates, terrible things happen.

Lorenzo lit another cigarette.

– Why was I telling you this? he said.

– No one knows anyone, said Marta. – Everyone's a mystery.

– I mean sure, added Lorenzo, – but it's not like you two don't know all this already.

Then he got up to be sick in the bathroom.

All this might be true, said Celine to Marta, as she watched him disappear into the crowd, it might be philosophically perfect, but still, it would be nice to know *someone*, after all.

– You know me, said Marta.

For a moment it was like all the noise around them was concentrated into a single point.

– Do you want to see the garden that makes our dictator mad? said Celine. – I mean, really it's more like a forest. Do you want to see our forest?

The next day they drove away together out of the city, into the countryside.

II

The garden Celine and Saratoga had constructed wasn't really a garden at all, but more a sequence of confusions. There was their studio or pavilion. And then around it was an increasingly entangled structure that wasn't entirely made by them at all. They intended it as a place of total experiment and mischling kinkiness, a series of green explosions. Everything was slow release and delay, as if to imagine how a landscape could be constructed involved choreographies way beyond the usual forms: into months and seasons and years. There were roses, laurel, eucalyptus. Everything was an exercise in transplantation and translation. Friends in America had sent them even more American seeds. Also Claude had put her in touch with the most recent exploration activities, so that now they were testing out seeds that had been sent in boxes from the port, along with little tubs of living plants. More and more they liked to take what was exotic and let it grow here, like the straggly flat spears of phormium. There were groves and forests and streams, then secluded areas with benches or signs that Saratoga had painted in ink. Whenever anyone came to visit, Saratoga made little sketches or maps to help them know where they were if they wandered away on their own. But also anyone could use the landscape, without an invitation, the way it had been many years ago – just to walk through it or around it or gather mushrooms or fruits. It seemed beautiful to them to make somewhere that could be inhabited in different ways.

In everything she did, Saratoga wanted to be modern. Celine observed this with loving admiration. Saratoga was excited because a paper had just been published proving that the giant American bones once in Marta's husband's former collection were not, as everyone thought, the bones of an elephant but were as different from an elephant as much as or perhaps even more than the way a dog differed from a jackal or a hyena. They seemed to be the bones of a giant animal that in some ways resembled an elephant but in many ways did not. And this, of course, proved not only that long ago there were animals of whose existence people living now were completely unaware, but also that at some point in history they had disappeared. It proved that something could end forever, said Saratoga, and for her this was a very exciting way of thinking.

– But why? asked Celine.

– Why what? said Saratoga.

– I just mean: that idea doesn't upset you?

– Not at all, said Saratoga.

Or it was like the way people were talking about Manhattan, she added, as if this might help explain things for Celine. There was a plan to make that city as a grid of blocks, she said. Celine asked her the question she thought was obvious, which was whether anyone would want to live inside a grid. But the question wasn't obvious to Saratoga at all. It just seemed beautiful to her, this idea of bigness, she said. There was nothing worse than preserving the past forever. And anyway, continued Saratoga, she wasn't saying that everything would have to be torn down. There was no reason why new things couldn't also exist beside historical things. Perhaps tension and contradiction were just the elements of a new quality, rather than the refusal of all other qualities. And if it could happen in a city it could happen in a forest.

Celine felt excited by her youth and newness. The trust that she displayed in the future was very seductive.

But with Marta something else was going on. When they first arrived they spent as much time inside as outside, reading books. Or in fact Marta read books aloud, and Celine listened. They tended to pick up anything they could find, like Saratoga's books of biology and astronomy. The earth was just another planet, they read in one textbook, it was just another planet floating in an infinite volume of air. Then they gave up astronomy for fictions. The stories they chose were adventures, fantasias. They described voyages to distant countries and especially other planets, like the one about the man who managed to make himself fly to the moon.

About the moon, Celine was silent. It was possible she could never tell anyone what she had seen on the moon. The moon was her interior.

Marta was concerned about the alien beings this voyage described. For how would a person even recognise an alien, if they were to see it? Consider the hippogriff. Would you know a hippogriff, for instance, if a hippogriff came lumbering towards you?

– I kind of understand, said Celine. – You mean: if an alien is on this planet right now, it might well be a tree? Or at least look like a tree to us?

– Something like that, said Marta. – I'm not really sure.

They were reading books and then talking about them

because they were trying to avoid any conversation that might be without an obviously defined subject – and which could therefore very easily become a conversation about themselves. They had been apart for so long, and it's always difficult, to come back to someone you've loved, especially when they've lived a different way to you and where you aren't even sure you could describe what precisely you have lived through without them. For now, they simply existed alongside each other, and discovered that they liked this way of living much more than they liked living apart – however much it was unexpected, not just to be making this new life together, but to have even found each other again. It seemed so unusual for anyone to find another person again. It was much more usual to lose forever and ever.

Then gradually they started to spend more and more time outside. They went out with Saratoga, into the green twilight. Then, while she worked on designs or went into town, they explored the forest themselves.

Maybe some things would always be impossible to understand, said Marta – like how this was the same place she recognised from long ago, when they had come here with Julia, and also a completely new place too. It was maybe because things looked so different now: so much had burned down or been replanted or redistributed.

Their plan was to create as much wildness and mystery as possible, said Celine. Like a world. Saratoga liked it just for this, she thought, its wildness and its craziness. Whereas she also had another private reason, she said. It would be something that would continue to be alive in the future after Celine was dead. And the reason it would be living was because it was a mystery.

Around them bees drifted and combined in clumps.

And also, added Marta, there was now this added bonus that it was hated by the dictator.

12

In the landscape that surrounded them everything was clearance, timber factories, empty devastation. The new dictatorship encouraged private property above all other concerns. It was an era of war and major money and therefore all the remaining laws protecting forests, the ones that Jacob and their friends had once argued for, were now being dismantled. Anyone who owned forest was bulldozing it to make money. It meant that there were flash floods, and plagues of goats.

Saratoga's idea was that one method of resisting would be to start growing crops as well as plants. She was messaging all the time with her agent in town about the correct conditions for growth. Everyone had always assumed that plants liked to be grown with other similar plants, but Saratoga was beginning to wonder if this was true. The principle of the forest was mixture and profusion and she wondered if it might be the same for any other plant too. She imagined a proliferation of differences, minute intensities of detail. But to test this, they needed more land.

It turned out that Marta had the brisk talent of a business manager. She surveyed the edges of their territory, working out what they might buy next. Everyone was selling off their meadows and fields, after all, and Marta went round, buying anything she could. One day she came back with a new proposition. There was some kind of house that belonged to a family who were now bankrupt. They had been ruined in the decade's chaos. Around it there was what remained of a very formal garden. But the reason she wanted to buy it, she said, was because it had a water source, a stream that began on the edge of the property – which they could use to make something wildly aquatic too, as well as providing all the power their improvised forest technology might need.

The only problem, added Marta, was that this was directly next to the house Napoleon had bought with his wife. There were security details all around, long rows of parked vehicles with sleeping drivers.

– Why should that matter? said Saratoga.

A week later, they signed the contract.

About a week after that, a member of the local police force came to inspect their drainage systems. It was unusual but perhaps not completely irrational. Then a woodland inspector arrived two days afterwards, to check on their system of poaching deterrents. Then followed permit collectors, provenance committee surveys, and finally health officials, testing the quality of the water. Then the armed violence began.

13

One day Celine and Marta were out walking in the forest, continuing their infinite conversation.

– It makes no sense, said Marta, – why Napoleon is so crazy about gardens. Why he is so crazy about *this* garden. I mean: why you?

– It makes no sense but it's how he is, said Celine.

– It's so old-fashioned, said Marta, – the way he thinks. Who wants neatness in the countryside? It's like he wants things from long ago. Whereas in fact it's super contemporary, the countryside.

Celine found conversation with Marta so sensual and so easy that it prompted her to do something she had never done with anyone else. She stopped, and Marta stopped too. Then Celine gestured largely at the tangled trees.

– Can I . . . I want to tell you something, she said.

– Say anything, said Marta.

For a while Celine looked into the trees for help.

– They sometimes speak to me, she said. – I know: it's crazy.

– Speak to you who? said Marta.

– I have these visions, said Celine. – As if the forest is speaking.

Marta thought about this for a long while.

– It doesn't seem crazy, said Marta.

And Celine was about to continue when they were interrupted by a vision of violence: a kind of vicious sign or message from the dictator. A man was lying in the road, with an arm that seemed to be at a terrible angle to his body.

They bent down to help him. The man couldn't talk. A lot of blood was moving out of him, pooling in a black area. Marta knelt beside the wounded man and held his head in her lap. She spoke to him very gently. Meanwhile Celine ran back to find someone who could drive them into town. There was black blood soaking the sleeve of his shirt and it was difficult to tell what had actually happened, how much arm was really left.

After they had reached a doctor and the doctor had

examined him and bandaged the wound as carefully as was possible, they talked to him. He had been walking in their forest, he said, and then a man had come up to him and shot him. It was terrifying. The man with the gun had said that he was on private land owned by the dictator – and before he could speak, he shot him. He had thought that he could walk anywhere in the forest, he said.

– Of course you can, said Celine.

– But look, said the man.

Very stiffly he pointed at his shattered arm, then fainted.

That night, Celine sent a long message to Julia. She explained what was happening – about the various permit inspections, and now this state-sponsored terror. Everything was crazy, she wrote. Julia messaged back urgently to tell them what was up in the city. It was much worse than she thought, she said. What had she done to Napoleon? Napoleon seemed to hate her. He kept talking about Celine in public. *How is this person still alive?* he was saying. *Can someone help me out here?* No one knew if he was joking or not, said Julia.

For a long while after reading this message Celine found it difficult to speak.

– *How is this still happening?* she eventually said to Marta. – Here I am, with a child who is now an adult, while everyone we know has died, or almost everyone. Everything I remember has disappeared. And still people want me dead. *Can you explain this to me?*

She felt the usual contemporary feelings: charged-up, delirious, vexed. But at the same time she had to admit if she thought long enough and precisely enough that these feelings were almost enveloped by something sweeter and more intoxicating, a feeling closer to relief. Finally it seemed that

Celine had an enemy who was equal to her. There had been Sasha, Hernandez, Yves . . . She had seen each of them as an individual to be vanquished or outwitted, but perhaps it was possible that these men were all shadows of a larger principle, and in the dictator this larger principle was at last visible: malevolent and frightening but also very clear.

14

The dictator was the absolute celebrity, and this was something he encouraged. His ideas and conversation were reported in every newspaper. He liked to see his image everywhere – on street posters and giant flags, or his name spelled out by formations of children holding flaming torches. This made it very easy to think of him as crazy but perhaps this was unfair. Around him there were psychopaths with slogans like War is the Supreme Hygiene of the World and he always found these irritating. He liked war but he preferred science. It seemed to him that he had missed his vocation. He had become famous for his military invasions, surging down through frozen mountains and over swamps, but what he now thought about wasn't the manoeuvres themselves but the rare plants he had driven past in his armoured vehicle, which he hadn't had time to observe.

He felt old and intelligent and lonely and misunderstood. Also his position was much more precarious than people thought. The state had no money and he had no money himself. This was why he was often meeting with billionaires like Rosen. They were constantly putting together international deals – deals that had to be done in secret, to stop the hedge funds betting against him. This secrecy and this fragility combined to make him paranoid. He wanted total war, and the war depended on money that seemed invisible and unstable.

He trusted no one. He kept around him a tiny cabal of people who gave the allure of independent thinking while always agreeing with him, however much they might grouch about this in the antechambers and courtyards, because it's always difficult talking with someone who is neurotic and also in possession of ultimate power.

Now, one of these people of course was André. And one day, after Celine had left him and it seemed left town for good, Napoleon asked André if he was still in touch with her. With Celine? replied André. Absolutely not. Of course, they had friends of friends, but still . . . There were revolutionaries across the border, said the dictator, who he had heard were plotting to kill him. He was trying to find information. He had this feeling that Celine was in some way involved too, said the dictator. She was friends with many people out there, because of her foreign connections.

It was true, said André, that her place in the countryside was something everyone wanted to see. He'd heard that it was becoming legendary, where people went to party.

It was always like this in the atmosphere the dictator created. It was an aquarium for stories to emerge in.

– Exactly, said the dictator. – I totally agree. The countryside.

André suddenly felt that in some way, while only trying to make conversation, he had also gone too far. But it was impossible to say anything. All language was corrupted. He tried to think of a way to erase what he had just said but it seemed he had created a little machine inside Napoleon which now could not be stopped.

Napoleon stared at André for a long while until finally the dictator nodded abruptly and said he had to work. He asked him to call in one of his assistants on the way out. Then he scribbled down a note.

Two days later, a more official version of this note was delivered to Celine, accusing her of international speculation and espionage, and ordering her to appear in front of the executive committee.

15

All the members of the executive committee were appointed by the dictator, so that what looked like a sober committee operated like a mini terrorist cell, carrying out Napoleon's orders. The charge of international speculation which they had levelled at Celine was the traditional one to attack the dictator's enemies. This was partly because it was vague enough to be useful in any emergency, but also because the dictator believed it. He needed money and very obviously there was vast money everywhere else, across the globe – just not for him. Therefore it logically followed, thought Napoleon, that there was illegal speculation occurring in realms he couldn't understand.

The meetings of the committee took place in a new administration building. It was magnificent and disgusting. There were empty or dead spaces everywhere, with sawn-off pipes and unplastered walls, among which were concierges and assistants trying to give the impression of manic preoccupation.

When she had received the message telling her to appear before the committee, Celine hadn't felt that it was serious. It was a document of hysteria, and therefore very comical. This was not the time of any larger moves, she thought. She had therefore not arrived with a lawyer, or rehearsed her answers, or considered what she could offer in a deal for her own safety, and this meant that she was very shaken when they immediately began talking rapidly and brusquely, asking her detailed questions about when she had last seen her friend Rosen, the Jewish billionaire, or how she had paid for the new land she had just bought, questions which were so detailed that she couldn't always give appropriate answers, however much she also understood that these questions in some way could never be answered because they were a veil that concealed a larger power.

She had spent her life inventing strategies, she thought, with sudden and total dejection, making moves and counter-moves and little feints, and maybe now all this was over. It was really stupid of her not to have predicted that this would be how it ended – in a room whose walls were infinite arrangements of square pigeonholes, each stuffed with heavy paper.

They kept on asking what was happening out in the countryside, on her little finca. Her what? she asked. Her estate, they said. She was living there, she said. What kind of question was this? They started listing people who had come to visit her, some of whom she knew but who she hadn't seen in years, some of whom she had never even heard of, but the more she tried to respond to each name they listed the more interrelated everyone's movements and networks seemed to become, so that it was almost impossible not to give an impression of a large and compromised sociability, however much she was basically living on her own. It was very important that she understand how serious these charges were, they said. But what charges? she said. Answer the question, they said.

They seemed in a hurry to get the meeting over or to reach a certain conclusion or at least to get her to say a certain form of words. In what ways, they said, did she think she would get away with plotting with outside forces? This was impossible, she said. Why? they asked. Because, she said, it was impossible to defend oneself against charges that were imaginary. They assumed, they said, she would want to remove that sentence from the record. Of course not, she said. Because it was treasonous, they said.

There were some conversations from which you could only extricate yourself by losing something very precious and which you would never be able to recover, thought Celine, because the language used in them was such a malevolent medium. And it seemed that this was one of them.

16

A week after their meeting, the executive committee wrote to Celine, saying that they had found her guilty of international speculation and espionage and had sentenced her to permanent exile. She had one week to prepare her affairs. All her property would be confiscated and would belong to the state.

The shock turned Celine insomniac. It was as if a child was being harmed, and not just a forest. She sat up in the night while Saratoga and Marta slept, trying to understand what had just happened, or how she might tell them that this utopia they were trying to construct was soon going to be over. It seemed impossible. It was of course not the first time she had been blacklisted or proscribed but this only seemed to make what was happening more impossible and more terrifying, because this time it felt like it was final. It occurred to her to write to Julia but then she suddenly felt too exhausted. There was no way out. She had always wanted to believe in herself as someone portable and international but it turned out that she could not imagine a life without this place she had created. It was the only idea of the future she had ever believed in, and she refused to abandon it. But on the other hand, power was absolute and implacable.

For two days and nights, Celine sat and thought. She felt evaporated. It was possible that the miracle of her survival was in fact the much more ordinary phenomenon of *outliving*, and this was a very different condition. She had simply outlived her own life.

As if to prove this, the next morning the newspapers reported that Claude, who had been ill for many months, had finally died. And because the dictator, who loved both science and empire, had made Claude a national hero, whose expeditions into the oceans were apparently as imperial as they were intellectual, it was ordered that he should be given a major funeral.

Meanwhile Celine had three days left.

She found herself telling Saratoga anecdotes about Claude, who was after all her father, however much Celine had always told Saratoga that fathers were irrelevant. She liked his curiosity, she said. There was a time when she had once watched Claude and Titere speak to each other, they were both practising the other one's language, and so Claude would speak in Titere's language and Titere would speak in Claude's language and she realised that she understood neither of them and at the same time also understood their conversation completely.

– What do you remember? she asked Saratoga. – Do you remember anything from when you were young? I mean really young?

– I remember going to sleep, said Saratoga. – I remember going to sleep, and being happy because I could hear you talking in the room next door.

Celine decided that she would go to the funeral on her own, as her last visit to the city she had once so delightedly loved. She arrived in town early, so she went to her apartment for the last time, to look at what was left behind. Everything seemed dusty and unlovable. Accidentally, she broke a porcelain plate. It was the final item left from the pieces Lorenzo had saved for her in America, and it shattered into triangular fragments. As she picked them up she noticed the little object Claude had once given her: the fish hook he had been given by Titere as a gift. She had taken it with her to every house or apartment she had ever lived in, but while she came and went between the city and the countryside she had left it here in the city. But now she felt that maybe she should keep it with her always. She held it in her hand. It was a little pulsing thing.

At the funeral, no one spoke to her. She stood there, inside a crowd. Then suddenly in the shuffling flow of people making their exit Celine saw Cato, her former assistant, and beautifully he smiled at her. It turned out that Cato now had a wine bar by the river. Of all the people she had ever known he was the one who always looked young, but now he had finally aged and the effect was very moving. He was glad to see her, he said, because he had always wanted to talk with her again, to discover what had happened. She wasn't sure, she said, she would be able to describe what had happened. For a long while Cato didn't reply. He was finding life very difficult, he said eventually. She was sorry, said Celine. She would come to see him, said Celine, just as soon as she was back in town – even if as she said this she knew that she would never be back in town again, and she would have spoken more but someone interrupted them and Cato disappeared into a crowd.

And suddenly there was Napoleon, standing alone beside a vehicle. Everything was dreamlike and horrific so that it seemed entirely logical to go up to him and try to talk. Various goons blocked her way. He turned to look at the commotion. She said that she had to see him.

He was staring at her, breathing heavily, with this unusual space between them, peopled by security. She felt like she was some statue or performance piece illustrating total suffering – and it seemed that he liked the idea of watching her suffer, because he could see her that evening, he stated, before being quietly ushered into his blacked-out and oversized vehicle.

17

Celine was moving through the planet and she felt like every day she was moving away and away. It was as if all the lights she had arranged around her were going out one by one, and it was very important to keep at least one of them alight so that there was some connection back to her past. But something kept interrupting her so that she lost little parts of herself every day, thought Celine, and the most violent was perhaps this office of the dictator, as if it might be the final element in a series – this blank space which you entered after a long sequence of assistants.

His office was in fact so blank that as you entered it you almost thought that there was nothing there at all. Its main element was paper: crumpled on the floor or in files or piled up in heaps. In the middle was a giant marble desk with almost nothing on it, just a porcelain plate of blood-orange slices and a porcelain pot of coloured pencils. There was a pile of old boots in one corner. The overall effect was so confusing that it made her feel even more afraid.

She was the person who left – but she would not be told to leave by other people, thought Celine. She wanted to move freely through the world. But to do that, it seemed, she would have to pass through this scene of absolute constriction and emerge unharmed. And it was not obvious to her how this could happen.

The dictator began very gently, talking about how terrible it was, the way people talked about her, the way people said that he didn't like her, because the truth was that he did like her very much. He was very interested to be speaking with her like this right now, in private, it was a conversation he had been looking forward to all day, ever since she had appeared in front of him. And Celine began shaking, very minutely, but a lot of her effort was spent in making him not see that she was shaking, and it felt terrible that the universe for her at this moment was entirely this effort to hide her own fear. If only she had come to him earlier, said the dictator, it might have made things easier. Whereas now the committee, he had heard, had made their decision, they had ordered her to leave, and it made his options very limited. After all, said the dictator, he was no dictator.

Celine was silent although she didn't want to be silent, she was silent because she had no idea if she could find a way inside this miasma of words, and also because she was feeling very fearful and very exhausted and did not trust that her voice would come out clearly and without the fear being audible in its tone.

Why hadn't she helped him out? he said. André always said that he was wrong about her. So why hadn't she helped him? If she'd helped him out then maybe he could have helped her. But she hadn't. She had been impossible.

Celine asked, very quietly, in what way she could have helped him.

Suddenly he was ferocious and it felt lethal, because there was no way of entering into the flow of words he was producing the way you can usually enter someone else's conversation. Like maybe by not plotting against him, he said. By not entertaining foreigners, in some wilderness of her own making, next to his own house. She didn't understand, she said. What he didn't understand, he said, was how they ever thought they would be able to bankrupt him. It was really insane of them. If he had more time, he added, he would have loved to listen to her explain the whole conspiracy.

– What do you want? he said with wild fury. – Do you want to stay friends with people who hate me or do you want us to leave you alone? What do you want?

And clumsily he banged his fist on the table and it scared her, this gesture, it was so theatrical but to see it in real life had its own specific terror.

– But I only want to disappear, said Celine.

– So disappear, he shouted. – What's stopping you?

– I mean, I want to disappear in a place that I choose, she said.

He got out some cigarettes and it seemed to distract or calm him. She could feel the fish hook from the ocean in her pocket and that seemed to calm her too. She held it tightly in her hand. It was from America, he said, this tobacco. He offered her a cigarette. She said no. It was super strong, he said. This was one thing he admired about Toussaint Louverture, he said. The way he organised production. She didn't know about tobacco, she said. That was a pity, he said. Anyway, he would soon have Louverture in prison. It seemed amazing, he said, that people had ever wanted to give liberty to people like him. It was irresponsible. Had she ever heard Kreyòl? Presumably not, he added, before she could reply, and he envied her for this because it was a horrible language. There was no possibility it could ever express abstract ideas. It was nothing like the kind of language she could use, in her famous conversations.

It was as if they had reached a very dangerous point in the conversation because it kept on approaching silence. And she did not know how to operate in this silence because it was a silence that was in fact transmitting too many messages. She felt like she had to do something to help him, a sentence that would be very clear and allow him to see her clearly.

She had no interest in power of any kind, she said. But she couldn't live if she had to go somewhere else. The forest was the only future she had imagined for herself, and for her daughter.

For a moment she thought that perhaps she had produced an effect she wanted because for a long time he didn't reply, and she hoped that she had maybe moved him with her situation and he was thinking about what she had said and contemplating how to help her. But finally he did speak and it was still a language she could not speak, made of transactions and relationships. It was nothing personal, he said. It was always so boring when people took business so personally.

– I can't speak like this, she said. – I don't know how to speak like this.

They were standing very close to each other. It was always appalling when a man was too close even if it didn't necessarily mean anything violent, but it was also obvious that he was enjoying this erotic insinuation.

– I mean, he said. – What would you do?

– I don't understand, she said.

– You keep on saying that, he said, – and I don't believe you.

It was difficult to know how seriously he meant this, the way it was always so difficult, understanding what men thought they wanted, and how much they wanted to frighten you rather than attack, and so she tried to think of something to say that would return the conversation to a less dangerous frequency, but before she could think of a phrase, a fragment of a sentence, she saw his hand moving towards her very slowly, as if to grip her neck.

– I'm fucking serious, he said. – You think you're so unique?

Her fear was so pure that it was washing over her or was like a light that enveloped her, and she very clearly had the sensation that she was about to die or something in her was about to die and so she did one final thing to try to resist, and it could not be in language because it felt like all the language had dissolved or disappeared. So that as he reached towards her as if to grasp her Celine punched him, still holding the little fish hook in her hand, this concentration of potential. She swung at him abruptly and because she was taller than he was the fish hook slashed him at the side of his skull, behind one ear. It happened so quickly, as if for the first time in her life, perhaps, there was finally just a present moment, with no anticipation or recollection embroidering it at all, so that she felt a pure surprise at what had happened, even if it seemed to surprise the dictator even more because he had amazement in his eyes as he swayed a little, then fell backwards. As he fell he hit his head again in exactly the same place, behind his ear, on the sharp corner of the marble desk, and even more blood was spurting out. From the floor he looked up at her. He seemed to be talking to her but not saying anything.

She could feel the fish hook in her hand, back in her pocket: a little electric shock.

There was a sudden random spill of coloured pencils from the desk around his body. One of them rested oddly beside his face. It was the most violent arrangement she had ever seen, she thought, this colourful disorder. And she felt a kind of pity watching him retreat from her even as he did not move, but something in him was retreating, it was returning to a location that perhaps was impossible to define. He had some kind of seizure or convulsion. Then his breathing stopped.

Celine could feel her nerves sending messages all over her body. She looked up at an assistant who had run in because of the noise.

– I think he's dead, said Celine.

Another assistant ran in. They looked at her.

– He suddenly fell, she said. – I think it was a heart attack. He fell and hit his head.

She had been expecting punishment and terror for so long now that to be in this situation felt absolute and inevitable, the way it might feel inside a dream. All she was thinking about was Saratoga, she felt such sadness that she might never be able to hold Saratoga again or listen to her talking, and the size of this sadness was so large that perhaps it wasn't even sadness but she was maybe dying too.

But then she realised with amazement that no one cared about her, or the explanations she was manically trying to prepare in her head. No one was arresting her or even questioning her. In their own terror and alarm all the office managers and workers had already turned their attention away – not so much towards the corpse on the floor but even more urgently towards themselves. People were coming in and out of the office and trying to calculate what would happen next. They were running out to communicate in secret with other people. Power was something liquid that could spill anywhere, and it was incredible how quickly that could happen and how irrevocable it was when it did.

The situation was scribbled over with cartoon lines of motion, but inside this situation was Celine.

It seemed suddenly possible that if she acted with a sense of purpose and of innocence she could do whatever she wanted. And she felt very certain that at the end of these grey corridors there was Saratoga, if she could only reach her, and so Celine walked in that direction.

Gently she walked out of the room. She walked down the stairs, as deliberately as she could manage, an avenging assassin, but it was only when she emerged onto the street and saw that no one was following her that she felt the delicious rush of absolute revenge surge inside her – the way a narcotic is delicious when it first begins to trickle through your kidneys and your liver and your heart.

18

The next day, Celine received a long message from Izabela in Warsaw. They had somehow continued their correspondence for over twenty years and magically another letter arrived, just as Celine was here in the bubble of her vengeance.

Everything was gateau and super-heavy pastry here, wrote Izabela. She would surely die very soon, and this made her happy. But that wasn't why she was writing. She had been thinking about something and she thought that it was perhaps only Celine who might understand what she was trying to say.

It seemed to Izabela, she continued, that people believed that everything could be expressed in writing. And maybe she had believed that too, certainly when she was at Celine's parties all those years ago. They always assumed in that era that language was everywhere. But more and more she felt that there was something that went beyond language, something which language was pointing to but which escaped it forever.

What if the true art of language wasn't literature but *translation*? wrote Izabela.

She had been thinking about the languages she had used throughout her life, and she personally liked it when people wrote to her or spoke to her in more than one language, but at the same time she was aware that she could only really express herself in one of these, the first one she had learned. And yet, she wanted to add, the fact that she trusted that Celine could understand her, even when she wrote in another language, seemed to prove something she had always suspected about languages, that they must point to something that was in between the languages or above or below the languages. She had no idea exactly where this reality which words produced was located but she also knew that it existed.

Everyone was hung up on descriptions. But she refused the idea that this was what truth was, wrote Izabela. She believed in fantasia instead: multicoloured, light and pure. In other words, she was sure that truth could be made on this chaotic planet, even if it was always made of falsehoods.

Maybe all this made no sense, wrote Izabela in conclusion, as if she felt suddenly embarrassed. She missed Celine. She missed those parties. It was amazing to think that if they met again it would probably now be in another world. Did Celine remember the way Izabela would sit in her favourite chair, talking non-stop – although it wasn't really Izabela who was inventing those sentences, it was the conversation at Celine's parties that produced them?

It was a long message and it took Celine a very long time to read it, because Izabela's handwriting was incredibly neat but also microscopic.

She felt a piercing sense of useless love for Izabela. It was very probable that Izabela was right that they would never see each other again, and she wished that she could tell her directly how much she loved her thinking. She too wanted to say *farewell writing*, thought Celine, but in a different way – to let all the objects stand there, very simply and naturally as themselves, the way a fern or a mushroom might stand there.

Then she sent Izabela a one-line message in reply. *If language is over*, wrote Celine, *that's OK with me.*

19

After Napoleon's death the executive committee declared a state of emergency. They refused to allow any autopsy on the dictator's body but instead organised a major funeral. Then they cancelled all current government orders, including every foreign deal and negotiation.

In the chaos, André was made diplomat in charge of international negotiations. He was super excited. His project was to set up a world congress, with representatives from every country, according to his new theory of international representation. There would be no central location or building for these congresses – it would travel around the planet, a sequence of moving centres.

The future was diplomacy, according to André and his backers, the finance crew of Rosen and his associates. It was an unending series of negotiated contracts.

André's first task was to supervise the withdrawal of all their troops from the Pacific and Atlantic Oceans, and all their claims on alien territory. The idea was that in exchange for this withdrawal they would negotiate trade deals with the Lakota and Dakota in the South, the Mohawks in the North, Toussaint Louverture's people in Hispaniola, the indigo planters on the Indian coasts, the green islands of the Pacific.

Many people thought that this was crazy, but there was a sudden atmosphere that was hopeful and vivacious and it was impossible to argue with an atmosphere.

Most things he saw right now, said André in a manic magazine interview, were totally outdated. He was sorry, but it was over. The monarchy was dead.

André felt immense. At night he studied the constitutions coming out of Hispaniola. What no one ever wanted to understand, he sometimes thought, was that there was nothing *constitutional* about making a constitution. It just had to get done, out of nowhere. And in Hispaniola they seemed to understand this pragmatic truth. He admired it very much.

It was as if everything he assumed would always be reserved for the future was suddenly happening in the present moment and it made him feel almost nauseous with possibility. And while it was presumably only temporary, this little climate, it was also and perhaps because of this all the more to be cherished.

20

For some weeks after she'd killed the dictator Celine lived in the countryside in a state of shock. She expected the secret police at any moment, but no one came and gradually it seemed that she was free to stay in the country forever. The story of the dictator's sudden death, a death caused, according to the newspapers, by manic overwork, was now so widespread and accepted that her presence at the scene was only known to a very few people, and even those assistants who knew she had been there had no wish to begin to suspect anything illegal because they had no appetite for complication. The story was over, and therefore they edited Celine out of the picture. Only two people knew the secret story: Marta and Saratoga. So that gradually what she thought would have happened and what did in fact happen became equally faded or dissolved, and she found herself in some wonderful and unexpected finale.

She had thought that certain obstacles were permanent forever, but maybe history was in fact made of a much more fluid material, full of ripples and dissolves – the way glass was suddenly revealed as liquid in a glassblower's workshop.

She felt more and more exuberant and reckless and excited, even while she understood that it was possibly delusional or misguided. It seemed that she was dependent on nothing and no one, that she needed no one's money or protection or good opinion, and this was a very rare condition, a condition to which she had aspired since she was seventeen.

There had been so many fractures and moments of absolute change in her lifetime that she had given up believing in any kind of continuous self. Instead she had this basic sense of jubilant survival. One day she found a note inside a book, which Saratoga had left for her as a message when she was four. When Saratoga had put this message inside the book Celine had assumed that it would be unbearably poignant if she ever found it again, but she was surprised to discover, now that she found it and read it – this little message from Saratoga telling her to have a happy birthday and a very happy day – that it was only joyful, the delight of one state being improbably pasted beside another, and not saddening at all.

After all, the habitat time invented for a person was always unreality. Every day you think nothing will change, that in the cafes the waitresses will be always the same or at least if replaced by new ones will always in some way be recognisable. And yet one day suddenly it's as if the cafe is only populated by aliens, and the menu is written in a novel language, and you have no idea at what point this change happened. It was possible to find this terrifying but it was also possible, she thought, to find it wonderful.

21

Every day she woke up and went out walking in the forest. It was as if it had become increasingly magical, with little colours made by flowers, like lights – with no beginning or ending. It was like a system of lights reflected in a system of mirrors.

Then she realised that although there was no one else there, something very strange was happening. All the stories she had ever lived through or just heard about began looping inside each other. The past was acquiring a fluid quality that she found very enticing, as if an event could be restored with all its apprehensions and mispredictions still attached to it like little roots or fronds.

Suddenly, for instance, she could hear Lorenzo, telling Jacob how he loved the way Beaumarchais used to talk. It was like Lorenzo was a beech tree, or certainly all she could see was a beech tree in front of her. He talked so fast, much faster than anyone else he had ever met, Lorenzo was saying, and this was how he made the actors talk when acting out his scripts – quicker and quicker so that it was completely unrealistic how they could have thought of such jokes in reply to each other and he was right to do this, said Lorenzo, because timing in comedy wasn't like rational time. It in fact depended on the actor replying faster than anyone could reply in ordinary life. But still, interrupted Jacob, unimpressed, couldn't he have found something more interesting to write about than desire?

None of this seemed too extraordinary, Celine was thinking, as she listened to the forest, and maybe it wasn't. It was as if the atmosphere were restoring some completely new idea of a family, enlarged and comical.

He didn't think people understood what Beaumarchais had been trying to do in his scripts, added Lorenzo. Everything in his writing was so unreal and extravagant but the real subject was power, not desire, said Lorenzo. Maybe, said Lorenzo, he didn't even understand that himself – and that wasn't so surprising, most writers had no idea what made their writing interesting.

Celine kept on walking. Everyone was talking at once. Somewhere her mother was talking to Saratoga. She seemed to be talking from a camellia and in fact she was discussing flowers too, she was asking Saratoga about the best way of sketching them without them looking blurred or confusing. And Celine could also hear Josef, a little further off, discussing the old studios, and also Izabela, talking to André about revolutions. For a long while she looked around her, not understanding what was happening. Somewhere in the dark trees Julia was complaining about Lorenzo, who wanted to discuss what had happened between them in the past, which perhaps in itself was not a problem, she said, but Lorenzo also seemed so angry. Still, if he felt such things then it was important for him to say them, she added, and Celine found herself loving her friend even more because of this talent

Julia had for not feeling anger at other people. It was easy to conquer meanness but to conquer anger was much rarer. And especially it was difficult to conquer anger at people who would not give up an image they had of you that had been formed many years ago, when you were different, in a different life.

Celine had been at the centre of a party. It had been the little ship in which she had set sail, years ago. But at the centre of the party it had turned out that there was no one. There was a void. But now it seemed that at the centre of this void was another party, and it was the voices she could hear around her in the forest. A voice, she suddenly understood, could happen anywhere.

Something could still be talking, it turned out, even if it wasn't speaking.

And so the party continued, and it felt increasingly like the forest produced the party, and the party then gave new life to the forest, even while the party didn't exist at all: it was just this constant murmur of voices that Celine could hear, a chorus that was spontaneous and miniature.

That night she lay in the bath, in the middle of an empty room. The window was open. She could see some stars. Some blue hydrangeas were drying out to mauve in a vase. Then Marta came in to talk with her, and it was amazing, thought Celine, how different she looked to the way she looked when she was twenty but also the same. It wasn't that she looked more beautiful than before. She was just beautiful in a new way that was also identical. Celine closed her eyes. She liked letting the water and her body become interchangeable things, just letting the water make her weightless.

Around them was the dark garden and the forest around it and the animals.

– Do you remember your dog? said Celine. – Do you remember that crazy tiny dog who lived with you?

– My wild dog, said Marta.

And it was of course happiness, thought Celine. The word for this was very simple and not in any way enough but it was happiness.

22

After the revolution had been successful on Hispaniola and nearly all the white people had gone, a minister came to Toussaint Louverture with a task for their republic. It seemed urgent to come up with an image that would represent the revolution. This image could then spread itself across the world, like a seed, he said. It would represent their victory for future generations. Louverture agreed to the idea. He was working on a revised constitution, and was worried that it was taking too much time. An image might be faster. A committee was appointed. It was extremely important to make a picture to commemorate this moment, said the minister. The problem would be in working out what exactly the picture should represent. It was very difficult, trying to represent the people, because the people were plural while the image was single.

Louverture himself found these discussions a little boring. After the first session he tended to come in towards the end. He liked action, he said. Art was necessary, he understood this, but it did not fascinate him. For him, it was the revolution itself that was the important thing, not any picture of it.

In fact, although he did not say this to the committee, he distrusted images intensely, the way they could be used against a person. He hated all the schemes for merchandise and memorabilia that people were pitching to him, with little reproductions of his face on mugs and posters and coasters.

The committee, however, was passionate in its attention to artistic theory. It considered various suggestions. 1. Toussaint Louverture in profile, against a black background, in his military regalia. 2. Louverture surrounded by his officers. 3. A single anonymous woman, breaking the shackles from her ankles. 4. A crowd of anonymous women, breaking the shackles from their ankles. 5. Louverture with the ghosts of other guerrilla heroes behind him. 6. Louverture riding his horse through a mountain gorge. 7. The tree of liberty, which would also be a picture of Gran Bwa. 8. A series of images of the white people in tatters: leaving the island, bleeding in the marshland, dying in exploding ships. 9. Louverture as Ogoun Fer, with his red handkerchief around his head, the corners tied in delicate knots.

After two weeks of discussion, they presented Toussaint Louverture with the options. He considered them for a while. It seemed impossible to decide. It was maybe not what they wanted to hear, he said, but maybe they should commission more than one picture? The committee thought this was a very interesting idea. Maybe in fact the revolution could not be represented in anything other than a sequence, or explosion – the way the jungle exploded on every side, in any combination. The committee started dreaming of murals, a vast sequence. A single painting would not be enough. They needed a *series*.

That day, Toussaint Louverture took himself off into the mountains. After riding for a few hours he stopped and looked down. There the island was, still coming out between the sea and the gulf, garlanded by keys and cays and fastened by its little seines to the ocean. Everything around him was growing and multiplying. Seeds were being scattered. All the plants were working together with the sun. They were working very hard to repair the terror of the indigo plantations, the fields that the white people had burned. The plants were the sun transformed into something luxuriant. So Louverture lay down among some laurels, and closed his eyes. A little wind investigated the ferns and it sounded like the sea.

23

It was so easy to exist inside nature that it was also easy to forget how alien it was as a force. One day Celine came across a kind of grove of aspen trees. She thought of them as aspen trees but it was impossible to know if it was one aspen bifurcating wildly or multiple aspens with a single soul. She stood inside the grove, trying to imagine it in five hundred years or even fifty years and realised that she couldn't. She stared at it or into it, its abstract lines and zigzags, the way she had once stared at arrays of porcelain or Tarot cards on a table.

It was only after a few minutes that she realised one of the trees she could see in the distance was in fact not a tree but Saratoga, who was standing very still. It was as if she was listening to something.

For a moment Celine was about to shout her name so they could walk together but instead she found herself saying nothing. There was no need, she thought. And she watched

Saratoga walk away, so that she was no longer looking at Saratoga but at the space where she had been standing.

It was a very heavy moment, like all moments, because it contained everything.

The forest around Celine was green. She walked inside it. Then Celine was green too.

A Note About the Author

Adam Thirlwell was born in London in 1978. He is the author of three previous novels, and his work has been translated into thirty languages. His essays appear in *The New York Review of Books* and the *London Review of Books*, and he is an advisory editor of *The Paris Review*. His awards include a Somerset Maugham Award and the E. M. Forster Award from the American Academy of Arts and Letters; in 2018 he was made a Fellow of the Royal Society of Literature. He has twice been selected by *Granta* as one of its Best of Young British Novelists.